MW0113556B

" R Lawson Gamble's paranormal murder mystery novel, Under Desert Sand, delves into the violent and bloody history of Hidden Springs, ...where Zack, Susan and Eagle Feather work together to unravel the mystery surrounding...two dead boys. Gamble's love of the Desert Southwest and Native American culture is apparent on every page of this marvelous and engrossing mystery tale... Gamble mingles the story of Zack's investigation with that of the two college boys who were experiencing a summer to remember when tragedy befell them, and living both the past and present creates a tension that makes the story work beautifully. Under Desert Sand: Zack Tolliver FBI, Book 5 is most highly recommended."
Jack Magnus for READERS FAVORITE

UNDER DESERT SAND

R LAWSON GAMBLE

This Book is Dedicated To Pixie, who never pawsed his dogged companionship.

Thank you Ann & Barbara for hanging in there with me.

MOJAVE DESERT
1450

His name, translated into English, meant Wailing Calf, from an unfortunate moment in childhood he would like to forget. Wailing Calf belonged to the Mojave tribe of the Southern Paiute. His name would change after his coming-of-age ceremony, when he would consume the root of the Datura plant, called "east root", the poisonous Devil's Trumpet of the desert. Only an experienced sachem could administer the correct dosage; too much, he would die, too little, there would be no effect at all. Administered correctly, he would hallucinate, perhaps even become violent; afterwards experience amnesia. The effects would remain with him for several days. Following the ordeal he would be considered an adult, ready for a new name. He was impatient for this to happen.

On this day Wailing Calf was camped with his family on a stretch of the Mojave Desert west of the Colorado River. The great river's rich flood plain provided sustenance for his tribe, an agricultural people. Often, as now, they journeyed west through the desert from seep to seep to trade mesquite beans and corn for bead shells with tribes as far away as the Pacific Ocean. The Mojave people commonly walked a hundred miles a day.

Bored with activities at camp, the eight-year-old boy drifted away unnoticed, his feet following his eyes until he found his way to a small pool where water trickled from a spring. He stopped and drank. The cooling liquid refreshed and relaxed him. He felt weary, his eyes closed and he knelt there, blind to the world around him. A

R LAWSON GAMBLE

feeling of dread enveloped him; a pervasive sense of malevolence came over him. Wailing Calf did not wish to open his eyes, but felt he must.

A great being, larger than the tallest tribesman in his village, stood upright before him. The man-creature wore no clothing; its weathered skin was patched with coarse dark hair. Long arms hung at its sides, its hands huge with claw-like nails, a heavily muscled torso, thick neck, large mouth with leathery lips, sharp teeth black near the gums, eyes red and hostile. A fearful stench surrounded it.

Dread and loathing swept over Wailing Calf. He leapt to his feet and fled in terror across the desert toward his encampment. He had never run so fast; he felt he was flying over the sand.

Wailing Calf's wish for a new name came true. From that day on, he was known as Lost Boy.

ARIZONA
1905

Jake Skowler was a bad man. There are two kinds of bad men in this world: bad like one turned sour from life's inequities and his own poor choices, or bad like a man born twisted, as a fallen oak branch lies gnarled and rotting on the ground. Jake Skowler was the second kind. When the frontier moved west from Arizona he drifted with it, like a dry leaf blown by the wind.

The lawmen of Arizona were happy to see him go. Skowler had been to court twice in that state, once in Cochise for robbery, once in Sedona for assault. He was acquitted both times for lack of evidence—it seemed no one wanted to testify against him.

Jake tended to take what he reckoned was his. Before departing, he demanded the wages he felt his employer owed him. When the rancher disagreed, Jake settled the dispute in his own way. He waited until the old man left for Rimrock on business and met the stage along the way, held it up, removed the rancher by force, tied him to a horse, and took him deep into the Mogollon Wilderness to a cabin hidden away in a deep canyon. He chained his former boss to a wall, made him sign his name to a chit. The next day he took the paper to the bank in Sedona and withdrew $1000. That worked out so well he went back the next day and did it again. The ploy exhausted, Jake dumped the old man back on the roadside where he'd captured him and moved on.

Skowler ended up in the high desert of Eastern California in Fairfield Valley, a place anything but fair with no fields. The town, if it could be so described, consisted of a few rough-board shanties. The valley was home to scattered settlers who scratched out a meager living from the dry soil, raised a few head of cattle, or worked in the mines. Fairfield Valley was in the high Mojave Desert, a land of blistering heat by day, chilling cold at night.

The region was home to the Winslow Cattle Company. Jake was hired on as foreman. The outfit ran a thousand head of cattle on thirty miles of open range. Sheep had come to the valley. They thrived on the scarce vegetation; their numbers proliferated. This caused consternation among cattlemen, who believed the loud wooly creatures ruined grazing for their cattle. The Winslow Cattle Company hired Jake to see to their interests. After Skowler's arrival in the valley there were numerous incidents of bullets passing perilously close to herders from an unseen rifleman.

Skowler didn't get along well with people in general. Within six months of his arrival, he was involved in a dispute with cowboys in the Winslow outfit and he quit. Jake set up a small ranch nearby, put together a modest herd of cattle, origins unknown. About this time there was a rise in misappropriated calves from the Winslow herd. All the settlers in the region came under suspicion, Skowler foremost among them.

The Cattle Company responded quickly. They brought in another known gunman, a bad hombre from Arizona named Curt Johnson, gave him the foreman's job. They placed him in a cabin by a critical water hole in the area, known as Hidden Springs. He squatted there like a spider in the center of its web. No one would have water without his say so.

Hidden Springs already had an evil reputation. It was situated on the old Mojave Road, traveled by the earliest desert tribes. The few water locations along this

4

ancient corridor were critical for survival, yet known places for ambush. Like mice drawn by cheese in a trap, travelers over the centuries balanced thirst against danger when approaching the springs. The army built a fort nearby in the 1850s to protect traders and travelers along the road. It was a harsh posting; the soldiers went crazy in this barren, isolated place, were eventually withdrawn, the fort abandoned. There was an overall sense of decay around Hidden Springs.

As a newcomer, Curt Johnson saw the spring only as a place to water cattle. Its reputation did not matter to him.

The tension grew in Fairfield Valley. Incidents of sniping increased. Johnson found 13 bullet holes in his cabin wall one day when he returned from the range. Jake Skowler had his hat shot off, his horse killed from under him. The honest sheepherders and small cattle outfits began to move away from the valley in fear for their lives. They believed it was only a matter of time before the dispute exploded into open war and someone was killed. They'd just as soon not be there when that happened.

Surprisingly, things quieted down again. A year went by without incident. Hope grew among the few remaining settlers for a return to the peaceful life before Skowler and Johnson arrived. They would soon learn the pot hadn't cooled—only simmered.

The pot boiled over on the day Jake Skowler and a hired hand drove a few calves to Hidden Wells to water them. Jake called to Curt Johnson in his cabin for permission to open the gate and let his cattle water. Johnson hollered back to go ahead, and invited Skowler to come on in. Jake left his hired hand to water the stock, walked over to the small building and entered. The sound of gunfire erupted almost at once.

Skowler's hired hand cowered by the fence, the cattle scattered. A long silence followed. The man gathered enough courage to walk up to the cabin. He found Skowler on the floor just inside, Johnson sprawled near his bunk. Both men had their Colt .44s gripped in their hands; each had multiple bullet wounds and a neat round hole in the middle of the forehead. Both men were stone cold dead.

CHAPTER ONE
Present Day

"Imagine this." Susan looked over the folded top of the morning paper, her blue eyes twinkling. A beam of morning light set her blonde hair aglow and ignited bright sparkles in the lenses of reading glasses perched low on her nose. "A man riding his OHV somewhere in the desert, in the middle of nowhere, comes across two bodies in the sand, two young men lying 100 feet apart." Her eyes scanned on down the page.

Zack glanced up from his own paper, mildly curious. "And?"

Susan's eyebrows lifted as she read on. "Both were dead from a bullet to the head. Both men were wearing gun belts around their waists, each had a six-shooter in his hand, as if they had just fought a classic western duel."

"Wannabe gun fighters?"

"Yeah, but wait. Here's the fun part. Both guns had been fired just once, five bullets remained in each pistol." Susan crossed shapely legs stretched out on the lounge chair. "Each man was struck by a single bullet in the exact middle of the forehead." She watched Zack's face.

"Not so mysterious. They were good shots."

"You don't think it's strange two guys standing 100 feet apart somehow put a bullet right in the middle of the other's forehead? At the exact same time?"

Zack tri-folded his own paper, laid it on the table next to him. "What paper are you reading?"

"The Las Vegas Review-Journal."

"Where did this happen?"

Susan's smile broadened. "Grabbed your interest?"

UNDER DESERT SAND

Zack didn't want to admit it, but yes. "I might know the sheriff in charge."

"There wasn't a sheriff. They found the bodies in the Mojave National Preserve down near Needles at the California border. A Park Ranger was first to respond, did the initial investigation. He was later backed up by BLM agents."

Zack reached for his coffee cup, tilted it back, peeked in, found it empty. "They might have missed something. Not all those guys are trained for crime scene management. They have a lot of other responsibilities."

"Your modest way of saying they lack the skills you and your buddy Eagle Feather bring to crime solving." Susan's eye went back to the article.

Zack spoke through a yawn. "Well, yeah."

The two were breakfasting poolside. Although Susan would have preferred the magnificent buffet in the Crystal Room, spread across several tables, smelling of bacon and rich coffee, Zack found the heavily mirrored space oppressive and the ornamented furniture annoying. It was pleasant in the shade by the pool; the early morning breeze was still cool, the air fresh.

The Southwest Press and Lawmen's Annual Conference was meeting in Las Vegas and Susan and Zack had been invited to offer a presentation. Their workshop on how to deal with inexplicable and seemingly impossible occurrences during homicide investigations had met with a mixed response. Crime reporters and lawmen attending the conference were less interested in potentially paranormal perpetrators than ordinary human criminals, a fact illustrated by the sparse turnout. Still, those few in attendance were eager front-row types, the usual Las Vegas fringe group, as well as a handful of hardened reporters and cops from around the southwest who in the line of duty had stumbled into situations they did not understand. Despite the small numbers, there had been active discussion and the evening went late.

Susan put her paper down, took a sip of coffee. "You know, among the kooks attending last night, I felt there were a few people who genuinely wanted reassurance. They needed to know they were not going nuts. Perhaps my theories allayed some of their fears, coming from an academic and published anthropologist. But those grizzled cops out there needed support from one of their own. The fact that you are an FBI agent with a reputation and career on the line, yet willing to talk about these things, seemed to give them a boost."

"Kind of like those airline pilots who confess to seeing UFOs even though it will cost them five months of psychiatric treatment and a loss of flying time."

"Exactly. Now take this article, for example. If we accept the facts as presented here, it's an impossible scenario. Yet they call it a double homicide and leave it at that."

"Why impossible?" Zack wasn't ready to give in.

"What are the odds? According to this, both men shot each other directly through the forehead with their first bullet. Consider the immaculate timing and deadly accuracy it took to do that."

"Susan, you're always trying to dredge up a puzzle to solve even when there isn't one. The men were marksmen."

Susan studied Zack with raised brows. "So you're saying both men had absolutely no fear, took careful aim, and fired simultaneously with incredible accuracy."

"Sure. Why not?" Zack sighed at Susan's grimace. "Susan, there are always many mitigating factors, things we don't know. Who were they? What was their emotional state? Why were they shooting at each other? It might just be both were great marksmen and all it took was one shot."

"Could you be that accurate?" Susan's finger tapped the paper. She wore her stubborn expression.

Zack threw up his hands. "Enough. The fact is, we'll never know." He peered at his watch. "We've got just a few hours before our flights. I need to think about getting ready."

Susan leaned toward him, her eyes accusing. "There's something wrong with that scenario, and you know it. That's why you changed the subject." Before Zack could respond, she said, "Let's go take a ride on the High Roller over there. We can get a great view of Las Vegas."

Zack experienced the metaphorical jaw drop he always felt at Susan's abrupt subject changes. He followed her gaze across the roofs to the huge Ferris wheel, the passenger pods glistening in the early morning sun. "That's what it's called?"

She nodded, swung her legs down, and slid out of the lounger. "C'mon, don't be a stick-in-the-mud."

"Is that how you view me?" Zack gave her a sideways glance but Susan was already walking away.

Zack Tolliver's first assignment after graduating from the Academy was with the FBI Liaison Office responsible for the Four Corners Navajo Indian Reservation, Tuba City Region. That had been nearly fifteen years ago. He'd gone through a change in bosses, watched several other colleagues come and go, apparently unable to withstand the solitude, vast emptiness, and boredom punctuated with isolated moments of extreme excitement. Zack thrived there, and under the tutelage of friend and hunting guide Eagle Feather came to know the Navajo People, the Diné, for the deeply spiritual and mystic people they are. More than one case had drawn him from the concrete reasoned world of the White Man to an amorphous spiritual reality seemingly without conclusion or resolution, to his mind. Eagle Feather helped him to understand.

Half an hour later, Zack and Susan were packed and checked out of their hotel, their bags left in care of the concierge. On the short walk to the High Roller, Zack felt the desert heat building in the concrete canyons of the city.

The ride cost them twenty bucks apiece. At this early hour the line was short. Each car had benches on both sides and plenty of standing space in the middle, capable of holding forty people. The pods were glass enclosed to promote great visibility and a superior sense of queasiness. An antidote was available in the Happy Hour cabin, a car with a bar running through the middle of it for those willing to pay the ticket upgrade. Several people were already taking advantage of this despite the early hour.

"Maybe these people are still there from last night," Zack said, winning a laugh from Susan.

They declined the "Calorie Car", as Susan renamed it, and stepped into a pod that was almost empty. After their car was loaded, with just the two of them, the wheel moved briefly and stopped to load the next one. There was a series of starts and stops before the ride began in earnest. The motion was smooth and slow, more like a rotating restaurant than a Ferris wheel. Once beyond the halfway point of ascent, the view was notable. At the apex, a full 550 feet above the ground, they could view the entire Strip and the distant mountains, brilliant in the bright morning sun.

The second time their car came around to the high point, the wheel stopped. An official voice interrupted the mellow music and advised passengers not to be alarmed; they were experiencing trivial technical difficulties already being addressed and the ride would resume after a short delay. A loud cheer floated up from the Happy Hour car beneath them.

Zack glanced at Susan with wry amusement, about to comment when his phone rang. He glanced at it. The area code was California; he did not recognize the name. He shrugged, looked apologetically at Susan, and answered.

"Zack Tolliver."

"Agent Zack Tolliver?"

"Speaking."

"My name is Butch Short. I work for the BLM. Is this a good time?"

Zack looked out at the cloudless blue sky, the sharply shadowed buildings stacked together, the glistening desert beyond. "At this moment I'm at the top of a stalled Ferris wheel with an amazing view of Las Vegas all alone in a car with a beautiful woman." He paused for effect. "Sure, this is a perfect time."

There was silence. "So it's okay?"

Zack laughed. "Sure. How can I help you?"

"Well, I attended a university class recently with a friend of yours, named Eagle Feather."

"Oh, yes, I know him." He looked at Susan, raised his eyebrows.

"He mentioned your particular interest in solving unusual crimes. He said you are receptive to, well, a wide range of spiritual possibilities."

"Yes?"

There was another pause. "To get right to the point, I'd like to engage you as a consultant to help us solve a crime out here."

"Out where?"

"The area of my responsibility abuts the Mojave National Preserve."

Zack's eyes went to Susan. "A double homicide?"

"So you've read about it?"

Zack winked at her. "Just a newspaper report."

"Would you consider helping us? What arrangements are required? Do I need to contact someone in the FBI administration?"

"Whoa, slow down, one step at a time. Why do you feel you need me, in particular?"

"This case presents some unusual elements. You might be able to help our investigators work past certain, uh, impediments."

"What sort of impediments?"

There was a sigh. "Agent Tolliver, this case is not all it seems on the surface."

"You mean the fact that both young men were able to shoot one another with such precise timing and deadly accuracy?"

"Well, that's part of it, for sure. But mainly we have strong reason to believe someone else was there."

"You found evidence?"

"No, that's just it, we found nothing at all. The only tracks belonged to those boys; their ponies were still tied to the fence. The old guy who found them never approached closer than fifty feet, not enough to disturb any tracks or other sign. It was obvious to him they were dead from the flies, and the scene spooked him. It's all desert sand out there; you can't get near without leaving some impression. But according to Ranger Davidson, there were none."

"So why—?"

"Will you come talk to us, at least?"

Zack was intrigued. His mind whirred. "This does sound like my line of work. What is your authority to engage me? Who is lead investigator in this case?"

"Sir, the case falls under the jurisdiction of the National Park Service. The shooting occurred on Preserve land, which they administrate. However, the BLM is party to the investigation and it is within my authority to hire a consultant."

Their pod began to move. Zack held Susan's gaze as he spoke. "I might be available."

There was an audible sigh of relief. "Of course, time is of the essence. What is your fee? We—"

"We'll need a longer conversation to work all that out. How far are you from Las Vegas?"

"Just a couple of hours down Route 95."

"Fine. Where are you located?"

"I'm in Needles, California, at the BLM office. We can work out the details of your contract here. But first I'd like you to see Ranger Tav Davidson at the Hole-In-The-Wall Ranger Station on the Preserve. He can show you the crime scene and fill in a lot of detail, including background."

"Is he one of the active investigators?"

"As best he can be while manning his station. There're just a few rangers on the Preserve, that's why the BLM and the local Sheriff's office are pitching in."

"Okay. I'll be there in a few hours."

"I should caution you in advance not to be put off by Tav's manner; he spends a lot of time by himself, if you know what I mean."

As Zack put away his phone, he looked at Susan and grinned. "How would you like to take a ride into the desert? It seems we might be able to resolve this morning's debate after all."

CHAPTER TWO

Zack and Susan cancelled their flights. Zack called his
associate Alex Brown at the office in Tuba City to explain
things, arranged transport from the FBI vehicle pool in Las
Vegas. It seemed all they had in the Las Vegas lot were
bright red Jeep Wranglers. Zack was okay with that. They
drove south on Route 95, following the Old Spanish Trail
between the McCullough and Eldorado Mountain ranges.
The scenery was stunning, if you like dry. Zack kept the
Jeep's fabric roof up to protect against the burning sun but
had removed the window and door panels. The wind
whipped through, streaming Susan's long blond hair as
they drove.

"Too hot?"

Susan flashed a contented smile. "No. After all that
air conditioning this feels real good." She had changed
from the sundress to shorts and a sleeveless blouse, kicked
off her sandals and sat cross-legged on the seat.

In half an hour they reached the small town of
Searchlight. Ice cream called out to them, and they found it
at the Nugget Casino. They took their cones out into the
parking lot as much to escape the constant bells and
whistles of the slots as to absorb the serenity of the ageless
desert hills. It was a pleasing contrast to the crowded city
they had left behind them, despite the hot sun.

"I've heard enough slot noise for a lifetime," Susan
said. She lapped her tongue against the waffle cone edge to
catch a drip of melting chocolate.

Zack was lost in reverie; the shimmering horizon
and hot sun contributed to a comfortable lethargy.

"I know what you're thinking."

Zack broke away from his thoughts, turned to look at Susan, his eyebrows raised. "Aren't you the omniscient one."

"You're thinking it should be Libby standing here with you right now."

Zack and his wife Libby were undergoing a difficult time, not uncommon to lawmen and their families. For Libby, it was not just the alternating day and night shifts, or the personal dangers her husband faced every day, or the additional time away from home he spent on the lecture circuit with Susan Apgar; it was all of it, resulting in his absence and her perpetual worry.

Zack understood this, yet felt a personal responsibility to support Dr. Apgar. He knew his presence added validity to her presentations and credibility to her theories. Susan postulated alternate beings could and likely did exist among humans, creatures one might pass in the street without notice yet who had evolved to possess different qualities. These were human-like bipeds devoid of conscience or ethical sense, predatory creatures that were a source of unsuspected danger, the cause of unsolved murders.

Libby understood the importance of their mission, she knew Zack's personal experiences made him invaluable to Susan—she got all that. She also knew she couldn't raise their boy Bernie by herself, while constantly worried for Zack's safety. The last straw came when Zack's work followed him home one night and nearly killed all of them. She issued an ultimatum after that—either quit his job and stay home with his family, or move out.

For Zack, it was an impossible choice. He could not abandon his mission, yet he loved Libby and little Bernie and saw them whenever he could. It was never enough. He grinned at Susan. "Nine out of ten times you'd be right, but just now I was simply simmering in the sun thinking nothing at all."

The ice cream disappeared quickly; they resumed their journey. They passed through to the town of Palm Gardens where the highway crossed into California. A short distance later a sign caught Zack's eye, he pulled to the side of the road and glanced at the map. After gazing left and right, he pointed out to Susan where a sandy track approached from the east and continued west beyond the highway.

"That's the Mojave Road, an ancient trail first traveled by the desert Indian tribes all the way west to the Pacific for trade, later by Spanish and American settlers headed for Alta California."

"Aren't those car tracks?"

"You can still travel sections of the road with the right vehicle." Zack started up the Jeep and they lurched forward. "Looks lonesome out there, though."

Susan didn't comment, simply gazed down the dirt track into the far distance, a pensive look on her face.

They turned west onto historic Route 66. The road was narrow by comparison to the more traveled Route 95; here the macadam crumbled along the edges and presented occasional potholes.

"This will take us south to I-40. After that, it's just a short hop to the entrance road to the National Preserve." He glanced at Susan. "You okay? Too hot?"

"Not yet. I love the breeze."

The Jeep came up on a camper, which slowed them, but Zack didn't mind. The desert spread out on all sides like a threadbare carpet with tufts of creosote bush, cholla and yucca. He saw occasional small stands of Joshua trees. The land rose gradually toward sharp-ridged desolate mountains slicing to the blue cloudless sky north and west of them. The Jeep tires clicked rhythmically along the road surface, the smell of dry sage and hot tar was in Zack's nose.

At the Interstate they enjoyed a fast interval of four-lane highway. The ramp to the Mojave National Preserve came upon them and Zack turned off. The access road was intimately married to the desert landscape, following the terrain contours up and down as it took them in a wide sweep north and west. Creosote bushes and Joshua trees stood tall along the roadside, hiding their view while in the dips. When they ascended a crest, like a surfer tops a wave, a vista opened toward the desolate range of abrupt sandstone crags. They felt like the only two people on earth.

Asphalt gave way to sandy dirt from time to time; finally it quit altogether. They came to a fork in the road. Zack slid the Jeep to a stop. A wooden sign stated the Providence State Recreation Area was straight ahead; the Black Canyon Road was to the right. A smaller sign said the Hole-In-The-Wall Campground was also to the right. Zack went that way.

Asphalt re-appeared; the road followed hollows and rises within thickening forests of Joshua trees. Susan had never seen such vegetation before, was fascinated by it.

"They look like little old men beckoning this way or that," she said, and giggled.

Zack laughed. "I never thought of them that way before, but you do have a point."

A large mountain of fragmented cliffs slowly rose beyond the roadside vegetation, crisscrossed with fissures and wind caves. The next sign they saw said Hole-In-The-Wall Information Center turn left, Hole-in-the-Wall Campground straight ahead.

"Well, I guess this is it," Zack said, and turned left.

The driveway to the Information Center was newly paved and shimmered black. The center itself, a simple wood construction with a porch the length of the building, nestled beneath a great rock overhang, dwarfed by it. Zack pulled into a parking space. A Range Rover packed full of travel gear was in the next one; two more vehicles and a motorcycle with a pack behind the seat were parked in a larger lot a short distance away. Several flat stones created a path that led off to a luminescent green toilet off among the trees.

They climbed out of the Jeep, stretched, and looked around. Zack immediately felt the weight of the heat on his head and shoulders.

"It seems a bit primitive out here," Susan said. She paused, stared at the outhouse for a moment, and started down the path. "I'll be back in a minute."

Zack stepped up on the wooden porch of the information center. No one was around; the owners of the parked vehicles must be off on hikes. He had noticed signs indicating directions to trailheads. His boots sounded hollow on the porch floorboards; there was a pleasant smell of warm sap from the unfinished wood coaxed out by the sun's heat. The walls held display boards covered by informative maps and brochures. While he waited for Susan, he studied them to orient himself. The area was vast. If he understood the map correctly, there wasn't much in the way of structures beyond this point.

Susan rejoined him. They walked down the porch to a pair of screen doors. Susan pushed, they groaned open.

Zack followed Susan into the cool interior. His gaze swept the room. They were in a small store; shelves lined the walls filled with colorful books of all shapes and sizes. Souvenirs and practical items such as hats and sun lotion occupied revolving racks. Another turnstile display offered pocket-sized instructional books on vegetation, animals and reptiles of the desert.

At the far end of the room, behind the counter, a thickset man in a khaki uniform shirt looked up. His face was broad and brown; his frizzled grey-black hair was pulled straight back and knotted, hung in a long braid behind thick muscular shoulders. Black eyes stared at them.

Susan moved from shelf to shelf, oohed and commented on each item in her melodious voice, sounding like a sixteen-year-old at her first prom. Zack watched her, amused. He'd observed this performance before, knew it invariably worked as an icebreaker.

Not this time. The man behind the desk simply stared, his expression unchanging, offered no comment. Zack stood in the center of the floor, surprised at the lack of greeting. As Susan's act began to falter, he walked directly to the counter and thrust out his hand.

"My name is Zack Tolliver. I'm looking for Tav Davidson."

"For what?" His face remained stone. He didn't take Zack's hand.

"You people asked for me, not the other way round. I'm with the FBI." Zack felt irritated, let his hand drop.

21

"Who asked?" The man's voice was low, gravelly, as if used infrequently.

"Butch Short, the BLM agent."

The man grunted.

Zack waited. The men eyed each another.

"Well, do you know where I can find this Tav Davidson?" By now, Zack was fully annoyed.

"You're lookin' at him."

"You might have said so right away."

"Sorry. We get some real kooks out here."

Still no smile; Zack wondered if the man's facial muscles were permanently frozen.

Susan put down a book on insects and came over to them.

Zack motioned to her. "This is my colleague, Dr. Susan Apgar."

"She FBI too?"

Susan offered a warm smiled. "Oh, no, one agent in our team is quite enough. I'm a teacher."

"Butch didn't say he was gonna hire two consultants."

"I come for free...if I come at all."

Zack saw the beginning of petulance on Susan's face. It took a lot to squash her natural ebullience. Tav Davidson certainly wasn't getting off on the right foot with either of them.

Zack glanced around the small, shelf-filled room. "Can we talk?"

"Yes, not here. We'll go out back."

Tav came around the counter, flipped over a "Back in a Moment" sign. He was shorter than Zack's five-ten by maybe an inch or so, yet appear larger, his erect posture and thick chest adding to the illusion. He walked around

22

them to a door marked private and motioned them to follow. They entered a tiny room with a cot and a chair, crossed it and passed through a screen door to a small porch. A towering rock cliff faced them no more than fifty yards from where they stood, its shadow a source of coolness.

Tav pointed to a pair of wooden chairs, pulled a short bench out from the wall and sat. He pointed to a water cooler with lime wedges floating in it on a stand nearby "Help yourself."

Zack was thirsty. He took a paper cup from the stack, tilted back the lever and filled it. The water was cold and refreshing. Susan, already tucked into one of the chairs, waved off his offer.

Zack sat down, sipped his water, looked at Tav and got right to the point. "Mr. Short says you had a homicide-suicide out here."

CHAPTER THREE

Tav leaned back on the bench, his back against the wall, legs crossed, half closed his eyes and seemed to assemble his thoughts.

"I'm half Mojave, a quarter Chemehuevi, and a quarter white. My people lived in this desert for a thousand years. Survival here is the first order of business for human or animal." He studied Zack, then Susan. "That has not changed. The preserve is 1.6 million acres of desert, includes much of the Mojave Desert, and some of the Great Basin and Sonoran Deserts. A man feels alone out here, beyond the law, beyond the support of society. If you get into trouble, you got to handle things yourself."

"What about a woman? Must she handle herself as well?" There was dryness in Susan's voice.

"Sorry, lady, no offense. There happen to be way more men living out here than women."

Zack jumped in before Susan could get going. "You requested my help for this recent homicide-suicide."

"Homicide-suicide, my ass!" Tav squinted at Zack. "This wasn't suicide." He raised his index finger. "First off, a suicide-homicide suggests one boy shot the other, then shot himself." Tav shook his head. "Didn't happen. Both shots were fired far enough away so no powder residue was around the wounds. So next you think, suicide-suicide or homicide-homicide, however you want to look at it." He shook his head again. "Didn't happen. Those boys were just plain murdered."

Zack raised his eyebrows. "A third party at the scene?"

"Well that's the question, isn't it? If they didn't shoot each other, there must have been a third person."

Susan glanced at Zack, turned to Tav. "According to the Tribune, the investigators found nothing to indicate the presence of a third party."

"That's true."

"In your opinion, were the investigators remiss?"

Tav starcd at Susan. "Lady, I was one of the investigators. We did not remiss nothin'."

"It's important to establish if someone else was involved." Zack said. "How can you be so sure those boys were murdered?"

Tav shifted in his seat to face Zack. "Those boys were greenhorns. Both had .44 caliber Colt M1873 Old West Peacemaker revolvers. Those guns have a kick. The boys were a hundred feet from each other, yet we're supposed to believe they shot each other right in the middle of the forehead at exactly the same time." Tav shrugged. "You tell me."

Susan sent Zack a triumphant look.

"Who was first at the scene?" Zack asked.

"Some old guy on a Honda quad. He was with a group traveling the Mojave Road. The old man had come over to see about water." Tav paused, looked at them. "Either of you know anything about this region?"

Susan shook her head.

"Not much," Zack said.

Tav stood, went inside, came back with a park information pamphlet, opened it to a map and passed it to Zack. "If you wanted to travel west through this desert from the Colorado River in the old days, you could head for Soda Lake and the Mojave River which flows southwest toward Los Angeles. To get to it, you'd travel through a natural corridor of valleys and passes, the Mojave Road. Trouble is, you're lookin' at seventy, eighty miles of dry desert. There were seeps, springs, just enough to get you through, but you had to know where to find them. When the Spanish traveled from Santa Fe to California the Mojave tribesmen guided them across. Later the Americans used the road, built forts to guard the water holes. After that the railroad came through a different valley, other migration routes became more popular, the Mojave Road was abandoned, and the forts deserted."

Tav walked to the cooler, poured a cup of water. He brought it back to his bench. He sat on the edge of it, leaned toward Zack. "The thing about these water holes was, they were very reliable. Americans lookin' to claim land and raise crops and graze stock came out here knowin' they were there, countin' on them. One of the most reliable springs is called Hidden Springs; been water there as far as anyone can remember. That water is critical. People have fought over that well for centuries. That's where the bodies were found."

Zack scanned the map. "Where's Hidden Springs?"

Tav leaned over, put a large finger down. "It's about 15 miles from here. Even today, its not marked. You still have to know where you're going."

"Okay, I see it."

Susan peered over Zack's shoulder. "Shouldn't we go up there?"

Tav nodded. "We will. No hurry, though. There's nothin' up there now but sand and yellow tape."

"How long since the bodies were found?" Zack asked.

"It's been about 48 hours. From the condition of the bodies we guessed they'd been lying there anywhere from 10 to 18 hours."

"Nobody could've stumbled on them before that?"

26

"Just isn't likely. Could only be people traveling the Mojave Road, like that old guy."

"What's happening now?" Zack asked, backhanding a bee away from his water.

"The coroner has the bodies, he's looking 'em over. Trick is, neither boy had any ID on him. We still don't know who they are and what they were doing at the spring, rigged out like a couple of gun slingers."

"Who's working the case?"

"Besides me? Two BLM agents, several guys from the county sheriff's office, a private detective."

Zack straightened at that. "A private cop? Why?"

Tav gave a humorless smile. "Told you it's a bit complicated. Thing is, there've always been mineral and ranch interests in the area. The private cop represents the cattlemen's interests." Tav caught Susan's look of surprise. "Yeah, I know, doesn't seem like a great ranching area, but in fact homesteaders and large ranching outfits have fought over the area all along. Like I said, there are fairly reliable water sources here and there's lots of room for cattle to graze, long as they can graze wide and free. Fact is, this whole area was once involved in a range war—you know, a large cattle company up against homesteaders, the kind of thing like you see in the old western movies."

Tav saw he had their interest, went ahead. "It's the story I wanted you to know before we go up to Hidden Springs. Back in 1905 there was a shootout between two gunslingers in that very same spot. Both men were killed, just like now. In fact, my first thought was these two young guys had gone up there to re-enact that gunfight and ended up killing each other by accident."

Susan leaned toward Tav, a glint in her eye. "What did those men fight about?"

UNDER DESERT SAND

Tav cleared his throat. "Legally, everyone in the valley had rights to water. Each of several court cases over the years ended the same way: every rancher, regardless of size, was entitled to access to the water holes. The big player in this drama was the Winslow Cattle Company, with thousands of head of cattle. It was all open range in the beginning; the small guys ran their small herds right alongside the Winslow cattle. Not surprisingly, there were mix-ups. Winslow would claim their cattle ended up with small outfit brands on 'em, the small outfits would claim the other way around. When the Winslow cattle wandered onto small farms and ate their wheat and trampled their gardens, well, that caused another stir. That's when fences started to go up.

"Sounds the same as Montana or Wyoming or anywhere else in the west at that time," Zack said.

Tav nodded. "That's about right, although it was all over and done with everywhere else by the time it happened here. No difference, though, other than water access was more critical here, maybe."

Susan raised her eyebrows. "In western movies people started hanging each other at this point."

Tav shook his head. "We know what Hollywood does to reality. But things grew tense here, for sure. When the Winslow Cattle Company brought in a known outlaw and gunfighter to be their foreman, name of Jake Skowler, you could 'a cut the tension with a knife. The man wasn't no Sunday School teacher. He was a gunfighter and a quick-draw artist. He made no bones about his past, which included a fatal shooting. After a while, though, Skowler quit the Rock Springs outfit and started up a small ranch of his own right there in Fairfield Valley—joined the other side, as it were. Word was he had a row with a Winslow

Cattle Company cowboy named Johnson, who had his own reputation as a gunslinger."

"What did the little ranchers do?" Susan asked.

"Nothin'. They had accidently acquired their own gunfighter, Skowler, to defend their interests." Tav leaned forward. "So the big cattle outfit places Johnson in a cabin at Hidden Springs, the most critical water hole in the area, and fences it off." Tav lifted his palms. "Now here's Johnson sitting at the water hole an' the whole valley buzzing with talk about who's got the fastest gun. There's real tension for you."

"So what happened?" Susan blurted.

Tav glanced at her, almost smiled. "In fact, nothing," he said. "At least, not for a long while. The two men ignored each other and went about their business. But the tension kept growin'."

Tav stared up at the rafter, as if to get his facts in order. "It was November 8, 1905 that Skowler shows up at Hidden Springs with his hired hand driving a small bunch of cattle. Story is Jake calls out to Johnson, who's in the cabin, can he have water for the steers and Johnson yells back to go ahead. Skowler and his hand, name of Vanderhoff, open the gate and let the steers go to the water. Right then, according to Vanderhoff, Johnson calls to Skowler to come on in to the cabin. It all sounded amiable enough to Vanderhoff, until minutes after Skowler stepped through the door when all hell broke loose; two Frontier Colt .44s banged away in that tiny cabin."

"And then?" Susan asked.

"Well, according to Vanderhoff, after things went quiet, he went to take a look. He found Skowler lyin' just inside the door, dead. He'd been shot through the forehead. Robinson lay beside his bunk eight feet away, also shot in the forehead. Two shots, two guns, two bullets."

Zack locked eyes with Tav. "What you're saying is these men died from bullets fired from Colt Frontier six-shooters over 100 years ago, and now these two boys died in almost the exact same way just a few days ago."

Tav's mouth creased into a thin smile. "I reckon that's why Butch Short wanted you in on this."

CHAPTER FOUR

The road north of Hole-In-The-Wall was old asphalt, pitted and worn with tractor tread imprints that sent vibrations up their spines every time the Jeep tires rode over them. Windblown sand piled across the road in the bottom of the deeper arroyos, a smoother but more treacherous surface. When the road ended at the Mojave Road they followed Tav's white SUV to the right. Any suggestion of pavement ended here, but the sand surface was firm and the roadway wide. Off to the north tan cliffs guarded the base of Pinto Mountain, with its rounded barren summit suggesting the top of a monk's head.

Ahead, Tav picked up speed, rolling up a cloud of fine dust the color of muddy coffee. It settled in their hair and layered on their clothing. Zack dropped back; it didn't help. The road deteriorated quickly, forming deep ruts. After a couple of miles it swung abruptly south over a rise, turned east again, and became hub deep sand. The jeep skated side to side; the tires slithering through it like water. Zack fought the wheel; tried to see through the dust, so thick he almost ran into Tav's vehicle, stopped in the roadway.

Tav climbed out, walked back to the Jeep as they pulled up. "You'll want to drop into 4-wheel drive," he said. "We'll turn off the main road here. This next road isn't traveled so much."

As he walked away Susan looked at Zack. "Worse than this?"

"I think that's what he's saying." Zack shifted all the way to low 4-wheel drive.

Susan felt a new respect for Tav's tendency toward understatement. They were glad they engaged the lower gears—the ruts were deep enough to bottom out the Jeep. They plunged down an embankment into a dry streambed, lurched and spun up the bank on the other side.

"At least there's not as much dust," Susan said, trying to look on the bright side. They were moving too slowly to raise any. The two vehicles lurched and slipped their way up a low ridge, leveled off into another set of ruts coming from the east and followed the combined roads south along the ridge spine. Occasional Joshua trees stood in scattered groups like guests at a party, blackbush lined the road. The sand glimmered white, the Joshua tree needles were a dark green, the sky deep blue.

Susan took it all in. "Who said the desert is drab."

They couldn't guess their destination; there was nothing out there. A few lonesome pinyon pine dotted the flats, and low bushes of black and grey scrub and white alkali playa lay as far as the eye could see. Susan saw no indication of human habitation. The road turned, dropped into a hollow, rose again and there was a fence, a gate, beyond it a circular concrete container four feet tall. They had arrived at Hidden Springs.

Ahead, Tav stopped, climbed out and walked back to the Jeep.

"I was expecting to see a cabin," Zack said.

"The cabin disintegrated years ago. You can find foundation stones in the brush if you look hard enough, and the old windmill is still there." He pointed up to a tall cottonwood tree. Susan had to look twice to see the structure of the windmill buried behind the limbs of the tree.

"People have dropped lots of junk here over the years." Tav kicked a rusted coffee can. "You see by the

32

yellow tape over there it's still a crime scene. Follow me;
I'll show you where the boys were found."

Susan and Zack climbed out of the Jeep, stretched,
and followed Tav through the gate. The yellow tape ran
around the well, up a rise, around a hillside of blackbush
and back to the well from the other side. Between the well
and the tree the sand was level for a couple hundred feet.

"That's where it happened." Tav pointed to the
level area. "The boys were lying at opposite sides of this
flat space"—he pointed—"there and there."

Susan studied the two spots, patches of dry sand
now imbued with horrible significance. The soft ground
was impressed with the shape of the bodies where they had
fallen, colored by small rust-like spots where blood had
seeped into the sand. There were footprints scattered in
between. Susan felt a shiver; something about the place
brought a sense of dread to her, something beyond the
recent deaths.

"They couldn't have gotten much further apart,"
Zack said, glancing from one end of the level space to the
other. "There's nowhere to go."

Tav nodded. "I got the feeling neither was real
aggressive. It was like they reluctantly played out their
parts."

"With incredible accuracy," Susan added, her tone
sardonic.

Zack began a long walk around the periphery of
the yellow tape. His moves were meticulous and glacially
slow. He studied the ground, examined creosote twigs,
holly leaves, dug under brush, even studied the sky once or
twice.

"What's he doin'?"

33

"He's looking for anything the others might have missed." She saw Tav's reaction, realized he was offended. "Don't feel bad if he finds something. There's just one better tracker in the entire country—Zack's friend Eagle Feather, the one who taught him." She gave Tav a cheerful smile.

Tav didn't reply. He stood with his arms folded across his chest, his eyes on Zack as he worked. The FBI agent didn't appear to notice their stares; he was totally immersed in his inspection. By the time he completed his circumnavigation of the yellow tape, a half hour had elapsed. He came over to them, looked at his watch; an apologetic look came to his face. "Sorry. I got caught up, lost track of time."

"What did you learn you didn't know before?" Tav demanded.

"Not much," Zack said.

Tav's face showed grim satisfaction.

"There's been so much traffic in and out of this place most of the original footprints are pretty much obliterated." Zack glanced at Tav. "There was the old guy on the ORV, you said? He apparently went back to get his buddies before he called it in. They parked their machines over there, walked up to within fifteen feet or so from the bodies over on that side." Zack pointed beyond the windmill tree. "Three machines, one carrying two riders, judging from tread depth."

He turned to Tav. "Who came next? Was it you, Tav? I found Vibram tread like yours in several places around the bodies, and up where the old guy had been."

Tav nodded. "I was first. Emmerson, the old guy, called me on his cell, waited for me over there. His friends stayed back beyond the hill. They were good about that.

When I arrived there were no other prints near the victims."

"None, eh?" Zack eyed Tav. "Just the victims' own prints?"

Tav nodded.

Zack stared at the sand. "After you there was a whole flock of people, probably all investigators."

"That's right."

Zack raised an eyebrow. "You must not get a lot of crime out here."

"Not at this level."

Zack nodded. "I tried to find footprints put there before the crowd came along. The investigators' prints, being more recent, have sharper edges, better defined. The older prints are a bit more windblown, blurred. I didn't find any of the older prints around the victims. I did find older prints up on the far slope there."

"Are they the victims' prints?" Susan asked.

"Maybe. Probably. There were sneakers and flat-soled cowboy boots in different sizes. There are hoof prints by the fence. Seemed the boys rode up from the south." Zack pointed. "The victims made a couple of trips here over time, tied their horses to that fence, and walked together over to the tree. After that they walked one after the other across that slope, then came down to the flat sand. On the first visit, they both walked over there." He pointed to where the victim closest to the tree had lain.

"Anything else?"

"There were some older prints made by two different cowboy boots back up on the slope, narrower, longer heels. One heavier guy, made a deeper impression, one a bit lighter, with a smaller foot."

"But only the victims came down to this flat area?" Susan asked.

"That's right." Zack put up a hand to shade his eyes, gazed out over the landscape. "Looks like we have company."

Susan and Tav swung their heads to look. Occasional Joshua trees or acacia protruded above the blackbush and sage like a pull in an old sweater. Beyond, out on the flatland, Susan saw a dust cloud. They watched it grow.

"The Kellogg Ranch is out that way a few miles. I'd guess that's Jim Hatchett's truck," Tav said. He glanced at his two companions. "Jim's the ranch owner."

"Has anybody identified the two victims, or know where they came from?" Zack asked.

Tav scratched his head. "Not for sure yet. None of the ranchers around here seemed to know' em. There are some sheep camps, though. The herders come from all over the place; run-a-ways, illegals—the owners hire whoever they can get, no questions asked, then send them out in the high country with the sheep and nobody sees 'em again for months at a time. Likely those boys worked for one of those outfits."

Fifteen minutes later a battered pickup skidded to a stop on the rise beyond the cottonwood. Two men climbed out, came and stood in front of the truck, one slightly behind the other. The second one had a rifle in the crook of his arm. They stood, looked down the slope at them.

"C'mon, I'll introduce you," Tav said. He led the way around the tape and up the slope. The newcomers watched their approach. Both were built like whipcord: skinny and long, their features burned almost black by the sun. The man in front had intensely blue eyes, startling in contrast to his darkened skin. He stood erect, the posture of a man accustomed to power. The face of the man with the rifle was weasel thin, his hair black, eyes coffee, lips a thin line slashed above a sharp chin. No laugh lines there.

"Hello, Mr. Hatchett," Tav said.

"Hey yourself, Davidson. Who you got with you there?" Hatchett studied Zack.

"This here is Zack Tolliver. He's with the FBI. That's Dr. Apgar, his friend."

Hatchett didn't offer to shake hands. "I'm Jim Hatchett. This here is Bronc, my foreman. I run a cattle ranch south of here. Why's the FBI interested in a couple of guys who decided to shoot each other way out here?"

"We're not," Zack said. He nodded toward Tav. "He is."

Hatchett turned to Tav. "Thought you had this all wrapped up with a ribbon around it."

"Not my doing. Butch brought Agent Tolliver in. He was thinking a few things didn't add up."

"Like what?"

Tav's eyes looked off across the valley. "You'll have to ask him, I guess. He asked me to bring Agent Tolliver up here to see the crime scene."

Hatchett stared hard a Tav for a few seconds. "An' you got no idea what Butch Short is thinking."

"Guess not."

Bronc stirred. His voice was raspy. "We got to get access to this well."

Tav put his palms in the air. "I can't authorize you to go in there until Short and Sheriff Connolly give the okay."

Jim Hatchett studied the ground, brought his head back up slow, looked at Tav. "Seems to me bringing the FBI in here is gonna stretch things out."

"I'm not here in an official capacity, just as a consultant. It won't be me holding anything up." Zack's voice was soft and steady.

Bronc stared at Zack. "See that you don't."

Hatchett reached a hand toward Bronc. "Easy, Bronc. These boys know our cattle need this water. They'll do the best they can. Right, boys?" Hatchett's smile was thin.

"We'll do what we can," Tav said.

"I'm sure you will." Jim Hatchett turned and walked back to the truck. After a long look at Zack, Bronc followed. The truck spun around, raised a large cloud of dust, and headed back the way it came.

"Nice folks," Zack said.

"Desert folk tend to be spare with their speech and maybe talk their minds more than most."

"Is that an euphemism for rude?" Susan asked. Neither man spoke. Susan looked off at the horizon. Where the sky had been a vibrant blue, it now held clouds. Was that a metaphor? She felt a strange desire to be away from this place. .

CHAPTER FIVE

They followed Tav back, kept on going to Interstate 40 after Tav turned off at Hole-in-the-Wall, then turned east toward Needles. The BLM office was in town just a mile south on Route 95, easy to find. The sun was still hot when they climbed out of the Jeep, despite nearly cocktail hour.

Butch Short came to meet them at the reception desk. He fit his name, at no more than five feet six inches tall, broad shouldered and stocky. He led them back to his office and waved them into a pair of metal folding chairs, settled in behind his desk.

"Thank you for coming on such short notice. I didn't realize you and your wife were on holiday." He smiled at Susan.

Susan made calf's eyes and grasped Zack's arm possessively.

"Oh, no, Susan's not my wife. She's my colleague. We had just presented a workshop in Las Vegas together when you called. I have a wife and child back home."

"My bad. Welcome, Ms. —"

"Apgar, Dr. Susan Apgar," Susan said.

"Welcome, Dr. Apgar. Are you with the FBI as well?"

"I'm a professor of Anthropology. I teach in the California University system."

"She's being modest," Zack said. "She's a department chair and she is well published."

Butch shaped his hands like a steeple under his chin. "So you met with Tav today?"

"Yes, we did."

"He didn't put you off too much?" Butch grinned.

"Not so much, really," Zack said. "He's taciturn, but seems a man with his feet on the ground."

"If not in it," Susan said.

Butch laughed.

Zack glanced at Susan. "We visited the crime scene. I've a few questions for you."

"No surprise."

"What evidence do you have those boys didn't shoot each other, beyond the improbability of it?"

Short gave a grimace. "Good question. It goes right to the heart of the matter. Some of us had a hard time believing those boys could shoot one another with such accuracy at that distance. They sure didn't look like professionals. Later, when we got the bodies back here to the morgue, the people over there thought the entrance and exit wounds were messier than a factory produced .44-caliber bullet ought to make. It bothered them. The sheriff and I went back up to the crime scene, spent a long time searching the sand for bullets."

Zack raised his eyebrows. "A needle in a haystack."

Butch nodded. "Still, we actually found a bullet in the sand where one of the bodies had been, a few meters beyond it and just a couple of inches deep. The slug was deformed, of course, so we couldn't tell much right then. Buzz Connolly, the County Sheriff, brought it to the lab. The lab boys test fired the victims' revolvers, compared the bullets. They couldn't get a match. They found intrusions in the lead material, imperfections that wouldn't be in bullets from a modern manufacturer. The technician figured it might have come from a home mold, the cartridge hand packed. That began to explain why it didn't travel as far as one might expect after passing through the skull. Powder loads in home packed cartridges can vary."

"If that particular bullet killed the victim."

Short smiled at Zack, nodded. "Right. The lab guys tried to determine the age of the bullet, but they couldn't tell. They began to think it might have been a coincidence, finding it there, a bullet left from the days ranchers couldn't order them from Sears & Roebuck. They figured the bullets that killed the boys were still out there."

Zack nodded. "So we don't know for sure."

"Maybe, maybe not." Short shook a finger. "They took a long shot and made another discovery. They found microscopic bits of other stuff on the bullet, tissue residue, maybe enough to run DNA tests with mini-STRs. They sent it along with DNA samples from both boys to the Sheriff's office in LA yesterday morning. Those guys have something called a 24-locus multiplex STR kit. The full results will take a while, however they believe the tissue sample is recent. That knocks out the idea of it being some random old bullet. Unless full DNA testing reverses this, it appears that bullet killed that boy." Butch raised his palms. "Now you see why you're here?"

Zack shot a glance at Susan, looked back at Short. "What do you make of it?"

Butch Short slowly shook his head. "I don't know what to make of it. The boys packed .44s, alright, but not a match to this bullet with the recent tissue stuck to it." He shrugged.

"You think there was a third person?"

Short stared back at Zack. "It's a very real possibility."

Susan glanced at both men. "How does that work? The guys walk together to the clearing after tying off their horses, split and walk in opposite directions, turn and face each other. They fire at each other and miss, then a third person shoots each of them in the forehead with an ancient .44 caliber pistol and walks away without leaving any footprints?"

Zack looked at Susan, his lips slightly upturned with amusement. "That works for me. Let's go home."

Susan ignored him, her eyes on Short. "Could that .44 bullet have been shot from a rifle?"

Butch gave her a long look, nodded slowly. "Interesting you should think of that—my thought as well. My firearm expert tells me the .44 caliber revolver was popular back in the day in part because the .44-.40 cartridges were interchangeable with the Remington repeating rifle. You could carry a pistol and a rifle and just one belt of cartridges."

"But wouldn't the longer barrel of the rifle increase the velocity?" Susan asked. "We're talking about a situation where velocity had to have decreased."

Short shook his head. "The barrel increases the accuracy, I don't know if that's true about the velocity. And there are a lot of possible variables, like the size of the powder load or the age of the powder."

Zack stood. "We've got to go find a motel room for the night, get some dinner. I'll make this easy for you. You've got an interesting situation here. We don't need to sign a contract, I'll agree to assist you for my costs and whatever donation you think I deserve at the end of the investigation. That way, since this is not yet an official FBI investigation, I won't be seen to be double dipping. If it does come to involve the FBI, I guess you won't need to pay me at all." Zack smiled at Short. "Win, win."

"And Dr. Apgar...?"

"I'll take responsibility for her costs, for as long as she remains involved." Zack looked at Susan. "That work for you?"

Susan nodded.

Butch showed them out. "Any idea where you'll start?"

"Not a clue. I'll need to revisit the crime scene and think some more about it. I'll be in touch."

They all shook hands.

Zack and Susan found neighboring rooms in a small motel, just steps from the highway, near a McDonalds. The motel manager put them on to an excellent Mexican cafe. After dropping off their things, they located the restaurant and began with a round of house margaritas.

Zack raised his glass to Susan. "You sure you have time to get involved in this?"

"What's the matter, you don't want me hanging around?"

"Hardly that."

"My next engagement is a week away, as it happens. It's good to be on sabbatical, set my own schedule. So, yes, I have the time." She arched her eyebrows. "For as long as it holds my interest, of course."

"What are your deductive powers telling you?"

"Not much. I require more data. For instance, the evidence we have so far strongly suggests to me someone else fired the fatal shots. Yet they found no shell casings, no other evidence other than the bullet to support that. Then there's the angle of fire. To kill both boys the murderer would have to stand directly between them, but you found nothing to support that, did you?"

Zack shook his head.

UNDER DESERT SAND

"So we need to resolve that. I'm also interested in the bullet they found. Mr. Short said they found just the one. If it was fired by a third person, where are the bullets from the victims' guns? When, why, and at what were they firing? Did they really shoot at each other and miss?"

Zack licked salt off the rim of his margarita. "I thought of that. To be honest, I find it amazing they found anything at all in that sand."

"I would think a thorough search with metal detectors set at the right depth might eventually meet with success," Susan countered. "It's a matter of diligence. How much effort did they put into it?"

Zack gave her a pensive look. "You may be right, although the bullets from the victims' guns, assuming they were wide of the mark, could have traveled a long way." He thought a moment. "Then there's the second victim. Where is the bullet that killed him? If I remember correctly, the ground behind the victim nearest the windmill sloped up. If the shot meant for him didn't go too wild, it might be buried there somewhere. A .44 or .45 caliber bullet shot directly into packed sand will penetrate about 6 inches. A bullet having lost much of its velocity shouldn't be that deep." He cocked an eye at Susan. "What do you know about using a metal detector?"

She laughed. "I'm not sure I know what one looks like."

"We'll be evenly matched, in that case," Zack said.

After dinner, as they walked slowly across the parking lot to the Jeep, they paused to experience the evening. The pavement was still warm, the air cool. The moon was bright overhead, almost full. There was the smell of sage in the air. Susan breathed deeply, impulsively grabbed Zack's arm. "It's perfect, isn't it?"

Zack stared into the distance. "It's a beautiful night. I'm going to call Eagle Feather. Maybe he can find something I didn't at the crime scene. A lot hinges on that."

Susan rolled her eyes. "You sure know how to blow a mood."

CHAPTER SIX

Colter Budster had no patience for musty lecture halls and bald professors who clearly wished they were elsewhere almost as much as he did. His ambiguity of purpose didn't help matters, either. He'd heard his parents argue the first year of college was often like this, generalized, repetitive, a rehash of his last year of high school. The focus will sharpen, they said. Your path will become clear to you. Well, it hadn't. Part way through his second term nothing had changed, no stir of motivation lifted him beyond this miasma; no epiphany set him upon a life road.

Col—no one ever used his full name—did notice a change, not in himself, but beyond the school walls all around him. It was spring in Madison, Wisconsin. The smell of it was in the air, sweet and seductive. The world beckoned and Col listened. One morning he wrote a brief note to his parents, thanked them for all they had tried to do, and headed west.

Col had a few hundred dollars; it saw him as far as Colorado. There he found work as a carpenter's helper. Tall, rangy and strong, he could easily do the grunt work. Brighter than most, he quickly learned the trade. When jobs disappeared in one town, he moved to the next. The summer solstice came and went, the days shortened, he reflexively followed the sun as he moved from job to job. By September, he was in Las Cruces, New Mexico.

In this town he found the classroom that had eluded him at the University of Wisconsin. The area's rich history, from Spanish miners and travelers along El Camino Real to Billy the Kid and Geronimo; the art galleries, museums and performing arts; the breweries and authentic Mexican food all called to him. He found kindred spirits among the diverse young people he met at performances and in coffee shops, restaurants and pubs, in his classes at New Mexico State University. Las Cruces was growing, and presented more than enough jobs for a talented carpenter. Col settled in for the winter, content with his life and 350 days of sunshine.

He met Julio while hiking in the Organ Mountains, dramatic needle-like peaks just beyond the city, on the trail to the Needle summit. Not a climber, Col did not expect the class-4 scramble up the last bit to the summit. Julio, resting from a solo climb, offered to set a top rope on the pitch as security and Col accepted, not at all content to turn back so close to his goal. The two rested together on the summit, marveled at the view, enjoyed the beauty of the day, and experienced all those qualities of youth and spirit imbued upon them by the moment, a moment that initiated a strong friendship.

Julio offered to teach Col to climb, who eagerly accepted. They spent the remainder of that winter on the crags, as work allowed. Col learned quickly, and as he did, more routes opened up for the team. Julio left his YMCA quarters and moved in with his friend in a small rented house. Col's sporadic carpentry contracts more than supported their lifestyle. The odd jobs Julio worked to support his climbing habit now became a luxury rather than a necessity.

With late spring came an influx of tourists, and warmer weather. The mountain peaks, comfortable in the 50's in the winter, became uncomfortably hot in the 80's and 90's. Discouraged by crowds and the heat, the young men discussed their options. It seemed serendipitous when a letter arrived from Julio's uncle in Mexico City offering a summer job. His uncle owned sheep in a remote area of southern California, in the Mojave Desert. The sheep needed to pasture in the high country for the summer. The shepherd who normally cared for the herd quit suddenly; the uncle would pay a good wage if Julio would take over.

"What do you know of tending sheep?" Col asked.

"I helped my uncle with his herds in Mexico as a child. I know all I need to know. I will ask him if he will hire you as well. In the high pasture with the sheep all summer there is nowhere to spend our money, and so we will have plenty for climbing in the fall. "

Julio's uncle agreed to pay two salaries, so long as the boys took possession of the herd immediately. Col and Julio left the very next day for Kelso Depot in California to collect the herd.

CHAPTER SEVEN

Zack didn't sleep well, something about the texture of the sheets. By six am he was at the desk in his small room inhaling the steamy aroma of the motel coffee, not daring to drink it. His phone on the desk vibrated. He glanced at it: Butch Short.

"Wake you?" Butch asked.

"Hardly."

"Like to join me for breakfast?"

"As long as you promise me some decent coffee."

"I can do that."

The pavement was still cool from the night before, the dry grass and damp sand smell of the morning desert fresh and pleasant. Zack decided to let Susan sleep in, climbed in the Jeep and followed Short's directions to the Wagon Wheel Restaurant.

The moment he stepped through the door bacon and coffee aromas surrounded him in a delicious cloud. He spotted Butch several tables away. A stranger was with him. Zack walked along between the rustic log chairs and the shiny pine-hewn tables to where they sat, coffee cups in their hands.

Short looked up. "Morning, Zack. Sorry to roust you out so early. Allow me to introduce Dan Singletree."

Singletree stood. He was tall, had the look of an Indian, high cheekbones and a broad face, brown eyes. Zack grasped the man's hand, got a firm grip in return. When Singletree resumed his seat, Zack dropped into an empty log chair, its seat carved from a single chunk of thick wood.

"Dan is a Chief of the band of Chemehuevi Indians living in the Colorado River Reservation, down near Havasu. He came to Needles to make inquiries about our investigation. I told him his timing couldn't be better."

"What is your interest in the crime, sir?" Zack asked.

"Call me Dan." Singletree paused when the waitress arrived, waited for Zack to order coffee, watched her bustle away, turned back to him. "To answer your question, it's not the crime that interests me, it's the location of the crime."

"Oh?" Zack was surprised.

Short spooned more sugar into his coffee. "The Chemehuevi people live down on the reservation south of here now, but before that they lived up in the high Mojave." He glanced at Dan.

Dan nodded. "I'll give you a little background."

The waitress was back, placed coffee in front of Zack. "I'll be right back to take your order," she said.

Zack reached for the milk, nodded to Singletree he was ready to listen.

"My ancestors came from desert tribes. The Chemehuevi are the southernmost branch of the Southern Paiute. They separated from the rest of the Southern Paiute way back. After that, they divided into the north and south Chemehuevi. My people were the southernmost tribe. Our land was the entire area of what today is the Mojave Preserve. The Mojave Indians were our neighbors on the Colorado River, but there was bad blood between us. So bad, each tribe had its own trails to the same places just to avoid each other." Dan gave a wry smile. "Sometimes the trails were just a few hundred feet apart, running parallel. My people and the Mojave traveled far across the desert to the Mojave River and beyond to trade, sometimes walking all the way to Cajon Pass and on to the

Pacific Coast. There is very little water along the trails between the Colorado River and the Mojave River. It was necessary for the Chemehuevi and Mojave to use the same watering places. That did not work well."

"They fought?"

Singletree nodded. "They often ambushed each another. It was necessary for all the desert people to approach the springs with great caution. Often the choice given them was die of thirst or be killed by the enemy."

"Yet they still traveled those routes?" Short's eyebrows arched.

"They had little choice. Each tribe needed resources from the western desert and beyond to survive. Neither tribe was very large. Most days the springs were deserted and quite safe." Singletree sipped his coffee. "Some were more dangerous than others. Of all the watering places, one called Coyote Spring had the worst reputation for danger. It was said Coyote himself used the spring and liked to play tricks on travelers. Some saw Coyote as a protector of the water, others as a schemer who liked to cause problems. Either way, people from both tribes knew the reputation of Coyote Spring. No one wanted to stay at the water hole after night fell. They would pack all the water they could carry to a camp well away." He paused, gave a brief smile. "Today Coyote Spring is called Hidden Springs."

The waitress hovered, ready to take their orders.

Dan was ready. "I'm having the Big Mess Omelet."

Zack raised an eyebrow.

"It's the best deal on the menu, if you like meat," Singletree said.

"Then I'll have it too."

"Huevos Rancheros for me." Butch said. He grinned at Zack. "That's what I always order.

The waitress busied off.

Zack turned to Singletree. "Are you suggesting Coyote had something to do with the murders at Hidden Spring?"

"Maybe, in a way. My people will tell you Coyote still guards the well. They believe a shaman buried an object of great power there during the Mystic Era, perhaps a "crooked stick" or Por̲o, and those who come to steal it meet death. Often there is truth to the old stories. It is true many people died there, long before the first white man came. You White Men believe history began when you arrived. You people don't look beyond yourselves."

Zack pondered the story. "Maybe this is more my kind of case than I first thought."

Butch didn't appear amused. "You came up here to tell me Coyote hangs out at that spring and caused the death of those boys? What am I supposed to do with that?"

"You need to do your history homework. You don't have to believe Coyote or a spirit lives at the spring. You do need to understand how such beliefs influence people," Dan said.

"I still don't get you."

Zack turned to Butch. "It's kinda like going into Iraq without understanding anything about the history of the tribes there, or their disparate beliefs."

Dan nodded his agreement.

Short opened his mouth to say more, but the waitress was back with three huge steaming plates and a scattering of side dishes. It was a good ten minutes before anyone was able to talk.

The first was Butch Short. "Dan, I get the general idea, but you're gonna have to be a lot more specific."

Dan put down his fork. "I will try to spell it out. If you believe something bad will happen, it is probably going to happen. Take the 1905 gunfight at Hidden Springs. Before those two gunfighters met up, there was a lot of talk around the valley about who had the fastest gun, the steadiest nerve. The Chemehuevi already knew the reputation of the spring. We knew when those guys found themselves face to face there they didn't have a choice. They were gonna die. Coyote waits there for fools like those gunmen, so it's no surprise to me." Dan turned to Zack. "What do you think, Agent Tolliver? They say you understand the power of Coyote."

Zack was surprised. "I didn't know my reputation made it this far. Let's just say I don't discard any possibility out of hand. I've learned to wait and see. In the case of those gunfighters, I can understand how everyone's expectations might have helped bring about the confrontation. But I'm enough white man to think there's maybe more to it than just Coyote."

Dan chuckled. "Well played, Mr. FBI."

Butch shook his head. "It's still gonna take a lot of convincing for me to see Coyote behind every Joshua tree. These two young men who died weren't there by accident. I double damn guarantee you something was going on to draw them there. An' someone else knows about it."

Zack looked sidelong at Singletree. "Why do I feel there's something you haven't mentioned?"

Dan gave a half smile. "There is, but it might be too steep a hill even for you to climb."

"Try me."

UNDER DESERT SAND

"Okay then." Dan sat back from his plate. "My people say Coyote still lives at that spring. People who have seen him describe a cross between a human and an animal, sometimes walking upright, sometimes on all fours. Some say it is partially covered in fur, some say it is hairless and thick skinned like a reptile."

Short groaned. "Oh, wonderful." He shook his head. "Maybe your ancestors claimed to see it to keep others away from the water at the spring."

"Mojave people have seen it, too."

Short became impatient. "Thanks for all the background, Chief, but we really need to concentrate on what's happening today, not ancient mythology."

"I do not speak of ancient mythology," Dan said, "unless you consider last month ancient."

CHAPTER EIGHT

Susan's cell phone roused her from deep sleep. She yawned, stretched an arm to the bedside table, exploring the unfamiliar surface with her hand until she found the vibrating instrument. "Hello?"

"Stay away from Hidden Springs."

"I'm sorry, what?"

"Stay away from this case. Go home."

"Who is this?"

"This is the only warning you get. Tell your buddy."

The voice was gone.

Susan was wide-awake now. Her pulse raced, her brain whipped from numbing sleep to adrenalin-charged reality. Her eyes swept the unfamiliar room, the chain-locked door. She checked for the caller's number: her phone said: "No Name, No Number".

A loud thump sounded on the door. Her heart flipped, her mind blanked. She fought through a fog of panic. She started to call Zack.

"Susan, time to wake up." The voice through the metal door came muffled yet familiar.

"Eagle Feather?" Oh thank God. "Wait a minute, I'll be right there."

Not bothering with slippers, Susan threw on her dressing gown and ran to the door. She opened to the chain, slid it off, and put her arms around the man waiting there.

Eagle Feather stood, his arms pinned to his side by Susan until she finally loosed her grip.

"I'm so glad to see you," Susan said.

"So it seems."

Susan tugged Eagle Feather into the room. "Come, close the door. I'll call Zack to come over."

"Don't bother, he is not there. I tried his room first." Eagle Feather gave a glance around the tiny room, looked a question at her. "What's going on?"

"Someone just called and threatened me. He said to leave this case and go home." She took a deep breath to calm herself. "I suppose you know what we are involved in here, since it was you recommended Zack to the BLM agent."

"Butch Short and the double homicide?"

"Yes."

"Zack called me last night. He said bring Big Blue, he needed our skills. Since I obviously don't have a life of my own, I came right out here, drove through the night." Eagle Feather's gaze stayed on Susan. "That call has upset you. Zack said there might be hostility; apparently he was right. What will you do?"

"I—well, I don't know. It just happened. I haven't had time to think about it."

"Is there a reason you have to be here?"

"No, not really. Zack invited me along. He thought aspects of this case might interest me." Susan was standing this entire time. Now she sat on the edge of the bed.

Eagle Feather removed his black reservation hat with its single feather, set it on the desk and sat down. "What did this voice on the phone say to you?"

"Just what I said. Go home. Stay away from this case. Stay away from Hidden Springs."

"What is Hidden Springs?"

Susan launched into a fast summary of events. When she was done, Eagle Feather nodded.

"I see now why Zack wanted Big Blue. He must think there was another person present during the shooting. He hopes Blue and I can find some sign of that person." He paused. "Do you know where Zack is now?"

Susan shook her head.

Eagle Feather took out his phone. "Hello, Zack. Blue and I are with Susan in her room. She has had a scare. Are you available for breakfast?"

Eagle Feather put his phone away, stood. "I will go get Blue. He will want his breakfast too." He gave her a sympathetic look. "Zack will come soon. We will talk about this at breakfast." He paused. "I could eat a horse."

An hour later they were all at the Wagon Wheel, full plates of steaming food covering the table. They left Blue, fed and watered, stretched across the front seat of Eagle Feather's truck in the shade. The big bloodhound had a joyous reunion with Zack, almost knocking him over while sloshing a large, wet tongue across his face.

Zack was happy to see Eagle Feather. "You two eat your fill. I'll have a cup of coffee. I already ate a Big Mess Omelet." He grinned. "That was more than enough." He turned to Eagle Feather. "I'm glad you came. This case may become interesting."

"How much do you pay, White Man?"

"A tall beer?"

"Sounds good to me. When do we start?"

"Right after you eat your breakfast." Zack's blue eyes took a mournful cast. "Have you seen Libby? How is she?"

Eagle Feather's fork paused part way to his mouth. "She's good, Zack, she's doing fine." Their eyes met momentarily, drifted away.

"Susan's got some news," Eagle Feather said, his tone brisk, moving on.

Between bites, Susan told Zack about her alarming wake-up call. No, she did not recognize the voice. It didn't sound angry or emotional at all, just matter of fact. Yes, it was a man's voice.

"Susan, there is no reason you have to stay," Zack said, "I don't want you looking over your shoulder the entire time."

Susan was angry. She was over her fright now, felt safe with two strong men and a dog to protect her. "No whacko caller is going to drive me away; just the opposite." She set her lip. "I'm here for the long run now."

Zack regarded her. "You are the stubborn one—but I'm glad to have you."

After breakfast, and a trip to the hardware store, they all piled into the Jeep. Three humans, a dog, and a metal detector were a tight squeeze, but with the top removed they were comfortable enough. Susan sat on the rear bench seat with Blue, insisting Eagle Feather have the more comfortable front seat to stretch his legs after his long drive from Tuba City. Blue sloshed a tongue over her face as a welcome. That sealed the deal, to her mind. She would stay.

Eagle Feather probed, Susan and Zack answered his questions about the investigation until the Hole-in-the-Wall turn-off appeared.

"You plan to stop by for the ranger?" he asked.

Zack shook his head. "I don't want anybody around when you and Blue do your thing. I know you have no stake in this, but I can't say the same for anyone else."

Susan leaned forward. "You don't trust Tav?"

58

"My instincts say yes, but I don't want anyone to influence our findings, even with a facial expression."

"He doesn't have any of those," Susan said. She leaned back, took in the surrounding landscape. It was mid-morning, the sun bright, the sky flawless blue. A slight alkali taste of dust was on her lips. The whipping wind was cool, but she knew it would become dry and hot later on. Except for clumps of sage, the land seemed completely empty.

The jeep bounced onto the Hidden Springs access road, dropped into the dry creek bed, skidded up the far bank. When they arrived at the gate, it was closed. A large padlock hung on it.

Zack stared. "That wasn't here yesterday."

"Someone trying to protect the crime scene?" Eagle Feather asked.

Zack shook his head. "I've been granted full access by Tav and Butch Short. They didn't mention a lock nor did they give me a key."

"Who else, then?"

Zack stared around at the higher land to the south. "There was a rancher who wasn't so keen on our presence." He slid out of the Jeep. "Well, they can't keep us from the crime scene. I think the spanner wrench might do the trick." Zack walked around and opened the back, located the tool under the floor panel, lifted it out.

Eagle Feather came back and put a hand his arm. "I wouldn't break through that gate just now."

Zack looked at his friend in surprise.

"Somebody just might be hoping you'll do that to give them an excuse," Eagle Feather said. "Don't look now, but there's someone near that tall pinyon pine to my

59

right at about one o'clock. I saw a reflection, something metallic was moving."

Zack kept his eye on Eagle Feather's face. "A set up, you think?"

Eagle Feather nodded. "Perfect excuse. Somebody breaking through someone's fence."

Zack put down the wrench. The two men walked back to the front of the Jeep. "Ideas?"

"We can make him come to us," Eagle Feather said. He glanced at Susan, including her. "We will wait him out; raise the hood of the Jeep and study the engine as if there is a problem, see what he does."

They played out the scenario as Eagle Feather suggested. It took a half hour for the would-be ambusher to give up and ride over to them.

The man on the horse was Bronc. He rode up as if he'd just happened along. A rifle was in a scabbard on the saddle.

"You folks need a hand?" he asked. He eyed Eagle Feather.

"No, Bronc, just letting the engine cool while we wait for Tav to open the gate for us," Zack said.

"Who's your friend?"

"This is Eagle Feather, a colleague."

"You FBI too?"

"No, Navajo."

"We ain't got Navajo around here."

"I guess you got one now."

Bronc stared, then climbed down. He wore a pistol in a holster low on his hip "I reckon I can open that gate for you. Tav don't have a key. This here is Kellogg Ranch land."

"I thought it was a government preserve."

Bronc eyed Zack. "That too, but we got a grandfathered lease on it. We try to keep strays away." He walked to the gate, turned a key in the lock and swung it open. With a mock bow, he waved them through.

Once they were inside, Bronc swung the gate closed again. He set the lock in place. "I'll just leave it unlocked like this; when you leave push it closed." He climbed back into the saddle, gazed at Zack. "We'd shore like you to finish up and move along. Ain't no mystery here, unless you spend time trying to make one." He reined his horse around and rode back the way he'd come.

Zack grunted. "If I were a betting man, I'd say that's the fellow made the call to you this morning," he said to Susan. "Does the voice sound familiar?"

Susan shook her head. "I really can't say. It all happened too fast."

Zack walked to the yellow tape, scanned the area. "Nothing appears disturbed. Let's get to work." He glanced off at the far trees. "I think we can assume we'll have an audience from now on."

.

CHAPTER NINE

The boys' truck died in Kingman, Arizona. Fortunately, they'd stored most of their belongings with a climbing friend in Albuquerque before heading west on I-40. After the truck wheezed its last, they sold it to a local in Kingman who had a friend headed to Las Vegas. They caught a ride. From there, they hitched south on Interstate 15. Their ride dropped them at Primm, Nevada. Once it grew dark, rides vanished. The boys booked a cheap room at Whiskey Pete's Casino and headed to the bar.

"Drinks here cost more than the room," Julio said, looking at the menu.

"Burgers cost more than the drinks," Col said.

The man next to Julio glanced at the boys. "You're in the wrong place. Go to the Food Court. There's a Mac's, Dairy Queen, all that stuff. If you want a drink, go into town to the liquor store. My advice."

It was good advice. At the food court, they each bought a five-dollar foot long at Subway.

"Wonder how hard it will be to get a ride tomorrow on I-15," Col said between bites. "The traffic really flies down that road."

Julio 's idea was to work a ride in Whiskey Pete's parking lot. "You figure everyone here is going either north or south, there's no choice, meaning fifty percent are headed our way. If we stand on the shoulder of I-15 nobody will even see us."

"Where are you boys going?" The man at the next table was pale white, his blue eyes watery.

"We need to get to Kelso Junction," Col said.

The man shook his head. "Good luck. That's down in the Preserve. You'll be lucky to catch someone happens to be going there. You'll end up dumped on the Interstate in the middle of the desert. You don't want that."

Julio moaned. "You're telling us we're stuck here before we even get started."

"Not really." The man wiped his mouth, leaned toward them. "I been where you boys been, more than once." He grinned. "Fact is, by tomorrow morning, I'll likely have less money than you got now." He leaned closer. Col smelled the whiskey even past the cheeseburger. "Here's what you do. I'll meet you here for breakfast; give you a ride across the highway over to the Union Pacific Railroad. You can hop a freight car."

"The train?" The boys looked at each other.

"Sure, why not? It slows to a crawl at the state border for a long climb up the grade. It goes directly to Kelso. Time was it was a major stop for soldiers during the war. It still stops there, and even when it doesn't, it's slow enough to hop off."

The man was true to his word. When they arrived at the food court they found him right where he said he'd be, smiling. He'd done well at the tables, as it turned out, and treated them to breakfast. Then he drove them on a dirt road along the Nevada/California border as far as the Union Pacific tracks.

"Just wait here," the man said. "Don't be fooled by the cool air, the sun is hot. Stay in the shade of these trees and go easy on those water bottles. You're gonna need all that water." As he started to drive off, he stopped, rolled down the window, called to them. "One more thing. Don't jump a flatcar; you can't get out of the sun on those. Grab a freight car, then you'll have shade." With a wave, he spun off, leaving a spurt of dust.

UNDER DESERT SAND

Turned out, it was easy. Julio had some experience hopping trains, and led the way. Soon they were established in an empty car with the sweet smell of wheat. They stretched out near the door to enjoy the breeze and the scenery.

Several hours later, they saw a cluster of small dusty buildings. "Think this is it?" Col asked.

Julio shook his head. "Remember that picture of the depot? I don't see it."

The Union Pacific tracks paralleled a ribbon of paved road. Desert plants, Yucca and cactus grew right next to the tracks; on the landscape beyond were increasingly large stands of Joshua trees. Dry as it was, they sensed they were at higher altitude. The breeze felt almost cold.

When the train next slowed there was no doubt in their minds they had arrived at the tiny town of Kelso. The depot roof rose above other buildings, its red Spanish tile distinctive.

The diesel engines a quarter mile ahead of their car ground to a stop. The boys jumped out. They were at the edge of town, a strange mix of deserted ghost-town buildings mingled with newer structures, with fresh paint and apparent attempts at upkeep.

They scrambled to the road, walked through town to the depot. The road shimmered in the sun; the cracked and weed-laced sidewalk was empty. No one stirred anywhere until they reached the depot parking lot. Here, people mingled among SUVs, BMWs, and motor homes, tourists making their leisurely way across the Preserve between Interstates 15 and 40. Kelso Depot itself was a large building, a throwback to the golden age of the railroad, with an expansive multi-arched veranda facing the tracks, walls that glistened white in the sun, palm trees and emerald green grass, all in the middle of nowhere.

Col's eyes searched the parking lot, the depot grounds. "So what now? Just walk up to someone and say, 'I'm little Bo-Peep, I've lost my sheep?'"

"Not here. These are all tourists, they wouldn't know. The depot looks like it's a museum. Let's ask someone in there."

An attendant glanced at their dirty, straw flaked clothing, sent them down the road west of town. "There are stockyards over there," she said. "I see cattle, horses, and such from time to time when I drive in to work. I don't remember ever seeing sheep, though."

Outside, Julio started to cross the lawn. Col grabbed his arm, pointed to a sign. It read, "Stay off the grass. Africanized bees come to the irrigation for the water."

"We're not in Kansas anymore," Col said. He had a feeling many things in this land might not be what they seemed.

Just beyond the depot, the main street ended at an intersection. The road here crossed the tracks and wound off into a Joshua tree-filled valley. Beyond it Col saw the high ridges of sand dunes against the pale blue sky. The smell of horses, dust and sage came to his nose. Directly ahead was a dirt service road, a few shacks, and beyond them, Col saw fences. They went that way.

Two horses stood in the corral. A man in a cowboy hat emerged from a shack nearby, stood in the doorway and watched them approach. "Can I help you boys?"

"Yes, sir, we're looking for a herd of sheep," Julio said.

"What's your name, boy?"

65

"Julio Castro, sir."

"Is Roberto Castro your uncle?"

"Yes, sir."

The man walked back into the shack, re-emerged with an envelope in his hand. "This is for you, then," he said. He pointed to the two horses. "Those are yours, too. The tack is in that building over there. It's got your name on it. Don't take nothin' that don't have your name on it. Sign right here, please." The man ripped out the receipt, handed it to Julio and went back into the shack.

The boys stared at each other. Julio slit open the envelope, began to read.

"What's it say?"

"Uncle Roberto says the sheep are being held at a place called Circle Ranch. We have to ride over there to collect them. He's drawn a map."

Col peered over his shoulder. The map amounted to a few inverted 'V's to signify mountains, a few squares drawn to indicate buildings, squiggly lines for streams. An arrow began at the word Kelso and pointed East with little dashes through the mountains. Col glanced up from the map, looked east at the panorama before them. A thick forest of Joshua trees stretched all the way to barren mountain ridges with sharp pinnacles thrust toward the sky. "You got to be kidding."

Julio peeked into the envelope, brought out a slip of paper and handed it to Col. It was a check for $500. "An installment on your first paycheck," he said, grinning.

Col looked at the wilderness around him and laughed. "What am I going to do with this?"

"Not spend money, like we planned. Hold on a minute." Julio walked over to the shack, disappeared inside for a few minutes, returned.

"The wrangler says there's a trail cuts through those trees to a mountain pass. It'll take us into a valley." He pointed to the squares on the map. "This here is Circle Ranch. It's in that valley next to a stream."

"What about supplies?"

"We just got to get there with the food we got. The letter says they'll have provisions at the ranch for us for the next couple of months."

Col shook his head, stared at Julio. "Did I mention I've never ridden a horse before?"

Julio chuckled. "I thought as much. Don't worry. I'll pick out the best horse for you and give you a few pointers. I don't think you'll have much trouble, the horse does all the work." He turned toward the tack building, grinning. "You're gonna have a very sore arse, though."

Col followed him to the building.

Inside, Julio glanced around. "Bring out everything with my name on it. There's blankets, bridles, saddles. Bring all that stuff. I'll fetch the horses."

Once his eyes adjusted to the dark, Col stared at a mountain of equipment. In addition to the tack he saw chaps, hats, bandanas, and wool shirts. There were rifles in saddle scabbards, a pair of binoculars, even belts of cartridges with holsters and pistols. "Holy shit," he whispered.

When he returned to the corral with his first armload of equipment, Julio had a horse at the gate. "That one is yours," he said. "The wrangler says his name is Rat."

"Rat? You picked a horse for me named Rat?"

"He's the gentle one. I don't know where the name came from, but I bet we'll find out."

UNDER DESERT SAND

The mountain of equipment grew near the corral until the shack had been emptied of the gear tagged for them. Then the instruction began.

Col's first lesson was how to saddle a horse and mount it. With help from Julio, he rode Rat around the corral a few times. Next Julio packed up their horses with the gear and rifles. He showed Col how to put on the chaps and the cartridge belt. The hat was large, but Julio rigged it with rawhide string to hold it snug. "Uncle Roberto didn't know your size, so he bought all the clothing to fit me."

Julio smiled and hummed as he worked, obviously at home with horses and the necessary paraphernalia. It was clear he enjoyed Col's bewildered attempt to transform from urban climber to cowboy.

Once Julio was dressed and outfitted, he turned to Col and helped him mount Rat, the act made more difficult by the gear packed behind the saddle. Mounted, his feet in the stirrups, Col felt compressed like ham in a sandwich. Rat turned his head to eye him with a puzzled look.

Julio laughed.

"You're having a great time at my expense."

"Well, yeah, I am." Julio mounted and led off. Rat fell in behind without any encouragement from his novice rider.

A month of riding lessons compressed into a few hours began right then. They followed the road across the tracks and clomped along the pavement until Julio found the trailhead described in the map. They followed it up through the Joshua trees, their fuzzy green branches raised like arms as if to warn them off.

CHAPTER TEN

Tav showed up around one. He pulled up behind the Jeep, climbed out, walked over and stood with hands on hips. He eyed the small mountain of metal artifacts piled up just inside the yellow tape.

"Jim Hatchett called sayin' people were messing with my crime scene. What the hell is that stuff?"

Susan pointed to the metal detector. "I've been looking for bullets."

"Any luck?"

"I guess it depends upon how many old can lids you want," she said, smiling. "But no bullets yet."

Tav grunted. He looked at Zack. "Who's that over yonder with the big dog?"

Eagle Feather and Blue were just visible among the creosote.

"That's my friend Eagle Feather and my tracker dog, Big Blue. We want to see if there is anything more we can learn from this place." Zack stepped over the yellow tape and stood next to Tav. "We met up with Hatchett's man Bronc this morning. He seems to be keeping an eye on this place."

Tav's eyes narrowed. "Any problems?"

"We maybe managed to avoid one."

Tav grunted. "The Kellogg outfit has always shown a proprietary interest in this water hole." His gaze swept across the landscape. "Seems strange, given their time here is growin' short. The government is pushin' grazing stock out as fast as they can, hoping the land will revert to how it looked prior to the ranches. Except for the Kellogg Ranch and several herds of sheep up on the high ground, they've pretty much accomplished that."

UNDER DESERT SAND

An insistent beep from Susan's metal detector caught their attention. She'd worked her way up the slope toward the windmill. They watched as she laid the instrument aside, used a trowel to sift through the sand.

"That's a right energetic little lady there," Tav said.

Zack grinned. "You don't know the half of it. She's worn me to a nub." He glanced at Tav. "You mentioned some sheep. That where the dead boys came from?"

Tav scratched his forehead, sliding his ranger-style flat brim hat back. "Likely."

"Maybe a look up there would help to identify the boys?"

"Been done. Butch and a couple of sheriff's deputies went up there yesterday, found an abandoned camp. They collected some personal belongings; took 'em to the sheriff's office. Forensics is working on them. We know the herd's owner; name's on the grazing lease—he's a Mexican citizen. We've begun inquiries in that direction."

The men's eyes returned to Eagle Feather and Blue, returning through the blackbush.

'Looks like they finished over that way," Zack said. Moments later, Big Blue came sprinting over to Zack and greeted him as if he hadn't seen him in weeks.

"Nice lookin' dog."

"Say howdy to Tav," Zack commanded.

The bloodhound immediately turned to Tav, rose up on hind legs, placed both front paws on the man's shoulders and licked his face. He dropped down again to greet Eagle Feather, just coming up.

Tav wiped his face with the inside of his shirt elbow, spit and grinned. "I swear to you, I already washed up this morning."

Zack turned to his Navajo friend. "Eagle Feather, meet Tav Davidson."

Tav and Eagle Feather shook hands. "Navajo, I hear?"

Eagle Feather scrutinized him. "Zack tells me you're mostly Mojave."

"Got a touch of Chemehuevi—and white man."

Before he could say more Susan was there, a pleased look on her face, something clenched in her hand. Her red cheeks and shiny face framed by damp blonde hair enhanced her attractiveness, a fact apparently not lost on Tav, Zack noticed.

"Found it."

"What did you find?" Zack asked.

"I found a bullet."

All three men stared at Susan. She slowly unclenched her fist. The bullet was on her palm, perfect, no distortions from impact.

"A third bullet," she said.

Zack took it from her hand. "It's perfect, almost as if it was fired into a test cylinder in a forensics lab. Just a guess, but it looks like a .44 caliber."

Tav studied the bullet. "It looks like a factory made bullet." He looked over Susan's head to the neat hole she'd dug in the sandy hillside. "You found it over there?"

She nodded, blue eyes glistening.

Zack studied the scene from the yellow tags where the victims had been to the sandy slope. "That was a wild shot, if the boys were trying to hit each other."

"If that slope hadn't been there for a backstop, you never would have found the bullet," Eagle Feather said.

"I know." Susan shrugged. "It confirms one of the victims fired his weapon toward the other. It also confirms there was a third weapon, since we now have three bullets but the boys fired just one bullet each."

"So what was going on? If they were shooting at each other, one missed badly, yet both ended up dead with a hole in the middle of the forehead. You got one modern bullet and one homemade bullet fired in the same direction, but the homemade bullet kills the boy." Zack wiped sweat from his brow, looked at Eagle Feather. "Did you and Blue learn anything to help us out here?"

"I'll tell you what I know." Eagle Feather squatted and drew some lines in the sand. "This is where the boys stood when they fired their weapons. Blue and I just backtracked them over to here." He drew a longer line at right angles to the position of the two boys, then back across toward the tree. "Seems they rode in together, side-by-side from the direction of that mesa, tied their horses way over at that fence, then walked down to the windmill. They'd come down here at least one other time. It's hard to tell which prints came from their most recent trip. We had to untangle 'em from other riders who came in the same way." He glanced down at the bloodhound at Zack's feet. "Blue helped out with that."

Zack turned to Tav. "Which direction is the sheep camp?"

Tav pointed. "Up beyond that mesa, sure enough."

"So they likely came down from there." Zack glanced at Eagle Feather. "Anything else?"

"Blue caught another scent, followed it to the tree, but I don't know what it was." Eagle Feather shrugged. "Then we walked over to the where I saw the reflection. Someone had hunkered down, left his horse in the gully behind." Eagle Feather pointed. "It is not very far. I checked the line of sight; it is clear not just to us but to the victims." Eagle Feather raised an eyebrow at Zack.

"I'm not sure how that helps us."

"Just sayin'."

Tav turned to Eagle Feather. "If you're suggesting one or both boys had been ambushed, it seems to me a rifle bullet would have done more damage to them."

Zack shook his head. "We thought of that. I checked it out. Seems a .44 caliber bullet is a .44 caliber bullet, whether fired from a pistol at 10 yards, or a rifle at 200 yards. There is no acceleration or de-acceleration to speak of past a certain point, so we can't rule out a third person with a rifle."

Susan handed the bullet to Zack. "I'll go get the metal detector." She turned away.

Zack called after her. "Flag that hole, please. My kit is in the Jeep."

She waved a hand.

"What now?" Tav asked.

Zack rubbed his chin. "I think we should go up to that sheep camp, let Blue sniff around a bit."

Tav shrugged. "If these bodies were the shepherd boys, those sheep will be all to hell and gone by now."

Eagle Feather shook his head. "Maybe not. Sheep have a strong herd instinct, and the boys likely kept a dog or two."

"True enough."

There was a cry from Susan. They looked up. She had dug a second hole, was kneeling over it, the metal detector on the ground next to her. She held up a clenched hand. "I found another bullet."

CHAPTER ELEVEN

At Susan's shout, Zack went over to her. He peered at the second hole in the sand, just a few feet from the first.

He removed his hat, scratched his head. "Four bullets, just two boys, just two shots fired from their guns. I think we can rule out double suicide for good at this point. What kind of bullet is it?"

Susan handed it to him. "It looks just like the other one."

"Looks to me like another factory produced .44 caliber bullet." Zack turned, looked behind him. "It could only have come from one place."

Susan nodded. "The second victim."

"So..." Zack studied the positions marked by yellow tags where the two murdered boys were found. "They both fired at something over here, not at each other."

Susan's eyes narrowed in excitement. "Exactly. We assumed they were fighting a duel because the location of their bodies gave that impression. It might not have happened that way at all. Maybe they happened to be in those two places for some other reason entirely when something threatening appeared here and both boys shot at it."

Zack's mind raced with possibilities. "The timing could be quite different from what we inferred. They weren't necessarily killed right at the moment they fired; they could have been shot later. In fact, one could have been shot well before the other."

Zack met Eagle Feather and Tav on their way over. He dropped the bullet in Tav's hand.

"The only thing not changed with the discovery of these bullets is the position of the bodies," Eagle Feather said. He studied the ground upslope from Susan's holes. "Whatever they shot at left no trace, unless they were extremely poor shots."

"Might have been a rattlesnake in that clump of brush over there," Tav said, pointing. "There's your motive for shooting, and the bullets didn't land so far off the mark in that case."

"That's as good as any other explanation right now," Zack said. "Well, this certainly shakes things up." He smiled at Susan. "Your idea of the metal detector was a good one."

Tav added, almost smiling, "Good work."

Susan might have blushed; Zack couldn't tell with her color already heightened by the heat.

"If we are done congratulating one another, maybe we ought to go take a look at the sheep camp." Eagle Feather had already turned toward the Jeep where Blue was stretched across the rear seat, enjoying the shade.

Zack turned to follow. "You coming?" he asked Tav.

"I'll lead the way with my truck."

"I'll ride with Tav." Susan glanced at him. "If you don't mind..."

"Sure, come along." Tav said.

Zack started up the Jeep, waited for Tav to turn the big SUV around.

Eagle Feather watched. "Something going on there?"

Zack smiled. "With Susan, you never know."

Eagle Feather grinned.

"I'm still not happy with our interpretation of that scene," Zack said, his thoughts dragging him back.

"Me either, White Man. I got to ask myself why those boys separated the way they did."

"You suppose they were searching for something? That patch of level ground is not like the surrounding terrain, almost as if it was made that way for a purpose." He slipped the Jeep into low 4-wheel drive, the engine roared, and they started off after Tav's vehicle.

Eagle Feather stared ahead, musing. "This area must get storms, maybe occasional high winds and rain. The terrain everywhere else is shaped by the weather into shallow arroyos and mounds. Like you say, there's nothing flat and level anywhere else, just there."

"Maybe there was a platform there once? Or a building?"

Eagle Feather shook his head. "Even so, the wind would have cut furrows in it by now."

"Maybe, maybe not. It's protected by the configuration of the land to the west, shielding it from the wind."

Eagle Feather shrugged.

The caravan drove east along the Mojave Trail on packed sand. Small dunes fingered in from one side or the other. The sun shimmered on white salt beds nearby. Blackbush and sage edging the road had coats of dust. Several miles along, the road bent right, traveled south for a time. When it swung east again, Tav turned off onto a narrow, rutted passage tightly bordered by creosote brush. He pulled in a couple of car lengths to leave room for Zack, climbed out, and walked back to the Jeep.

"Step out a minute. I'll show you the lay of the land."

Zack and Eagle Feather joined him in front of the Jeep. They looked south across a flat valley to rising hills.

"Where's Susan?" Zack asked.

Tav grinned. "She's loving the AC. I gave her the tour as we drove along anyway. She's got her head buried in a map right now."

"Are we headed toward those mountains?" Eagle Feather gestured toward the purple peaks piled up in front of them."

Tav nodded. "Those are the Woods Mountains to the right, and Hackberry Mountain is that tall one to the left. Our road will take us to Watson Wash at the base of Hackberry, then left along its flank. At this time of year I'd expect the sheep camp to be somewhere near Hackberry Spring, up on the mountain's shoulder. We'll need to watch for any sign of sheep as we go along."

Tav grimaced. "If they had sheep dogs, they'll find us first; they'll be hungry by now."

The caravan moved on. The road was no longer gentle; hidden gullies and shifting sand kept Zack busy, bumps often lifted their heads toward the canvas roof. When they reached Watson Wash forty-five minutes later, their muscles were sore from hanging on.

The road, such as it was, turned left and the SUV slowed to a crawl. Eagle Feather leaned out and scanned the mountain slopes as they rode. Bright deposits of gypsum far up the mountain shoulder fooled them more than once, appearing as sheep-like dots. The rounded summits were mostly bare, pinyon and juniper filled the upper washes and patched the slopes lower down, scrub filled in toward the flats.

"It'll be hard to spot them through all that vegetation." Zack's face was close to the steering wheel, peering out and up. But when they did find the sheep, there was no mistaking them. They covered the hillside like white dots on dominoes.

Ahead, the SUV turned off the rough track into a sandy wash, climbed it until the wheels spun. Zack pulled up behind. Everyone climbed out. Blue ran circles around the vehicles, expending his pent up energy.

"We walk from here," Tav said, and started up the deep sand.

All four were in good physical shape, but it wasn't long before they were gasping.

"How high are we here?" Susan asked, when they stopped to grab a breath.

"No more than 3500 feet or so, it's a bit over 5000 feet at the summit," Tav said. "It's not high, but steep. There's a psychological effect here in the high desert. You don't expect it to be as high as it actually is."

They left Big Blue off lead. The dog disdained rest and disappeared beyond the head of the wash through a clump of sagebrush.

"If they had sheep dogs, Blue will find them for us," Eagle Feather said.

He was right. Ten minutes later Blue's baying voice floated down to them.

"That's what Blue says when he's found something," Zack said.

Near the head of the wash they heard thrashing in the brush and Blue bounded out accompanied by two Shetland sheepdogs. They looked like miniature Collies to Zack, sable and white, one a smaller version of the other. At the sight of the four humans, both dogs sat still and eyed them cautiously yet expectantly. Their fur was matted with dirt and coated with seeds, and their ribs showed.

"Oh, you poor little things," Susan said. "You've had no one to care for you." She started toward them, but as she neared they moved a few steps away, looked back at her. "Oh, they're afraid."

"Maybe they want us to follow them," Zack suggested.

"It seems funny to see Shelties out here. You associate them with Scotland, places like that." Susan stood hands on hips, admiring them.

"If you're a shepherd, these are the dogs you want," Tav said.

They advanced; the dogs retreated in front of them through the brush. They broke free onto a slope of grass-like vegetation, Indian rice grass according to Tav, with boulders scattered about. All around them were the sheep.

Susan studied the black and white mottled creatures spread across the slope. "What kind of sheep are these?"

"Painted Desert Sheep," Tav said. "These sheep are a rare breed, particularly adaptable to the desert. They're hardy, able to withstand the extremes of heat and cold."

Zack glanced at Tav. "How is it you know so much about sheep?"

"Used to be a lot of sheep over in Fairfield Valley. Your average woollies had a hard time of it but these guys did fine. They're a double-coated breed and cast their wool in the spring, in nice big clumps. They've got this layer of hair underneath, rather than wool, so's they survive the heat well. Then, in the fall they grow back that thick wool coat. On top of that, they lamb twice a year, so your herd grows real quick. Didn't take the other sheep owners long to see the advantages and switch over."

"That one looks like a mountain sheep." Susan pointed to a large ram with curled horns eyeing them from a boulder.

"That's one of the Painted Desert Rams. They can grow to two hundred pounds and almost three feet at the shoulders."

"There must be a lot of money tied up in this herd," Zack said.

"No doubt."

Eagle Feather inspected the slope. He pointed to an arroyo that divided it. "I would put my camp above that arroyo near those pinyon pines, if it were me."

Tav nodded. "The runoff from Hackberry Spring comes down there in the winter season."

Zack strode toward the pinyon grove, the other three fell in behind, the dogs running ahead. Sheep baaed and grunted and scampered out of the way.

At the lip of the arroyo, Zack stopped to stare, hands on hips. There was a camp there, or what was left of one. The remains of tent fabric fluttered in the breeze on a wooden platform, held there by stakes. Cans of food, shredded sleeping bags, ripped clothing, personal items were scattered all up and down the rocky sides of the arroyo.

Zack lifted a bent utensil, dropped it. "Either someone had a large fit of temper or they're looking for something important.".

CHAPTER TWELVE

Col's bottom and inner thighs were afire before the first hour had passed on the trail. Their path led upslope, the incline gradually increased as they neared the abruptly rising granite ridges. They rode through a continuous forest of Joshua trees, 15 to 20 feet tall. At the occasional high point, the boys looked out over a forest of green sentinels thick upon the slope all the way to the far horizon. Scattered among the Joshua trees were Mojave mound cactus with round, bright red flowers, and the yellow-flowering threadleaf groundsel. Fallen limbs lay decaying underfoot on either side of the trail, sprouting new growth of their own. The sky blinked deep blue through the trees. Somewhere a kestrel cried.

"Pretty fucking awesome," Julio said over his shoulder.

"If my butt didn't hurt so much I'd agree with you."

"I told you to relax, just flow with the movement of the horse like floating on a wave."

"Hard to relax when everything hurts. Besides, I never know when Rat is going to do his thing." The boys discovered the origin of Rat's name when the horse suddenly lunged forward trying to bite Julio's mount from behind. They maintained a half-horse interval after that.

"How about we climb down and take a break?"

"Negative," Julio said. "If you dismount now, you'll stiffen up and the pain will be ten times worse. Best to keep riding."

The way steepened. They emerged from the Joshua tree forest onto a rocky slope, here and there house-sized boulders loomed. The trail swung north along the flanks of the sharp ridges, difficult to find on occasional rocky stretches. The horses had to negotiate loose stone that tumbled and slid underfoot.

Julio pointed ahead. "I think we're headed for that canyon up there."

Col's eyes followed Julio's finger but saw only a slice of shadow down the face of the mountain. It grew wider as they neared, at last revealed itself as a deep narrow slash between the mountain ridges. The trail worked gradually east, dropped back into Joshua tree forest for a short time, re-emerged into a wash and on into a canyon laced with Juniper and pinyon. The canyon walls quickly grew precipitous. Tumbled logs and caches of brush here and there gave hints of the power of the water that roared through in the wet season.

After another hour of riding up the steepening canyon floor Julio stopped, swung down from the saddle. Col rode up next to him.

"There's a pool of water in the streambed at the base of those rocks. Hold the horses here while I go check it out." Julio saw the question in Col's face and grinned. "Yeah, you can get down. We all need a rest now."

Col half climbed, half fell out of the saddle. His legs were so stiff he could hardly move them. As he waited, holding both reins, he shifted his weight from foot to foot to get the blood flowing again. Everything that could ache did ache.

Julio was back. "Water's good, there's insect life on it, and I found a salamander in the mud. We'll take the horses down to drink." Julio took his reins from Col and led the way. While the horses drank, the boys sipped from their canteens and chewed on trail bars. Neither wanted to sit, instead strode about stretching their legs.

At the end of the break, when Col climbed back into the saddle, he understood why Julio had cautioned him not to dismount earlier. He thought for a while he would be physically unable to withstand the pain surging through his legs. He set his teeth and urged Rat forward. The canyon narrowed, solid rock ledge closed in and overhung them, left barely room for the trail that in places became the riverbed itself.

"This is not a good place to be if there is a thunderstorm upstream," Julio said.

"Does that ever happen in the desert?"

"From the debris in the river bed, I'd say yes."

The narrow passage hooked left, widened slightly before twisting right again. After another tight section, the canyon widened, the walls eased from vertical, and they faced a wide steep slope.

They reigned in.

"The head of the canyon," Julio said. He looked at his watch. "I'd like to make it over this pass and down the other side before nightfall."

"How far do you figure to the ranch?"

Julio shrugged. "I can't tell from this map. If darkness catches us, we'll have to find a place to camp."

Col stared up at the trail winding up the slope until it disappeared from sight high above. "We better get started, then."

The brief rest seemed to refresh both horses and men. The trail was well graded and their progress was good. At the top of the incline they faced a landscape of blackbush. Col reined in, looked behind them. A magnificent vista greeted him; the vast Joshua tree forest blanketing the entire western slope, the whiteness of the Kelso Wash, the purple rise of the Marl Mountains beyond. Far to the south, just in his view were large sand dunes bathed in yellow by the lowering sun.

Julio put it into words. "What an incredible place."

Col nodded. "The strange part? It's all ours. I mean, there's no one else here."

"I think Uncle Roberto has sentenced us to a lonely summer."

"You regret leaving all of your girlfriends behind, no doubt."

Julio laughed, urged his horse ahead. "It's just you and me, baby."

A blanket of Goldenbush and Indian paintbrush extended for most of a mile across the divide summit, then they were back in the pinyon forest. Darkness came quickly as they descended, the sun blocked by the mountain ridge behind them. Far below was a valley, maybe a mile wide, mountains rising on the far side.

When they stopped to rest, Julio studied his uncle's map. "If I'm reading this right, The Circle Ranch should be in that valley." Col looked down at it.

Julio swung around in the saddle. "What do you think? Maybe another coupla miles?"

"I can't stay on this horse much longer than that."

"If we make it to the ranch tonight, you'll sleep in a bed." Julio smiled, glanced over his shoulder at the dusky sky. "I think we've just enough light to make it."

The trail still had a few surprises for them, steep sections with several layers of switchbacks. Col found riding downhill involved other muscles, adding new pain to the old. He was pretty sure he'd never walk again.

The light faded to grey, objects beyond the nearest vegetation blurred, but the trail widened and flattened. They were in a yucca scrub flatland, in the valley they had seen from above. Alkali soil reflected the disappearing light enough to aid them on their way. A fence line appeared, took form as they neared. They saw it followed a road. A gate obstructed their passage.

"Almost there, amigo."

Col knew now he would make it.

Julio dismounted to open and close the gate. Col let him. He knew once he was down, it was for good. They rode on, past dark mounded shapes of cattle barely discernible from the yucca and barrel cacti.

A pinpoint of light appeared ahead of them.

Then there was another gate and the shadowy shapes of buildings, one with light in the windows. As they approached, a porch light came on. They rode into its glow. A man stepped out on the porch, then a girl.

Julio called a greeting.

"You would be Julio Castro and friend," the man said.

"I am Julio. This is Col Budster. We have come to collect the sheep."

The man smiled. "You are welcome, then. Roberto told me to expect you. Climb down—come in. My daughter Kella will see to your horses."

Even in the poor light, Col could see Kella was a beautiful girl. He was badly in need of rest, food and drink, his entire body ached, but seeing the girl almost made him forget it all.

Julio dismounted, handed the reins to Kella. "Gracias, senorita."

She smiled, moved to Col's horse and took the
reins. Flustered, Col smiled at her, tried to dismount, but
his stiff muscles would not respond. To his horror, his
foot caught in the stirrup and he fell hard to the ground on
his back. He lay there, looked up at the girl, unable to
move.

She laughed, her teeth white against the shadows.
"You have had a long ride, poor man. Let me help you."
She extended a hand.

Embarrassed, Col took it and managed to stand,
mindful of the softness of her skin even through the pain.

Kella led the horses away, still smiling.

"I'm Frank Darnell," the man said, and shook their
hands. "Glad to meet you boys. Come inside." As he led
them toward the door he called out, "Debby, we have
guests."

Frank Darnell was an energetic man; Col felt his
vibrancy through his handshake. Tall, over six feet, the
sleeveless T-shirt he wore revealed a farmer's tan dark
against white skin. His shock of red hair was apparent in
the full light of the house interior.

Frank led the way into a short hall, adorned with
hats and boots, jackets and leather gloves. The hall opened
into a large room. A counter lined with stools segregated a
kitchen space from the dining room, with a comfortable
living room beyond. Large windows and wide glass doors
lent a feeling of openness.

The woman behind the counter smiled, teeth white
against cheeks rosy from stove heat. "Come in, boys. How
about a bite to eat? Something to drink?"

"Debby, this is Julio Castro, Roberto's boy."

Debby came around the counter. Julio offered his
hand but she ignored it, pulled him into a hug instead.

Debby was the physical opposite of Frank; short, with delicate features, raven black hair worn long, and dark brown eyes.

After the hug, she stepped back to look at Julio. "I grew up near your uncle in Concepcion, a small village near Monterey, Mexico. We were friends as children but I have not seen him for many years."

"When he wrote to ask us to mind his sheep until he could find another herder, we were happy to do it," Frank said.

Debby smiled. "Next he wrote to say you would come to collect the sheep. I could not wait to meet you"— she looked at Col—"and your friend."

"This is Colin Budster, but everyone calls him Col."

"You must have a hug also," Debby said, and gave him one. Col had difficulty standing, for his legs were numb.

Debby noticed. "Come, sit down and rest. You must be very tired." She led him to a chair. "How was your journey way out here?"

Col sat, feeling great relief. Julio settled into an overstuffed sofa and began the long tale of their journey to the ranch by truck, train, and horseback. Debby bustled about in the kitchen finding plates, serving chili on steaming rice. Frank grabbed chilled beers from the fridge for all of them.

Julio paused to catch his breath and sip his beer.

"What a wonderful adventure," a girl's voice said.

Col looked up. Kella stood in the doorway, her eyes on the boys as Julio told their story. She had her father's red hair, although hers flamed more softly with many golden hi-lights. Her features were delicate, her skin lightly tanned. To Col, her face was angelic, her green eyes hypnotic. It was all he could do not to stare.

"Come boys, eat. Your meal is ready," Debby insisted.

Everyone gathered on stools around the counter. For a long time the only sounds were spoons on crockery as the boys ate bowl after bowl of chili and drank beer. After they had their fill, the entire party moved to the living room and chatted away the remainder of the evening. It felt as if they had known each other all their lives.

CHAPTER THIRTEEN

Tav studied the remnants of the camp, hands on hips. "Why would anyone do this?"

"Maybe someone doesn't like sheep," Susan said.

"Then why not just shoot them?"

Zack rubbed his chin. "This may have nothing to do with sheep. This destruction is very thorough. I think they were looking for something."

Eagle Feather raised an eyebrow. "What could anyone want from two lonely shepherds?"

"That's a good question. The destruction is so complete, it could mean they never found what they were looking for." Zack moved down the slope toward a tattered sleeping bag. "Maybe we will be luckier."

Zack looked at Tav, who shrugged his shoulders. "Worth a try."

The four spread out across the arroyo. Even Big Blue sniffed around amongst the litter, although likely on his own quest for something he could eat. The two Shelties sat and watched. The arroyo was completely littered, yet there were pathetically few belongings. A half hour later they all came together.

"These boys lived a sparse existence," Susan remarked.

"Here's something." Eagle Feather had a small spiral notebook in his hands. "This was stuck between the wooden planks of the platform." He leafed through it. "It looks like a journal, there are dates on the pages. Some are ripped out. It's written in English."

"What's the date of the last entry?" Zack asked.

Eagle Feather handed the small book to Zack. He glanced through it, saw it was written with pen in careful cursive as if for a school paper. There was no date on the last entry. He flipped back a page. "Here, this one has the date August 12 at the top of the page. The final entry could be the next day, August 13, but he never got the chance to finish."

"Well?" Susan said.

"Well, what?"

"Well, what does the final entry say?"

Zack grinned at her, began to read. "Very cold during the night. I was glad Junior came to cuddle with me. Beautiful morning, with the clear light that comes just before the sun rises, a new freshness to the air."

"A romantic," Susan said.

Zack read on. "Later today we'll go to Hidden Springs and try our luck. If we leave mid afternoon we can be there and back before too late. Julio says we won't find anything; the map is too ambiguous. But I think I see a pattern. I am excited to try it."

"And?"

"That's all. It ends there."

"So. He mentions a map," Eagle Feather said.

"A map suggests an entirely different purpose to their presence at the spring," Zack said.

"It suggests something different might have been going on there, not necessarily what everyone thought," Susan said.

Zack turned an eye toward Tav. "Was anything resembling a map found on their bodies? It could have been anything, it might not have looked like a map at all."

Tav shook his head. "No one mentioned anything like that, as far as I know."

"I think we'd better double check."

Tav looked at his watch. "It's time I got back anyway. I've left my store locked up too long. I'll call the sheriff's office with that question, let you know what he says." He looked at the two dogs. "I'll take the Shelties with me, get them something to eat, see about someone to watch the sheep."

Zack nodded. "You go ahead. We'll stay and sort through this stuff a while longer"

Tav whistled, motioned with his arm. The two dogs came and trotted along with him.

Zack watched them go.

"No rifle."

Zack turned to Eagle Feather. "What was that?"

Eagle Feather waved an arm at the demolished camp. "We have not found a rifle. A shepherd would have a rifle. A pistol is no good at long range against varmints."

Zack nodded, thought about it. "No one mentioned finding rifles at the crime scene, either."

"Maybe whoever did this took their rifle, if they had one," Susan said. "Maybe whoever wrecked this camp killed the boys. Maybe they wanted the map mentioned in the diary."

"Whoa, there, slow down. We need some evidence to make those connections."

"If we find the rifle, maybe we find the killers," Eagle Feather said.

"Any ideas?"

Eagle Feather shrugged. "If the boys bought rifles in this area, the store might have a record."

Susan nodded in agreement. "Zack, I know it's a big leap from assuming the boys had a rifle to assuming the person or persons who wrecked their camp stole the rifle, but even so, what could it hurt to inquire? If we find one or both boys had bought rifles, we now have a solid line of inquiry."

Zack put up his hands. "Okay, okay. It's a good idea." he gazed around the littered slope. "Let's give this place one last thorough search before we go."

This time they went about it in a more organized fashion. Eagle Feather began his search at the downhill extremity of the debris, Susan at the top. Zack worked across the middle, and Blue went where he wished. The sun was high, the arroyo exposed to its rays. In another hour, Zack was damp with sweat, ready to call it off. A glint of silver caught his eye. It looked like a torn piece of packaging. He picked it up. There were red letters across it which read: "Winchester Super-X High Velocity—". The rest was torn off.

Zack called to the others, handed the fragment to Eagle Feather.

"Winchester Super-X High Velocity Ammunition 22 Long Rifle 40 Grain," Eagle Feather said, finishing it. "I recognize this. I use this ammo myself." He handed it to Susan with a grin. "They had a rifle."

"Your idea to check local gun shops looks even better now." Zack looked at the sun. "I think we're done here."

They trudged back across the slope, hot, sweaty, and tired.

Susan looked at the sheep. "I get the sense these fellows would remain right here forever just munching away, oblivious to all the drama around them."

"I envy them," Zack said. "Life can have too much drama."

Eagle Feather caught his tone, glanced at him. "Think you and Libby might get back together anytime soon?"

Zack grimaced, shrugged. "Nothing has changed, really. I can't promise to give up my work, she doesn't want me to move back until I do." He gave a resigned grin. "I drive out to see them every chance I get. I probably see them more now than before we separated." He sighed. "I get it, though. She couldn't live with the constant threat of danger, not just for me, but for her and our child."

They emerged from the scrub. The red Jeep was below them in the wash. Zack glanced at it, stopped and stared. "Oh, shit," he said.

All four tires were flat.

CHAPTER FOURTEEN

Sunlight woke Col from sound sleep. He felt its warmth, blinked, let his eyes wander. He was in a strange bed, strange place. Memory came slowly. He sat up and immediately emitted a groan of pain—every muscle ached.

His clothing lay heaped on the floor. Across from him Julio was asleep, sprawled on an identical platform bed. They were in the bunkhouse, he remembered. They were at the Darnell Ranch.

The thought of Kella came to him. He flushed with embarrassment at his behavior the previous night, hoped he hadn't created a lasting impression as an utter fool. He vowed to remedy it this morning, somehow.

He yawned, stretched, felt the universal ache but otherwise felt rested and for once, clean. The bunkhouse had a wonderful hot shower; Col had monopolized it before bed. He dug in his pack for the clean set of jeans and shirt he'd set aside for civilized occasions. He had just pulled on his boots when the ringing clang of a metal triangle sounded. It was time for breakfast.

Col nudged Julio through the blanket with the toe of his boot. When his friend's eyes opened, he said, "Breakfast," and without waiting clumped across the bunkhouse floor toward the bright sunshine framed in the doorway. He crossed the packed dirt yard. Mrs. Darnell, white aproned and smiling, was on the porch.

"Morning, Col. Is Julio awake?"

"Just now," he replied. "He'll be along."

He followed her from the morning chill through the kitchen door into snug warmth smelling of fried bacon and coffee. Mr. Darnell was seated at the long plank table, filling his plate from a heaping platter of sausage, bacon and scrambled eggs. A tall pot steamed on the wood stove, potatoes crisped in a skillet. No Kella, he saw at once.

"Sit, boy. Eat your fill," Frank Darnell said. "Those as are late must meet their fate, as my dad used to say." His eyes twinkled.

Col pulled back the bench and slid in front of an empty plate. A hot cup of coffee was set before him. He held it under his nose; let its steam enliven him before venturing the first burnt-tongue sip. The moment was delicious.

The bench moved, shifted as someone's weight settled in next to him. He dared not look right away; her fragrance, the warm brush of her arm announced her presence. Before turning toward Kella, Col first lowered his very full and hot mug to the table. He was careful, determined not to make any slips in front of the girl. He turned to her. Curious green eyes met his glance.

"Good morning," she said, her voice sleepy and soft.

Col opened his mouth to reply.

"Buenos dias." Julio's loud salutation came before Col could speak. His friend stood dark against the brightness of the doorway.

"Come in, come in," Frank Darnell said.

"Good morning," Mrs. Darnell and Kella said in unison.

Julio sat at the table opposite Kella, smiled at her, looked at Col. "How do you feel this morning, amigo?"

Col groaned. "I am searching for a muscle that does not ache."

Everyone laughed.

"I think you did wonderfully well for someone who never rode a horse before," Mrs. Darnell said, her eyes crinkled and kind.

"When I first met him, he couldn't climb either. Now it's all I can do to stay with him." Julio grinned fondly at Col.

"So you boys climb, do you?" Frank Darnell said. "I did some climbing back in the day." From there, the conversation moved to climbing experiences and on to other explorations with the discovery of the inevitable similarities and differences. All assembled were adventurers—two young men footloose and happy, and a family of pioneers living in the final vestige of unexplored and seldom seen wilderness. Common threads abounded.

After a long, leisurely breakfast, the group left Mrs. Darnell to her chores, mounted up for the ride to the pasture where the sheep grazed. Col felt anxious as he saddled Rat, but surprised himself with the ease with which he managed to mount, and his relative lack of discomfort in the saddle. He was becoming an old hand quickly, he thought.

"Your uncle is a savvy man," Frank Darnell said to Julio as they rode. "He studied sheep breeds and selected the perfect combination of hardiness and yield in his sheep. Few know the type—Painted Desert Sheep, bred by a relative unknown from Far Eastern breeds. They lamb twice a year; produce a good weight of wool each spring. Your uncle's herd has already doubled in size, even with predator loss and sales to locals." Frank swung sideways in his saddle to smile at Julio. "Better yet, they are great scroungers and can find forage in even the sparsest conditions."

"How are they when water is scarce?" Julio asked.

"No animal does well without water," Frank said, "but these do better than most."

Behind Frank and Julio, Col and Kella rode side by side, appearing to listen to the conversation in front of them, yet with a mutual awareness of one another.

The riders passed through the two gates the boys had negotiated the night before and traveled on north toward the head of the valley. The baaing of sheep came to them long before they saw the creatures spread out on the gentle slopes of the mountain foothills. With their black and white coloring they were difficult to see against the shadow-speckled hillside.

"What keeps them from wandering?" Julio asked.

"...Or from predators?" Col added.

"Two things," Frank said. "First, there is a fence line beyond this first range of hills to keep them in this valley. As for predators, the answer to that is coming toward us right now." He pointed. Two dogs were sprinting toward them, joy written in every movement.

Kella laughed. "They are happy to see us, but even more happy at the prospect of breakfast."

Julio had already dismounted to greet the dogs. "Are these your dogs? What are their names?"

Frank laughed. "No, these are your dogs. Their names are Shep and Junior. Your uncle purchased them along with the sheep. They will go along with you when you move the herd." He looked at Julio, then at Col. "Believe me, you'll be happy to have them. They know more about herding sheep from instinct than most people ever learn from experience."

Kella swung down from her mount and extricated bowls and dog food from her saddlebag. "They're mighty cute, too."

The two Shetlands sat side-by-side, tongues lolling, waiting for the bowls to be filled and put before them. They politely ignored Julio's advances.

"They'll be happy to meet you, but not until after breakfast," Frank said, with a laugh. "Meanwhile, why don't you mount up and I'll show you the herd."

They left Kella with the dogs and rode up the pasture. At their approach, a large ram, horns thick and curled, stepped forward to challenge them.

Julio reined in, surprised. "I've tended plenty of sheep, I've never been challenged by a ram quite like that before."

"You've never tended this breed of sheep before. They originated on Texas game farms, more for hunting than wool. Your uncle tells me they are Mouflon crossed with Rambouillet, Merino, and Texas Blackbelly."

"Look at the beard on that big guy," Julio said.

Col stared. "Those horns are massive. He's like a mountain sheep."

"These sheep are self sustaining to a very high degree," Frank said. He grinned. "That will make your job easier."

"Speaking of our job, where are we supposed to take this herd?" Col asked. He scanned the hillside. "There must be a hundred of them."

"Roberto leases an area of mountain grassland around a spring at a place called Hackberry Mountain. It's about twenty miles east of here." He waved an arm off in that direction.

"You mean we've got to walk this mob twenty miles?" Col was shocked.

Frank laughed. "Ordinarily that'd be nothing for a shepherd, but it's pretty near impossible from here, what with mountain ranges and private holdings and BLM land in between. We'll truck 'em." He sat quiet for moment, calculating. "You've got maybe 85 head here, rams, ewes and lambs, give or take any birthing that might have happened last couple of days. We might make it in two trips with my cattle truck." He sensed the boys' eagerness. "Plenty of time, though. Let them feed a bit more here, fatten up. Where you're goin', forage is a bit scarce. Besides, we haven't had company in some time." He looked at both boys and smiled.

The man's smile was infectious; you couldn't help but grin back, Col thought.

"Guess the dogs are done eating," Frank said, looking behind him.

Col looked, saw the two dogs coming toward them like rockets. Kella wasn't even in sight yet.

"Told you they'd be wanting to meet you, " Frank said, laughing.

CHAPTER FIFTEEN

Zack inspected the front tire. Eagle Feather walked a wide arc around the vehicle, his eyes on the sand. He came full circle, looked at Zack.

"No footprints here but our own."

"This tire was not slashed," Zack said. "It was shot."

"Shot?" Susan said, alarmed.

Zack nodded. He looked at Eagle Feather.

"They've all been shot," the Navajo said.

Susan looked puzzled. "I didn't hear anything."

"We may have been too far around the face of the mountain to hear the shots."

"Tav's vehicle was spared, apparently—it's not here," Susan said.

"How long ago did he leave, do you remember?" Zack looked from Eagle Feather to Susan.

Susan looked at her watch. "He had at least an hour head start."

Zack studied the tire marks where Tav's SUV had been parked. He shook his head. "Tav's tires were all inflated when he drove away, apparently before the sniper arrived—or perhaps the sniper wasn't interested in him."

Eagle Feather gazed up the wash. "The shooter would have had to change position and angles to shoot all the tires from up there."

Zack stood at the left rear tire, looked at the hole in it, glanced up the slope following the angle of shot in his mind. He walked to the right rear tire and did the same. "He shot at a sharp angle, didn't move all that far, would have been somewhere around those bushes." He pointed up the wash.

"That's good shooting."

Zack rubbed his chin. "The sniper could of left off after shooting the front tires, and have accomplished the same thing. I sense some anger there."

Susan had her phone in her hand. "You two can admire the sniper all you want, I'm going to get us a ride home."

"You got a signal out here?" Zack asked, surprised.

Susan smiled, nodded, pushing numbers.

Zack reached into the Jeep for the metal detector.

"You think the bullet went all the way through the tire," Eagle Feather said.

"This front one did, anyway. I saw the exit hole on the backside. The bullet passed just above the rim, it should be in the sand here somewhere." Zack turned on the detector, moved it over the sand behind the tire. The beep-beep came almost immediately. He set the detector aside and dug into the sand with his hands.

"I hate to bring up an unpleasant thought," Susan said, "but what if the sniper is still around and decides to practice on us instead of tires?"

"Keep moving or low," was Eagle Feather's advice.

Susan immediately crouched behind the Jeep.

"Did your call go through?" Zack's voice came muffled from under the vehicle.

"I called Tav. He's arranging for a tow."

Eagle Feather raised an amused eyebrow, had begun to speak when a loud "Gotcha!" came from Zack. He crawled out, opened his fist. A rifle slug lay on his palm. "It's a bit flattened from the impact, but a lab should be able to identify the caliber, and maybe even the type rifle."

Eagle Feather glanced at it. "Why shoot our tires, and not Tav's?"

"Maybe because we're the strangers," Susan said.

Zack gazed up the slope. "If the shooter left prints, they'll be up there. Let's take a look."

Zack and Eagle Feather started up the wash.

"Hey! What about me?" Susan called.

"Wait in the Jeep," Zack said over his shoulder. "I wouldn't worry, though. The shooter is long gone."

"But what if he isn't?"

"If he's still here, he'll shoot Zack or me first," Eagle Feather said."

"Well, that's alright then." Susan climbed into the back of the Jeep.

The first thick brush that could serve as cover was two hundred yards up the wash at a place where the sandy bed narrowed and turned toward the right. At the dogleg someone could cross the wash and still remain out of sight.

Eagle Feather got there first, inspected the ground. Zack came over.

"There are his prints. He crossed the wash twice." Eagle Feather's eyes followed the impressions. "He shot first from this side, behind that creosote bush, then crossed over to that side, shot again, came back when he was finished and went across the slope that way." He nodded his head in a westerly direction.

Zack stood in the center of the wash where he could see the Jeep. "That's not all that far for a marksman, but still good shooting."

"Yah, I would not want to be in his sights."

Zack knelt next to one of the prints. "This is a rather small foot, looked larger because of the loose sand. It's at least a couple of inches shorter than my foot."

Eagle Feather measured the shooter's stride with his own. "Short steps, too." He glanced at Zack, eyebrow raised.

"He's a she," Zack spoke both their thoughts. "I admit I had Bronc in my head. I guess I'll have to put that notion aside."

"He stays on my list," Eagle Feather said. "I will not forget he tried to ambush us. Maybe this woman is with him."

Zack scratched his head. "How many people here resent our presence enough to shoot up our equipment, do you suppose?"

Eagle Feather shrugged. "I have been places where every stranger is treated like this."

Zack studied the site where the sniper fired the first shot. The marks in the sand told the story. The shooter had stretched full out on her stomach, steadied the barrel with one arm supported by an elbow, taking her time.

"She picked up her spent shells," Eagle Feather said.

Zack nodded. "Professional, or at least smart."

They followed her tracks to where she'd left a horse tied to a juniper branch. The hoof prints led on downslope, off into the barren desert.

Zack gave his head a shake. "People appear out of nowhere around here."

The colleagues walked back down the wash to the Jeep.

Susan climbed out. "What did you find?"

Zack was about to respond when Eagle Feather said, "Someone is coming."

They all looked. A dust cloud moved along the road toward them.

Zack reached into the back of the Jeep, brought out the rifle. "I'm a little tired of feeling like prey," he said. He stood next to the front of the Jeep, planted his feet, leaned over the fender with the rifle barrel resting across the hood, and waited.

CHAPTER SIXTEEN

The boys happily accepted Frank's offer, seconded by Debby Darnell, to stay on in the bunkhouse. It was a smart decision, as it turned out. Frank Darnell knew a lot about livestock, horses and riding, working dogs, and just about everything else they needed to know once they were on their own. He had a way about him, teaching without appearing to do so, with a quiet comment here, and demonstration there. The boys learned fast. In return, they helped Frank finish projects he had put aside until he could afford to hire a hand.

Part of the payback for the boys was the down-home cooking Debby served up at meals. Julio was to be cook in sheep camp; he had some experience at his uncle's camps. Col had none and preferred to leave it that way. Their meals would be basic. One glance at the stack of tins of pork and beans and spam lining the storage shed, purchased by Frank on Uncle Roberto's authority, was sufficient to encourage them to delay their departure and continue to enjoy Debby's cooking. They lingered on.

Col was especially happy to stay, for Kella's charms attracted him more each day. She was natural in her ways, always herself, ready to leap into the saddle or wrestle down a calf without a moment's hesitation, yet all with unconscious grace. She seemed to enjoy the company of the two boys, treated them like brothers, but Col's growing feelings for her were not those of a sibling.

Kella seemed unaware of Col's adoration, although to everyone else it was obvious, and so a misunderstanding grew between the two. If she asked Col to help mend a fence, or ride out to locate a missing calf, he took it as her desire to be with him, a reciprocation of his feelings. When she asked the same of Julio, Col was immediately consumed with jealousy.

Julio was aware of Col's feelings toward Kella, found the situation amusing. He took particular joy in accepting Kella's invitations purely to watch his friend's face. For Col, those times were agony. Neither boy ever spoke aloud about it, and so Col's suspicion and distrust festered.

Several weeks passed. The sheep fattened on grasses greened by late spring rains, and the boys did the same on Debby's cooking.

One night Frank's eye rested on Julio across the dinner table. "I hate to see you boys go, but I believe it is about time we moved your sheep. It's best they change feeding ground while there is still good grazing up on the mountain. What say we take them over tomorrow?"

There were immediate sounds of disappointment around the table.

"Must the boys leave so soon?" Debby asked. "Why, they've become members of our family."

Kella said nothing, but unhappiness was written all over her face.

Col felt as if someone had stabbed him to the heart.

Frank gave a sympathetic chuckle at their reactions. "I know, I know, but its not as if they're moving to Timbuktu. We'll see them often enough." He smiled at Debby. "If i know my wife, we'll be traveling over to the mountain frequently with baskets of food." He gazed at his daughter. "Kella, you can ride over to see them any time."

Somewhat mollified by this, the family and Julio began to plan the order of things for the next day. Col simply sat and stared, stunned.

They stayed up late that night, enjoying one another's company one last time. Morning came early; the boys clawed out of bed and rode sleepily to the far pasture to round up the sheep. Frank drove the vintage cattle truck. Kella and Debby remained at the ranch house to prepare food for the trip and a bit more for the boys' first night out alone.

Col used his new skills to set the dogs to gathering the sheep. With the truck backed up to the corral and ramped, the dogs funneled the woolly, complaining creatures up and in until no more would fit. They left the balance of the animals secure in the corral for the next trip. Frank drove the truck back to the house, the boys followed on horseback. There they all had breakfast. After the meal, Frank presented his plan.

"I'll drive the truck with Julio," he said. "Debby will follow in the Subaru with Col and Kella. Everyone ready?"

Kella and Col packed the ancient Subaru's rear hatchway with packages of food and thermoses of drinks while the dogs joined Frank and Julio in the cab of the truck. The caravan started down the long dusty drive to an intersection with a dirt road. Here the truck turned south through a narrow canyon. They passed the Vulcan Mine with it's scattered, deteriorating outbuildings. The ride was long and dusty.

They reached a second slightly better maintained road and turned east. More traveled, it had fewer ruts, permitting greater speed. But it wasn't until they reached the paved roads of the National Preserve that they actually made good time. Black Canyon Road took them north beyond Hole-in-the-Wall. It was much hotter here than the canyon where the Darnell's lived.

They came to the old Mojave road, turned east past Rock Spring; there they took another unimproved road south.

In the Subaru, Kella pointed toward a high ridgeline. "That's Hackberry Mountain. Hackberry Spring is on the eastern slope. That's where we're taking the sheep."

"This all looks very dry," Col said, staring out the dusty window.

"It won't be like it was at our ranch," Debby said over her shoulder, keeping her eyes on the road. "We're at a higher elevation, it's not so hot and there's a bit more rain. You'll find plenty of forage for the sheep here on Hackberry Mountain, though."

Now the road bent east and followed the contour of the mountain. It was another half hour before the truck came to a stop. Julio, Frank and the dogs climbed out. Kella and Col walked over to join them.

Frank pointed toward a rock strewn sandy wash scarring the mountainside. "The cook wagon is up at the head of that wash. After we've transported all the sheep, we'll stock it and go through the equipment, check everything out. Roberto said to go ahead and replace anything we need."

"I'll stay here with the sheep and the dogs," Julio told Col. "You can go back with Frank to get the rest of the sheep and the food supplies."

"I'll stay here with Julio and show him the cook wagon," Kella said.

Frank nodded. "That's a good idea. Show him around." He smiled at Col. "Col and I can get the job done at the ranch."

108

Col forced a smile to hide his unhappiness with the plan.

It took the remainder of the day to collect the rest of the sheep, load the food and camp supplies, and drive back to the campsite. Debby said her good-byes at the ranch; there'd be no need for her to drive back again. Col felt as if he was leaving his own mother behind.

When the truck returned to Hackberry Mountain, Julio appeared with the dogs. They all worked together to off-load the remaining sheep, letting Shep and Junior round them up and move them up the draw to join the rest of the flock. The men began the laborious task of hauling cartons of food and equipment up to the campsite.

Col found Kella sitting at a large camp stove, both burners flaming, heating pots of water and homemade stew.

She smiled up at Col. "Dad and I will join you for dinner before we go home."

Dusk had already begun to mute their surroundings.

"Won't it be dangerous to drive back in the dark?"

Kella laughed. "Not really. Those roads are like an extension of our driveway; we use them all the time anywhere we go." She waved a hand toward the two tents set up near the cook wagon. "Besides, there isn't room for all of us to spend the night."

A plan for accommodating everyone flashed into Col's mind, but he kept it to himself.

The stew was delicious, washed down with several cups of hot chocolate, but already Col missed the cheery warmth of the Darnell dining room. Julio had a fire going nearby and Col contented himself with storing away passing glimpses of Kella.

UNDER DESERT SAND

"Watch out for snakes," Frank said. "The Mojave rattlesnake inhabits this area. It's most active at night; it's very aggressive and one of the most venomous snakes in the area. There's not much else to worry about in the way of dangerous animals. The few mountain lions stay at the higher elevations up among the pinyon pine."

"What about the sheep?" Julio asked.

"The rams help guard against snakes, they kill them with their hooves, although you may lose some lambs before they are old enough to learn to look out for them. There are coyotes around, of course, but the dogs keep them at bay. A mountain lion might wander down, attracted by the sheep, but you'll know 'cause the dogs and the sheep will set up an unearthly racket." Frank eyed the boys. "You've got powerful torches in your gear with plenty of batteries, and you've got rifles. Just firing in the air should be enough to scare away most predators."

Frank paused, grew thoughtful. "Old Juan, the last shepherd Roberto hired claimed he had some night visitors. He never saw 'em, never knew who they were. They did no harm, but you should know some people around here still have hard feelings about sheep." He shook his head sadly. "In the end, the most dangerous predator is man."

"What happened to the last shepherd?" Col asked.

"Old Juan? Nobody seems to know. He just up and disappeared one day, took off, left the sheep and dogs on their own. He was a quirky old guy. Probably just got it in his head he wanted to be somewhere else, that's all."

CHAPTER SEVENTEEN

"Well, I don't believe it." Susan stood hands on hips, stared in disbelief. "Look at that."

They watched the large flatbed truck with its shiny white cab and great red letters AAA on the door pull up behind the Jeep. A man in a greasy service uniform climbed out.

"You folks need some help?" he said.

Zack lowered his rifle. "Where the hell did you come from?"

The man looked at his notes. "A man named Tav Davidson called this in, set it up with his membership. He said you'd need a lift to Needles. I happened to be over on the Fairfield Road, got here pretty quick." He looked at their amazed faces. "We perform assistance pretty much anywhere, you know."

"I'm joining AAA tomorrow," Susan said.

The man looked at Zack. "First time I've been greeted with a rifle, though."

"Oh, sorry about that. We were expecting less friendly visitors."

The serviceman reversed his truck, backed it up to the Jeep. The powerful winch pulled the deflated vehicle up onto the truck bed, where the man chained it down. Everyone piled into the large cab. Blue stayed in the Jeep, stretched out on the seat, quite content.

The ride to Needles took less than an hour using the Fairfield Road to access Route 40. While the service station went about locating and mounting four new Jeep tires, Zack called Butch Short and arranged a meeting. Eagle Feather and Susan opted to catch a ride back to the motel. They agreed they'd all meet at the Wagon Wheel Restaurant for dinner.

When Zack walked into the BLM office the agent was shuffling papers around on his desk.

Short looked up. "Come in, grab a chair."

"I thought I'd report on our progress."

Butch pushed the papers aside, nodded. "Shoot."

Zack winced. "I wish people wouldn't use that expression."

The agent gave a lop-sided grin. "Sorry."

"Someone is disturbed by our presence here, it seems," Zack said. He went on to list the incidents as they had occurred; the menacing call to Susan, Bronc's apparent attempt to ambush them, the discovery of the boys' bullets, the destruction and apparent search of the shepherd camp, and the shot up Jeep tires.

"Jesus!" Butch said, when Zack had finished. "You've had a helluva day."

Zack grimaced, nodded.

Butch was full of questions. "You think the location where you found the two .45 caliber bullets means the boys were shooting at someone or something else, not each other? Who do you think shot up the Jeep tires—Bronc? You think we're after murderers now, rather than some suicide pact?"

Zack held up a palm. "Whoa, slow down. We've got a lot of stuff to sift through. You now know what I know. I'm meeting with my team later and we'll go through it, bit-by-bit, step-by-step. You should close the loop with the other investigators, see where it leaves you." He looked at his watch. "It's after three right now. I'm meeting my friends for dinner. I'll give you a call after that."

"I may not get hold of everybody by then, but I'll call and let you know what I've got." Butch laid a hand on the stack of papers. "I've got enough to keep me chained to my desk all afternoon anyway."

Zack was about to climb into the loaner car when his phone buzzed. It was the garage saying the Jeep was all set and asking where to charge it. Zack gave them the number of the FBI vehicle pool manager in Las Vegas. Susan's right, he thought to himself, the Agency will never issue me another vehicle again.

Zack stepped out of the car in front of his motel and dug for his key card. The door of a big black Buick in the next space swung open on the driver's side. A very large man climbed out. He spoke across the roof to Zack.

"Say, may I have a word?"

The man looked close to 300 pounds. His large head was perched directly on his torso without benefit of a neck. A good-humored smile stretched the fat cheeks of his fleshy face, but dark penetrating eyes above it hinted at purposeful intent.

"About what?"

The man moved around the front of the car to Zack with surprising dexterity. "About your case, Mr. FBI Agent."

Zack closed his car door, faced the man. "What case is that?"

The man's grin broadened, as if they shared a great joke. He waggled his finger at Zack. "How many cases have you taken on in this little town, FBI man?"

"I guess my affairs are none of your business." Zack tried to move past him.

The man stood firm. "Oh, but they are, sir, they are."

113

"Mister, I don't know who you are, or what you want. I've had a long day, and—"

"You don't really think two nice young men simply decided to kill each other one fine day, do you?"

Zack stopped, stared.

The stranger smiled back, waited as if for a child.

"Who the hell are you?"

"Well now, that's precisely why I'm here, to tell you that very thing. If we could just step inside your room out of public view for a moment, I will do just that."

"You'll tell me here and now, or this conversation is done."

"That would be a shame. What I have to say will truly interest you, I believe." He didn't move, still blocking Zack's path. "There's a lot more to this than a couple of dead boys."

Zack gave in. "Okay, I'll walk over to the McDonalds with you. I'll give you the time it takes to drink a cup of coffee, Mr.—"

"Jones. Bob Jones."

Zack had turned to lead the way, stopped. "Not good enough."

The fat man sighed, dug into an inner pocket. "I don't mind telling you my name, what I mind is having to haul all this crap out every time to prove it."

Zack watched the man struggle to reach a hand across his massive chest into the inner pocket of his jacket. The silk lining was torn at the pocket edge suggesting this struggle occurred frequently. He extracted a wallet, opened it, found a card encased in plastic, and held it out to Zack. It was the official I.D. of a private investigator, credentialed and authorized in the state of California. The fat man's photograph was there; the name given was Robert Ezekiah Jones.

"No kidding," Zack said, and cracked a grin.

Jones flashed him an annoyed look. "If I had a nickel—. Never mind. Can we talk now?"

"The offer of a cup of coffee stands. My treat." Zack walked toward the McDonalds, Jones shuffled along behind. Inside, the P.I. went to select a table while Zack ordered two coffees at the counter. He brought the cups, napkins, sugars, milks and stirrers to the table.

"Just black for me, thanks," Jones said.

Zack dumped the sugars and milks on the table, sat down. "You're the P.I. Jim Hatchett hired."

Jones nodded.

"Why?"

The fat man's lips twitched. "Why am I a P.I., or why did Mr. Hatchett hire me?"

Zack stared, not amused.

"Okay, here's the story. Jim Hatchett's a long time rancher in the valley, third generation. His grandpa came there to work for the Winslow Cattle Company, gradually put aside enough money and bought cattle to start his own little spread. Out in the high desert in those days everything had thorns—bushes, critters, the weather, and men. It was pretty much survival of the fittest. Water was king; if you had it, you made it. If you didn't, you moved on." Jones grinned. "It's still pretty much that way, it seems."

He sipped his coffee and continued.

"Anyway, there were some bad hombres living in the valley alongside Jim's grandpappy, men who'd as soon shoot you as look at you, men who came there to get away from somewhere else. They were bank robbers, highwaymen, back-shooters; you name it. Grandpappy Hatchett worked alongside these guys at the Cattle Company, lived as neighbor to them once he got his ranch. He somehow managed to walk that fine line, keeping friendly enough with the lawless element not to get shot, but never crossing over to become one of 'em. There were some honest settlers living there, sheep men and miners, but they kept mostly to themselves. It was a lonely existence for grandpappy Hatchett, at least until he found a woman willing to live out in that desolate place and raise a family with him.

"To make a long story short, which I'm not, the Hatchett family survived the range wars and droughts and every other devilish thing the high desert threw at them. Eventually the bad men drifted away, were shot, or were hung. A little town developed, name of Fairfield, even had a church and a schoolhouse, but it didn't last. Once the mines petered out, all you had left were holdouts raising a few cows or sheep, or hermits living off government checks. Grandpappy Hatchett died, passed his holdings on to his son. Things never got any easier for the family. Although Jim inherited the family holdings and the house, it was a creaky old thing. Jim set about upgrading it. He tore off one side to add a new wing, and found stuff in an attic crawlspace nobody knew about, stuff his grandpappy had left."

Jones gave Zack a dry smile. "It was just the kind of thing everyone secretly hopes they'll find in their attic, an old trunk with a treasure map in it. Hatchett guessed the map indicated a place where one of the robbers hid his ill-gotten gains. The map was crude, on the backside of a page ripped from a book, looked like it had been sketched in a hurry. The landmarks shown were things like trees and posts and stuff that were no longer there, but the terrain contours, hills and such, gave clues. Well, Jim looked it over, made a few half hearted attempts to locate the place, but no luck."

"Are we going somewhere with this?"

Jones put up a chubby palm. "Hold your horses, FBI man. There's a point to all this. You see there was an old shepherd up on Hackberry Mountain. Hatchett met up with him while searching for stock there one day. The old guy was pretty lonely and they got to talking. Somehow the subject came around to the treasure. Jim always carried the old map with him in case he came across some features to match it. He pulled it out, showed it to the old man, thinking a shepherd spends his whole life out there and might recognize the place. But he didn't. Least, he said he didn't."

"But now Hatchett thinks he did?"

Jones nodded. "That's right. But he didn't figure that out for a long time."

"How did he figure it out?"

"Jim Hatchett believed he had the only copy of the map. A month or so later he was in the hardware store in Needles buying supplies. The storeowner told him the old shepherd had come in, talked about a map, said it showed where robber's loot was buried, and could he have a pick and shovel on credit? The storekeeper turned the old man down of course, but now Hatchett realized the old guy must have recognized the features on the map after all, copied them down from memory after Hatchett was gone." Jones squinted across the table at Zack. "Say, I could eat a cheeseburger or something. You want anything?"

"Finish up your story. I'll get you one."

"Thanks, partner." The fat man wiped his mouth with his sleeve. "So, anyway, Hatchett is right pissed, as you can imagine, so he rides right up to the old shepherd's camp, but he's too late."

"Too late?"

"Yeah, the old guy was gone; lock, stock, and barrel. Jim searched around the campsite, but all he found was a few empty tin cans and food wrappers. The shepherd, his mule, tent, clothing—the whole ball of wax––gone."

"So what'd he do?"

"Nothin' to do. Either the old guy found the money and took off to Las Vegas or somewhere, or he simply got tired of hanging around sheep." The fat man shrugged. "Who knows?"

Zack eyed the private detective, chewed on what the man had just told him.

"That can't be all of it."

"It is, mostly," the P.I. said. "There were reports people saw the old man here and there before he disappeared, mostly down near Rock Creek and Hidden Springs. That would be natural, though, being the best sources of water. Mr. Hatchett sent his man Bronc down there to check around both places, look for any recent sign of digging or the like, but no dice."

Zack stared at Jones. "So why'd he hire you?"

The P.I. opened his squinty eyes wide. "Why, the dead shepherd boys, of course. He asked me to check into their back story."

"Why?"

"Couple of reasons. First, he didn't believe they shot each other any more than anyone else did. He guessed the next thing to happen would be people figuring the

118

boys died because they were sheep men; you know, the old range controversy raising its ugly head again. Hatchet wanted to stop that before it got started. Second, he wanted to know if there was any connection between the boys and the old shepherd, Juan."

"Meaning had the boys learned about the treasure from Juan."

"Yeah, that kind of thing. And last, Hatchett wanted me to learn what really happened to the boys, so suspicion wouldn't fall on him and Bronc, as he figured it likely would."

"Why would he figure that?"

"The Kellogg Ranch cowboys have always had a somewhat proprietary attitude toward Hidden Springs. It's the only viable water source for their cattle, and maybe they over reacted from time to time when someone seemed ready to jump in there. The old shepherd was seen there before he disappeared. So naturally, people might—"

"Was he seen there more than once?"

Jones nodded, stared back at Zack. "Fair exchange, FBI man. I've given you everything I got, how about you answer a few questions."

Zack shrugged. "Okay."

"Why are you here?"

Zack smiled. "If you've done any back checking, and I'm sure you have, you've discovered my speciality tends to be cases that are, shall we say, somewhat unusual. Butch Short decided this case was unusual, and asked me to act as consultant for the investigators."

The fat man's eyes narrowed. "Consult, not actively investigate?"

"That's right."

"Do you believe there was a third party involved?"

"I do."

"Who do you think it was?"

Zack smiled, put palms up. "We're very far from an answer to that question. At this point, virtually everyone is a candidate."

"What's the motive?"

"Again, if we knew that, we'd be able to narrow down some suspects."

"Are Hatchett and Bronc on your list?"

Zack nodded. "Along with everyone else in the area."

"How'd they do it? I mean, there were no prints near the bodies, each holding pistols with factory loads, but one of 'em killed by a homemade .44 caliber bullet."

Zack's eyes narrowed. "How do you know all this?"

"I'm a private investigator, it's what I do."

"Answer to your question is, I don't know." Zack put his palms on the table. "Look, I got to go. I've got people waiting to meet me for dinner."

"What about my cheeseburger?"

Zack pulled a few bills from his wallet. "Here you go. Enjoy yourself."

The fat man took the bills. His eyes narrowed as he watched Zack turn to go. "I'll be in touch."

Zack waved a hand as he walked away. When he entered his motel room, the amber message button on the room phone was blinking. He listened to the message.

"Hey, Zack, it's Butch. I just heard from Buzz Connolly, the sheriff. He says Roberto Castro, the guy who owns the sheep, is on his way here from Mexico. Turns out, his nephew is one of the dead boys. Sheriff says this Castro is a high roller with a lot of bucks and influence. Just wanted to give you a heads up."

Just what we need, Zack thought to himself.

CHAPTER EIGHTEEN

Col woke to sun streaming across his face through the open tent flap. The air was crispy cold, his nose felt like an ice cube. He let the sun play on his face to warm it while he remembered things.

Frank and Kella had left after eight last night, Frank promising to return next day with their horses. Kella was home-schooled, had studies and couldn't come. Col remembered Kella's goodbye, a shake of the hand but her eyes seemed to say more. At least, that's how Col read it.

He glanced at the still sleeping form of Julio as he quietly slipped on his pants inside the warm sleeping bag. He stepped out of the tent, his sandals in his hand, and stared off across the flatland below where the first rays of sun drew black shadows behind the Joshua trees. The land stretched for miles to the rim of the New York Mountains far off on the horizon. The impact was stunning, the vista with it's play of light and shadow incredibly beautiful. The dogs, curled together at the side of the tent, watched Col with just their eyes, not ready to move from their warm positions.

I'm going to like it here, Col thought. He walked across dry crumpled earth to a cluster of tall bushes, the designated bathroom, almost stepped on a rattlesnake stretched full length across the sun-patched but still frosty ground. Col walked carefully around it. It didn't seem to notice, still sluggish until the sun could revive it. The encounter did not dwindle his enthusiasm. There was something about waking up outdoors at the cusp of the day that invigorated him.

Col returned to the campsite, found the driest wood in the stack and built a pyramid over the ashes of last night's fire. He set in some fire-starter and soon had hungry flames lapping up the sides. Then, still barefoot, he walked out to a hillock and tried to count the sheep all gathered close together around a rock formation below him, guarded by the big ram. He tried several times, but always before he finished a lamb or ewe moved, scattered the others, and his count was lost. Col contented himself with an approximation.

When he returned to camp, he found Julio at the fire, setting water to boil. His friend looked up as Col approached, and smiled.

"We won't have good coals for a while, but we can get started with boiling the water. We need a rolling boil of at least four minutes to trust it." The water had come from Hackberry Spring; they kept it stored in a re-purposed oil drum.

Col came to the fire, rubbed his palms together to warm them. The sun felt good on his back. The dogs had deserted their position by the tent for the warmth of the fire, and settled near their new masters. Junior licked Col's hand; Col smiled and looked at Julio. "Think you can handle this for a summer?"

Julio grinned. 'Pretty darn nice, isn't it?"

The smell of fried eggs and sausage filled the air. Col's appetite had always been large, but now it was all consuming. The boys went for second helpings despite knowing they should spread out their resources. They no longer had a grocery store just down the street.

The morning was spent in organizing camp, structuring their daily tasks, generally preparing for life as shepherds. They found two sturdy trees near camp, far enough apart to set up a picket line for their horses when they arrived later. They made plans to build a shelter for the horses for protection from the sun and as a place to keep their tack.

By late morning, they were ready to explore their surroundings. Col found himself puffing as he moved about; he'd have to adjust to life on a slope, always uphill or downhill. They made a wide, leisurely circuit around the sheep grazing range. The best grazing, they noticed, was in a bowl-like area defined by a perimeter of up-thrust rock ledge, almost like a shallow volcano crater on the side of the slope, a half-mile wide. It made a great natural fence; they could walk along it every so often and look for escapees. Beyond that, the dogs would take care of things.

They found evidence of old Juan everywhere. The shepherd left monuments to his dedication with stone corrals, small shelters of stone and brush for injured sheep, a lean-to for shearing. They discovered strands of rope tied to trees near the camp where he likely picketed his horse.

"He picked a perfect place," Julio said, gauging the distance between the trees, "close enough to camp to keep an eye on the horses, yet a good place for them to graze while hobbled."

"Don't you get the feeling the old shepherd felt something for this place? You know, all the careful construction, the thoughtful placement of things. It's like he created this home for himself. Why would he leave so abruptly?"

Julio shrugged. "Who knows why anybody does anything?" He shaded his eyes, looked out over the flats. "Looks like our horses are coming."

Col turned to look, saw the plume of dust along the arrow-straight road. "Let's go on down and meet

Frank." He didn't share the hidden hope Kella might have changed her mind and come along after all.

She hadn't, it turned out, but the day was filled with work and left no time for dreaming.

Within a fortnight Col and Julio were completely comfortable in their surroundings. The two dogs, Shep and Junior, lavished the kind of love on their new masters that comes only from recently orphaned animals. Even the sheep responded to them, some trotted over to greet them when they arrived each morning. Col gave them names, a habit Julio tried to resist.

"One day we'll have to leave them, or worse we'll have to send them off to their fate. Giving them names will just make it harder."

Col was adamant: that was then, this was now. After a while, even Julio found himself thinking of the sheep by the names Col assigned them. It did make it easier to have discussions about individual animals.

With the arrival of their horses, their world on Hackberry Mountain expanded. When the available water in the natural meadow all but disappeared, they rode to Hackberry Spring, lined with its namesake trees, and filled large waterproofed sacks with the fresh water, slung them over their horses, and brought them back to camp to fill the metal trough, left there by Old Juan. They enjoyed daily rides, only after they checked on the sheep and finished the morning chores. The expanse surrounding Hackberry Mountain seemed endless, and exciting.

Their camp grew in size and comfort. The boys enjoyed the challenge of creative improvement; a solar shower made from an extra water bag, hammocks they braided from rope and hung in the shade of pinyon pines, hot and cold running water for cooking and washing. They rarely used their tent for sleeping now, except in the windiest of times, when dust sifted into every crevice. They slept in their hammocks, snuggled in warm sleeping bags, washed by bright moonlight, an eye on the horses and their ears listening to the sheep.

So it was the morning Bronc came to call; the tent empty, the boys gone. He was emerging from their tent when Col and Julio rode up after riding a circuit around the sheep. They reigned in their horses, stared in surprise.

"Hello," Col said. "Who are you? Why were you in our tent?"

Bronc stood by the tent flap, said nothing, his sinewy form taut, his arms hanging at his sides. Col noticed the pistol in its holster worn low on the man's right hip. The stranger's face was expressionless.

There was an aura of danger around the man. Col stared, unable to think of anything to say, afraid somehow that any movement, even dismounting from his horse might mean risking his life.

It was Julio who spoke next. He seemed to know how to disarm the situation. "Had your coffee yet?" he asked. "Why don't you join us?"

Bronc stared at Julio for a moment, as if taken by surprise, finally nodded.

Julio dismounted and led his horse to the picket line. Col followed suit, the tension in the air now abated. They saw Bronc's mount tied to a branch in a pinyon grove farther away.

Bronc waited by the fire. When the boys returned, he stuck out a hand, spoke for the first time. "Name's Bronc."

Julio took the lead. "I'm Julio, this here's Col."

He poured hot water from the big kettle through the coffee strainer and into a cup. "We're stretching the grounds a bit this morning, but it should still be strong."

He handed the cup to Bronc, who nodded thanks. He handed a second cup to Col. They sat on the large logs around the fire, sipped in silence for a few moments.

"You must be from the Kellogg Ranch." Julio's tone was pleasant.

"I ramrod the outfit." Bronc looked from one boy to the other. "That's why I'm here wondering what you and your sheep are doing on Kellogg Ranch lands." His voice was soft, flat, his eyes slits.

"Must be some mistake," Julio replied, his tone level. "We're on my uncle's lease. He's had this lease from the Preserve for years now."

Bronc stared back at him without responding. The silent moments seemed loud. Then Bronc shrugged. "We got grazing rights to this whole valley. Cattle need a lot of space in land like this."

"I expect so," Julio said.

Col spoke for the first time. "Did you know Juan?"

Bronc turned his head to stare at Col. "The old shepherd here before you?"

Col nodded.

"He moved off kinda quick, didn't he?"

"We never did know why," Julio said.

"Likely the territory didn't agree with him."

"We did wonder why he left so suddenly." Col pursued the matter.

Bronc showed a mirthless grin. "Lots of things in the desert can spook a man. You boys need to be careful. Everything around you has sharp teeth or thorns or is poisonous."

"Thanks for the warning," Julio said.

Bronc stood, poured the remains of his coffee into the fire, handed the cup to Julio.

"Appreciate the coffee, boys." He started to walk away, turned back. "Say, did the old shepherd leave any stuff behind? He had some papers of mine, I wondered if he left them for me."

"Papers?" Col asked.

"Yeah, papers." Bronc eyed Col, watched him close.

"He didn't leave anything behind at all," Col said.

Bronc stared a moment longer, turned and walked toward his horse. A moment later they heard hoof beats moving off toward the draw.

Julio and Col looked at each other.

"We need to watch our backs around that man," Julio said.

CHAPTER NINETEEN

It seemed to Zack he had just dozed off when something large and wet sloshed across his face. He ducked away from a second Big Blue kiss and sat up in his bed, sputtering. Susan broke into gales of laughter. Even Eagle Feather was grinning.

"Time to rise and shine, sleepy boy. It is time for dinner at the Wagon Wheel."

"I expected to meet you there."

"We never agreed on a time, so we came here to pick you up," Susan said.

Zack stretched, stood, straightened out his clothing. "How about you all ride with me in the loaner car so we can go pick up the Jeep."

They left Blue stretched out on Zack's bed. It took just minutes to reclaim the fully inflated vehicle. Minutes later they were seated in one of the few booths still available at the Wagon Wheel. They ordered drinks.

Susan looked at Zack. "So, what's new?"

"I met the private eye today."

Eagle Feather looked puzzled. "What private eye?"

Susan answered. "Tav told us there was a private cop involved, hired by the Kellogg Ranch."

"Interesting character, name of Jones, shared a bit about Hatchett and his involvement in the case with me." Zack went on to relate what he had learned.

Susan's eyes glowed with excitement. "So that's the map the boy mentioned in his journal."

"Apparently. It couldn't be the original, of course, it has to be whatever Old Juan drew up."

"Did any of the investigators find a map?"

Zack shrugged. "I don't know. I've arranged to meet with Short after we eat. You two are welcome to come along."

"It doesn't seem likely," Eagle Feather said.

"What?"

"It doesn't seem likely any investigators found a map. We'd have heard about it."

Zack nodded. "Maybe."

"Unless one of them found it and kept it to himself," Susan said.

Zack put palms up. "Let's put the map aside for the moment. I'd like to get your thoughts on what we've learned so far. Give me a scenario."

His two friends pondered. Their drinks arrived and they clinked glasses in a silent toast.

Susan was ready first. "Everything points to hidden treasure," she said, eyes glistening. "Bronc is the link. He's there when Hatchett finds the original map, probably has his own outlaw connections so he knows the buried loot story is authentic. He watches Hatchet, sees him go to Old Juan's camp. He somehow learns Juan has tried to buy tools for digging, goes to visit the old shepherd but fails to find a map. He's probably non-too gentle, likely precipitated Juan's departure. He believes the map is hidden somewhere in the camp, keeps an eye on the two young shepherds when they arrive. When they begin to show an interest in Hidden Springs, he watches them closely. Finally, afraid they might find the loot before he can, he murders them and returns to their camp to search for the map, but fails."

Susan grinned at her companions. "There! How's that?"

Zack smiled. "Not bad. Quite exciting, really; buried treasure, murders—where's the dragon and the beautiful maiden?"

Susan's spirits would not be dampened. "They'll turn up, sooner or later."

Zack looked at Eagle Feather.

The Navajo coughed, and began. "This is an old dispute involving sheep, cattle and water, nothing more. Bronc is very loyal to Hatchett. He was with him during the sheep and cattle wars. When he sees the two shepherd boys measuring distances around Hidden Springs, the critical watering place for the Kellogg herd, he thinks they plan to bring down their sheep, an act he sees as hostile. One day he uses his rifle and ends the threat." Eagle Feather looked at Susan. "No more, no less."

Susan pouted, shook her head.

"Neither of you have explained the mystery of how the two boys died."

Eagle Feather shrugged. "What is not apparent now will be soon enough."

Susan glanced at him. "That's a major cop-out." She grinned at Zack.
"This is where the dragon comes in. One dark night—"

"Okay, okay, enough," Zack said.

The waitress appeared at his shoulder. "Are you folks ready to order?"

"Oh, yes, thank God." Zack placed his order, and the others followed. The waitress hurried off.

"As fanciful, and again mundane as your two theories are, I think there may be elements of truth in both. Somehow, they fit together. Maybe our meeting with Butch Short will shed more light."

UNDER DESERT SAND

Zack glanced at Susan as she ate. Her energy, her unquenchable good humor turned his thoughts to his estranged wife. They had been like that once, each revitalizing the other. Every moment was a precursor to something new and exciting. What had happened? Libby's objections had been about the dangers of his job, to him as well as to his family. Zack couldn't simply dismiss her fears; they were well founded. Yet until little Bernie came along, Libby had involved herself in many of his cases. An extraordinarily strong and self-sufficient woman, she had never shied from danger. But a baby changed all that.

Butch Short was waiting for them in his office. He nodded toward the empty chairs. When they had all taken a seat and greetings were exchanged, he spread his palms apart. "So, what's the consensus?"

Zack chuckled. "We have two scenarios, quite far apart. They have one commonality: they favor Bronc for the shooter."

"Motive?"

"That's where they differ. One says hidden treasure, the other a cattle vs. sheep feud."

"What's this hidden treasure idea about?"

Zack told him about his conversation with Bob Jones.

Short crossed his arms, leaned back and regarded them. "I could go with either motive. As for Bronc, well, he's a pretty easy target. He's got a lot of rough edges."

"He's also got opportunity, motive, and access to the crime scene," Zack said.

"So does just about anyone who lives out there. It's gonna be hard for a guy who works by himself out on the range all day to establish an alibi."

132

"It will be equally hard to prove anything against him," Susan pointed out.

"What's our next step?" Short asked.

"We believe the shepherds would have had at least one rifle between them, but no rifle was ever found." Zack raised his eyebrows. "Am I right?"

Short nodded.

"We propose to search gun shops, second hand stores, pawn shops, anywhere a rifle might have been sold or dispensed with. Maybe a shopkeeper will remember who sold it. We could get lucky."

"I can help you with that," Short said. "But why wouldn't the murderer simply keep it?"

Eagle Feather eyed Short. "Would you keep the rifle of a man you just murdered?"

"Uh, no, I don't guess I would. But I might bury it."

"If he buried it, Blue will find it," Zack said. "By the way, I expect you've had a chance to chat with the other investigators."

Short leaned forward, moved some sticky notes to the center of his desk, looked at them "Sure did. I got to tell you, none of 'em are happy we might have a murder case." He glanced around, was met with silent stares. "Anyway, Connolly and the other guys at the County Sheriff's office are happy with your progress. My bosses are pushing for resolution, the sooner, the better." He peered at another note, looked up. "Seems like Tav is tickled to death by what you've accomplished so far." He shrugged. "I haven't had contact with that private cop."

"He's following the treasure theory, mostly. He thinks Bronc might be responsible for the old shepherd's disappearance, but that's as far as he went," Zack said.

Short's eyebrows shot up. "He suspects foul play with Old Juan?"

Zack shrugged. "Maybe, or maybe Bronc just scared him off."

Short's eyes narrowed. "If this private dick, this..."

"Bob Jones," Zack said.

"If this Bob Jones finds out something, are we gonna hear about it?"

"We struck a deal," Zack said. "I'm pretty sure he'll honor it. He wants to keep track of where I'm going, so he'll trade."

Susan glanced at Zack as they stepped off the wide porch of the BLM building. Heat still radiated off the asphalt parking lot. "What's our next move? I know you've got more in mind than checking hock shops for rifles."

Zack's lip twitched. "You've got me pretty well figured. I'd like to take another look around the sheep camp. I can't help but feel we missed something there. I agree with your thought the boy's were working from a map. What happened to it? And how did they come across it?" He glanced at Eagle Feather.

"I wish to take another look at the crime scene. There is something bothering me about that place," the Navajo said.

Susan gave them both a sly smile. "If there is a treasure out there, it came from somewhere. I'll go to the local library and jump on the Internet, see if I can find out anything about it."

They parted at the motel. Eagle Feather and Zack would take Blue and the Jeep and head out early the next morning for the Preserve. Susan planned to spend some time on her computer, catch up on her business Emails, and later visit the local library.

Zack was dead tired. When he carded his door it seemed to push open even before the click. He paused. So that's how Susan and Eagle Feather got in this morning, he thought. He tossed his hat on the bed, shrugged off his jacket. The wardrobe was a stand-alone unit, with drawers on one side, a hanging rod in the other with a shelf at eye level. His jacket in one hand, Zack pulled the wardrobe door open with the other. In that millisecond his eye caught movement on the shelf; something had coiled, constricted, tensed. He heard a dry rattle. His brain registered the bunched face, beady black eyes, and poised head of a rattlesnake.

CHAPTER TWENTY

After Bronc had gone, and after the breakfast utensils were washed and stored, Julio and Col mounted up and rode down the slope to the sheep pasture. The dogs rushed to greet them, tails wagging, tongues lolling. The sheep had grazed eastward as they exhausted the greener, softer vegetation.

The boys dismounted. Col had a biscuit for each dog, as he always did, and the animals came to sit near their masters while the young men surveyed the sheep.

Julio pointed. "That yearling is still limping."

"He seems to be doing better, though."

Each shepherd's eyes tallied the sheep, inspected each, one by one, the ritual at a subconscious level by now. The morning was warm, the boys felt dozy, letting down from the anxious meeting with Bronc. The sound of hoofs from behind caught them by surprise.

The boys spun, their eyes widened when they recognized the rider working down the slope toward them. It was Kella Darnell.

Kella wore a mischievous smile on her face. She rode up and dismounted. "You look surprised to see me."

"Well, yah," Julio said.

Col said nothing, simply stared.

In the weeks after they established the camp, Frank Darnell had driven over several times, once or twice with Debby and her fresh pies and strudel, and often with Kella. The girl's relationship with Col had grown. There were no more pretexts on her part; she enjoyed Julio's friendship but her feelings for Col were of a different nature. They grew closer with each visit. Col often pinched himself to believe it was real and languished like a puppy in her absence. This was the first time she had come alone on horseback.

Kella went to Col and gave him a big hug and a quick kiss, and turned to Julio and hugged him. She laughed at Col's look of amazement.

"Dad let me ride over to visit for a day. I have to return tomorrow."

"That's a long way. How long did it take you?" Julio asked.

"It's about a day's ride."

"But..." Col still couldn't get his mind around it. "It's morning. Did you ride through the night?"

"No, silly. I camped out." She saw the faces of both boys. "Don't look so shocked. I've camped out alone in these hills for years. My parents know I can take care of myself." She laughed. "You boys spent too much time in the city." Her eyes narrowed. "Or is it a gender thing?"

Both boys threw up their arms, shaking their heads in denial. Everyone laughed.

"I don't care," Col said. "I'm just happy to see you."

Julio's expression turned solemn. "You didn't cross paths with that Bronc character, did you? I'd worry more about him than a sidewinder or a scorpion."

"No, I didn't see him. Why?" Kella saw both boys wore a serious look. "Did something happen?"

Col described the morning encounter. "We found the man coming out of our tent."

"I don't trust him," Kella said. "My dad ran into him several times when he came here to check on Old Juan for your uncle. He said he always wished he'd carried a rifle those times. He said Bronc reminded him of a coiled rattlesnake."

Col gave Kella an inquisitive look. "He said something funny just as he left. He asked us if Juan had left any papers behind."

"Do you know why Juan would leave any papers?" Julio asked.

Kella shook her head. "I can't imagine."

"You remember the camp when we first arrived. There was absolutely nothing here. Juan had packed and gone, lock, stock and barrel." Julio gave a shrug.

"I heard he vanished virtually overnight," Kella said.

"He never said a word to my uncle." Julio glanced from one to the other.

Col shook his head in bewilderment. "We've found signs of Old Juan everywhere around here: enclosures made with stone, dams on creek runoffs to water the sheep, old picket lines, trenches. He seems like a careful, methodical man who cared about his job, not a fly-by-night."

"It's a mystery." Julio reached down for a pebble and tossed it. "Here we have this hard-working conscientious man who just evaporates. Then we have this strange visit from Bronc, asking if he left anything behind."

"Maybe he did."

Kella and Julio looked at Col.

"Maybe Old Juan had something Bronc wants, like cash, or a deed, or..." Col struggled to think what else.

"Maybe a map to something hidden or buried, like a treasure map," Kella finished for him, grinning.

"Or a treasure map," Col said, and grinned back.

"Why don't we do a search?" Kella grew excited. "We can have our own treasure hunt."

Julio was doubtful. "We've looked this area over very thoroughly since we arrived."

"Yes, but you weren't looking for something specific, like a treasure map."

Col chuckled. "It would be fun."

"How could any papers still be here? They'd be destroyed or be part of a bird's nest by now."

Col nudged Julio. "Come on, grumpy. You never know. Old Juan could have buried something in a cigar tin."

Julio shrugged, put up both arms in surrender. "Okay." He turned to Kella, gave a mock bow. "Lead on, Omniscient One."

Leaving the dogs to guard the sheep, the three rode west to the place they had first found remnants of Old Juan's camp. He had set up on a sheltered slope near an area of alkali playa close to the boys' current camp. Col and Julio had made use of some of the stone pens until the sheep migrated, there were large boulders scattered about, and the original trenching from Juan's tent remained. The trio left their horses to graze, and wandered about near the old encampment.

"What are we looking for?" Julio asked.

Kella's eyes roamed the ground. "If we suppose he hid papers, he must have put them in a cylinder or a box of some kind. I think we can assume Bronc has searched the area, so Juan didn't leave a container around in plain sight. He would most likely have buried it. I intend to look for an area of disturbed dirt."

"Makes sense to me," Col said. "Let's spread out and work outward from the camp."

139

UNDER DESERT SAND

They divided the search area into three quadrants and began. There were several false alarms almost immediately—rodent burrows, places scratched by coyotes looking for grubs, and other natural disturbances that seemed likely places. They found sticks to dig with and to use as probes in case a snake was sheltering in a crevice where they looked. After an hour their search perimeter had moved a hundred feet out from the campsite.

Julio called a halt to rest and talk it over. The sun was hot on their bent backs and progress snail-like. Kella passed around her water bottle.

Sweat trickled down Col's face. "We can't cover every square foot of ground. It will just take too long."

Julio agreed with a nod.

"Maybe we should try to think like Old Juan might have thought," Kella said. Her face was red and dotted with perspiration but her spirits seemed un-dampened. "If he didn't bury the container near his camp, how would he have decided where to hide it?"

Col stood with hands on hips and cast his eyes at the surrounding area while stretching his aching back. Below them, the salt bed of the alkaline playa glistened. Beyond it to the west, the mountainside sloped toward Watson Wash. Nearer them, scattered juniper and pinyon opened up to an expanse of cactus and yucca, with tumbled boulders scattered here and there like marbles.

"If I wanted to bury something out there, I'd want it near a marker more permanent than a juniper tree or cactus. I think we should search around those big boulders."

"Good idea." Julio stood, grimaced at his aches. "Let's work together this time. We can select a boulder, search around it, and move on to the next."

"We should search a few yards out in case he paced a certain number of steps away from the stone," Kella suggested. She sighed, giggled. "Did someone say this would be fun?"

Julio grinned at her. "That would be you, I believe."

"Let's give it another hour," Col said. "That's about all the fun I can stand."

They went to work. About ten minutes later, Col heard Julio give a grunt. His partner had migrated to a slab of rock a few yards away. "I think I've found something," he said, staring down at it.

Col and Kella went to where he stood, looked down at the slab partially buried in the ground. All around the perimeter there were fresh cylindrical marks in the soil, as if made with a pry bar.

They gazed in silence.

"I'm afraid to look," Kella whispered. "I didn't really expect we'd find something."

"Are you worried Old Juan himself might be under there?" Col asked.

"I guess we all thought we might find more than a map," Julio said.

No one made the first move toward the stone.

"Well, we know we can't leave without trying to move it, so we might as well get to it," Julio said, finally. "If we all grab one end, we might shift it a bit."

They lined up along the uphill end and pushed fingers as far under the stone as they would go. Once all six hands were inserted under the lip, Julio counted off. "One, two, LIFT..." The slab tilted up. "Don't let go. Now, shift right." In a single motion, the three pushed as directed. Grudgingly, the heavy stone moved six inches to

141

the right before it came out of their hands and dropped with a thud that vibrated the ground. Col barely got his foot out of the way in time.

Julio knelt to look into the exposed depression. His face showed disappointed. "'There's no pit here that I can see. It's just flattened earth underneath." He rocked back on his heels. "Maybe the dig marks are from someone else trying to do exactly what we're doing." Sweat dripped down his face. All three were soaked in it.

Col put hands on hips. "Well, look. We've gone this far. Let's try to move it out of the depression. There could be a hole directly under the center of this slab, just large enough for a tin box." He wiped the sweat from his forehead. "We might as well finish what we started."

There was reluctant agreement. After a short rest, they positioned themselves as before and lifted and shifted. This time, the stone moved more easily, exposing much more of the area beneath. Again, they found nothing but flattened earth.

Julio prodded with his fingers. The dirt was hard as iron. "No one has dug into this soil, I guarantee you."

"One more push, and we'll know for sure," Col said.

Kella gaped at him. "You're a glutton for punishment." But she lined up with the boys. This time, they lifted from the side. With one long concerted effort they hefted the stone until it stood on its edge. It teetered for a moment, fell on over to expose its underside.

"Damn," Julio muttered, looking at the undisturbed earth. "Nothing."

Col prodded at it. The ground was consistently hard everywhere on the exposed surface. There was no hole. Both boys squatted, disappointed but also relieved.

"At least we didn't find a grave," Julio said.

Col stood, wiped his face with his sleeved arm. "I'm done. This is too much fun for me. Let's go back to camp and have a glass of wine."

Kella didn't respond. She was staring at the exposed surface of the stone. Bits of soil clung to it here and there; a dirt film covered it. She wiped an area clean with her palm. "Look."

The boys crowded close. Under the dust were scratches, deliberate etchings in the stone, dotted lines connecting crosses and squares and other markings. It was a map.

CHAPTER TWENTY-ONE

Even as his brain registered the image of the snake and its threat, Zack's hand had begun to close the wardrobe. His reflexes could not match the speed of the snake's strike, but his effort to close the door was just fast enough to nudge the snake's head with its protruding fangs aside and alter its course by inches. The smack of the door unbalanced the rattler and it fell. Zack threw himself backward against the wall, watched the snake land on the carpet with a thump and disappear under the innermost twin bed.

"Jesus!" Zack's heart pumped in his ears, his pulse raced. With one eye on the bed, he reopened the wardrobe to check for any other surprises. Finding none, he picked up his jacket where it had fallen to the floor and hung it up, walked to the table near the door, and picked up the phone.

"Hello? Front desk? I have a snake in my room I'd like you to remove."

The motel Jack-of-all-trades arrived at the door within minutes, armed with a snake stick. It didn't take him long to secure the snake and deposit it in his bag. He gave Zack a lopsided grin.

"We don't see this very often," he said.

Not sure if it was an apology or simply a comment, Zack gave no reply. As the man left he handed him a five-dollar bill, wondering how much of a tip one should give for rattlesnake removal. It was a full hour before he could settle down enough to fall asleep.

Zack was still sleepy when he stepped outside his motel room next morning, but the crisp cold air jarred him awake. The post dawn sky was deep blue, still framed with red. The Colorado River basin remained in shadow. Where the river notched through the mountains the sky was a purple V, like the tip of a spear. The sight lifted his spirits.

His eyes on the distant horizon, he did not at first notice the two figures standing near the exterior stairwell. The taller one approached Zack.

"Hagaruaji, FBI?" It was the Chemehuevi Chief Dan Singletree.

"Hello, Chief."

The large man nodded toward his smaller companion. "I have brought Veronica Nimri to speak to you."

"The thing at the well you mentioned?"

Singletree nodded, motioned the girl forward.

The young woman stepped up to them. She was slim, dressed in T-shirt and jeans with a woolly vest against the chill. Her hair was cut short, draped across her forehead. If not for her deep brown eyes and high cheekbones, Zack would not have thought her a Native American.

Singletree glanced at her, back at Zack. "Veronica did not wish to talk about the creature she saw at the well, but I convinced her."

"I was just going to meet Eagle Feather for breakfast. You could join us."

Chief Singletree shook his head. "Veronica will talk about it to you only."

Zack shrugged, waved toward the McDonalds. "Okay, fine, let's go get a cup of coffee, anyway."

Zack and Singletree walked side by side toward the restaurant, Veronica following in their wake. The Chemehuevi chief was a larger man than he had seemed when seated at their last meeting, several inches taller than

Zack, broad at the shoulders. He was an impressive man, Zack thought.

There were no other customers this early, they quickly received their order and sat on stools at a table. Chief Singletree spoke softly to Veronica in their dialect. He seemed to be encouraging her. Her voice was soft, a little timid.

"She'll talk to you," Dan said. "She doesn't want her name mentioned, for fear of...well, angering spirits. Or white men," he added with a grin.

Zack gave Veronica an encouraging look.

The girl began in perfect English. "My friends and I go four-wheeling along the Mojave Trail once or twice a year."

"You know the area quite well, then?"

She nodded. "We pick a different section of the road each year and camp in the wilderness, visit together away from everyone else."

"To reclaim her roots," Dan said.

She glanced at him. "In a manner of speaking."

"What about the creature?"

Singletree turned his gaze toward Zack. "Patience. She will get there."

The girl gave a timid smile. "This past June we decided to travel the Fort Piute section. Our third night, we camped near the New York Mountains road junction. We have stayed there before."

"Where is that, exactly?"

Chief Singletree used his finger on the table surface. "Here is Rock Spring. The road junction is just east of it, right here. Over here is Hidden Springs, the crime scene."

"What's that, a couple of miles?"

Singletree nodded.

"How many were you?" Zack looked at Veronica.

"Just three this time— my girlfriend Ellie and her friend Tom."

"One vehicle?"

"Yes. My old Bronco." She rolled her eyes at Zack.

"Okay, no more questions. Please go on."

Veronica glanced at Dan and continued. "We hung around at our camp awhile, with a fire going, talking. It was our second night out; we had stayed at Piute Canyon the night before. We thought it would be good to replenish our water supply before traveling the next day, because the filtering system would take several hours to make the water potable. Ellie came with me but Tom decided to stay by the fire and enjoy his beer."

"What is Tom like?" Zack asked.

"He's a real sweet guy, kind 'a tall and skinny, but also athletic, you know?"

"How well did you know him?" Zack saw Veronica's expression shade toward annoyance and spoke hurriedly. "Okay, okay, no more questions."

"It was dusk by now. We knew the way; we'd gotten water from Hidden Springs many times before. The gate was open, like it usually is, and we drove the Bronco right up next to the well. We had to skim leaves and stuff off the water surface before we dipped our jugs to fill them, so it took a while. It grew dark quickly, we didn't realized the time, I guess." Veronica glanced at Dan. "Those roads are fun in bright sunshine, but they can be kind of tricky in the dark, so we loaded up in a hurry. I backed the Bronco around to go back the way we came, but I suddenly remembered I'd left my bracelet at the well. I took it off so it wouldn't get wet," she explained.

147

Veronica lifted her left hand to show a turquoise and silver bracelet with dangling charms of some sort. "It's pretty expensive."

Zack admired it. "Very pretty."

Veronica smiled. "By now it was dark enough everything was shadowy, harder to see. As I turned to go back to the well, I thought I saw movement near it. I stopped and looked, but saw nothing. I finally decided I was imagining things so I went to the well, found my bracelet, and fastened it on my arm. When I looked up, it was standing there."

Zack saw Veronica's eyes were watery. Whatever she had seen scared her even now. "Go on."

"It was about ten feet away from me, up the slope toward the tree; you know the one with the broken windmill?"

Zack nodded. "Can you describe what you saw?"

"It was like a man, but not a human man, at least none I've ever seen. It had no clothes, just a lot of hair. Not as much as bears and stuff, though. You could still see lots of skin, and, well...stuff" Veronica blushed, paused.

"Physical details," Singletree prompted.

Veronica nodded. "Its arms were bare but the skin seemed tough, you know, kind of like a monkey's skin. It was very tall, way taller than you, Chief Dan, and its arms and chest were big and strong looking." Veronica paused to explain. "I didn't notice all that right then, it came back to me later as I thought about it. Right then I was just frightened."

"Understandably," Zack said.

"The other thing was its eyes, they were very scary, kind of a reddish glow, like you see when you shine a flashlight at a dog's eyes. But there was something in them

148

that made me feel afraid, like real anger, or hate, or..."
Veronica searched for the right word.

The men waited.

"I think what scared me was the coldness, its lack
of feeling, like it saw me as, well, dinner. I've never felt that
sort of thing directed at me before." She shivered.

"What happened?" Zack couldn't help himself.

"I just stood there, I was frozen. I...I don't know
how long. Then Ellie called to me from the Jeep to come
on, what was the problem."

"She didn't see it?"

"No, she was in her seat listening to the radio. She
just called something like, "Are you coming, or what?"
When she called, I turned to look her way, worried she
might be coming and I wanted to warn her. When I looked
back again, just seconds later, it was gone."

"Do you know where it went?" Dan asked.

Veronica shook her head. "No. There was no place
to hide where it was standing. I guess it somehow blended
into the shadows, or something like that."

"Then what happened?" Zack asked.

Veronica's face was white from the memory. "I ran
to the Bronco. I never looked back. I didn't want to know
if the thing was coming after me. I got to the Bronco, got
it in gear and got out of there."

CHAPTER TWENTY-TWO

Susan found the Needles Branch Library on the corner of J Street and Bailey Avenue, across from a large baseball diamond and next to the Needles Aquatics Center, which shared the parking lot. Before she climbed out she paused, rested her chin on both hands on the steering wheel and stared at the expanse of desert nearby, thinking an aquatics center in this place made as much sense as a beach umbrella in the Artic, until she remembered the Colorado River with its strong currents and dangerous whirlpools. Maybe it was smart to safeguard local children by teaching them to swim. Beyond that, a cooling swim in the center's pools during the heat of the desert day sounded pretty nice.

Susan locked the Subaru. It was on loan from Butch Short. She'd asked him where to find a rental and he'd told her go ahead, take his car. "I'll be here in the office all day, it won't be used," he said, insisting. Susan thought the vehicle could use a good interior cleaning, and it smelled vaguely of cigar smoke, but it would get her where she needed to go, and she was grateful.

The librarian, a serious looking young man, peered up at her from his work. After listening to her request, he led her to the stacks. There was just one other person in the entire place, at a table reading a newspaper.

"We don't get a lot of people doing research in the mornings, most people, the school kids and their teachers, come in during the early afternoon. You'll have everything pretty much to yourself." He waved his arm toward a row of shelved books. "These are local history. We have an excellent base for local historic research right here. We are also part of the San Bernardino County Library System, which is huge. You can tap in from computers over there," he waved toward the phalanx of computers on a long table, "and if you need anything else, just let me know." He moved off.

Susan oriented herself, found several likely volumes and hauled them to a table. She quickly learned the Mojave Desert was littered with buried treasures, weird creatures, mining for a wide variety of minerals, and, strangest of all, ships—if one were to subscribe to everything written about the place. Several legends were quite persistent. A story about a Spanish ship buried in the desert sands somewhere west of the Salton Sea, once discovered but never relocated, rang true enough to some people to launch an expedition from Los Angeles in 1870. A member of the Juan Bautista de Anza expedition had first discovered the galleon in 1774 and claimed it was filled with pearls. As a scientist and educator, Susan was aware the Salton Sea was the remnant of a far larger inland sea formed by the vagaries of the Colorado River delta over the centuries. It was entirely possible an early explorer might have sailed into this waterway and become trapped by the capricious ebb and flow of the great river's course— but the pearls, not so much. In any case, it was never found again, and for Susan's purposes lay too far south.

Another legend that refused to die was the story of an underground river discovered in a cavern beneath Kokoweef Mountain, said to flow over a bed of black sand permeated with gold. Susan studied a map, realized Kokoweef was in the Ivanpah Mountains in the Northeast corner of the Mojave Preserve, no more than fifteen miles from Hidden Springs. She creased open the book; this was more interesting. It was the usual story of discovery, sudden riches, the only access dynamited to hide the hoard until the prospector returned, and, of course, he never did. There were other mines in the area, she read. In fact, traces of a ghost town named Kokoweef still existed at the end of Zinc Mine Road, which was no more than a set of ruts and tire-shredding rocks, according to a guide. Could some gold laden sand have been transported to Hidden Springs where water was more plentiful, perhaps to rinse the soil, or even build a sluice? Had the resulting gold been hidden there?

Susan discarded the idea. It seemed unlikely; there were closer water supplies than Hidden Springs. Besides, why not use the water from the reputed underground river itself?

She flipped pages, scanned more legends, including one about a seven-foot deer reputedly seen by hunters in the Kelso Valley region of the Preserve that left no tracks. She grinned. This story probably came from an embarrassed hunter attempting to explain his lack of luck.

Near the bottom of her stack she had a loosely bound book containing a series of newspaper articles with notes written in ink. It looked like someone's personal scrapbook, no doubt a gift to the library from a community member cleaning out a closet. The articles were from a newspaper now extinct: The Kelso Times. She scanned through it, careful not to tear the yellowed pages. An article written in 1930 caught her eye. The title was "The Iron Door" and it related the story of two partners, settlers from Fairfield Valley seeking mining prospects on Table Top Mountain, who discovered an iron door to a mineshaft. It was another "find it and then lose it" story. One prospector slipped on a steep slope, grabbed at something as he fell, couldn't hold on, and careened to the bottom. When his friend reached him, the man said the object he had tried to seize, which he had barely glimpsed, was a partly open iron door to a shaft. In among the rocks that slid to the bottom with him they found an ore sample that proved to be rich in gold. But, of course, neither man was ever able to find the iron door again.

Susan chuckled at the oft-repeated story line, and looked on her map for Table Top Mountain. She found it about four miles from Hidden Springs. It was directly south of the crime site, just across the Watson Wash from Hackberry Mountain where the boy's shepherd camp was located. Her amusement turned to surprise. She sat back in her chair for a moment, thinking. After a few moments, she continued her research with increased interest.

$$* \quad * \quad * \quad * \quad *$$

At the Wagon Wheel Restaurant, Zack spun his spoon in his coffee cup and watched Eagle Feather for his reaction. They were seated across from each other with plates strewn with remnants of egg and biscuit crumbs in front of them. Zack described his meeting with Dan Singletree and related Veronica Nimri's extraordinary account.

Eagle Feather cocked an eye at Zack. "This creature sounds much like others we have come across in the past. A sighting such as this can not be confirmed, but it should not be dismissed, either." He gave Zack an amused look. "Especially not by us."

Eagle Feather was referring to past joint investigations. For good, or sometimes for ill, Zack's reputation for dealing with the "unusual" crimes often led them to cases where ancient myths and legends received new life from sightings or sounds on tribal lands. They were difficult to affirm. Tribal members outwardly discounted these stories despite their beliefs, to minimize controversy. Zack soon learned not to dismiss reports of strange creatures from the standpoint of his logical processes; too often events led to situations he could not explain. Stories of one such legendary creature spanned several tribes and reservations, a bipedal giant very similar to Veronica's creature.

"I agree," Zack said with a nod. "But for the moment, the thing Veronica saw does not seem to play into our murder investigation. Unless Native American lore has changed greatly, none of their legends involve gunslingers."

"According to the Chief, the reported sightings were all at Hidden Springs—you think that is a coincidence?"

Zack shrugged. "I'm content to attribute it to something entirely different, and much older, from the sounds of it. The murder of these two boys is a modern mystery, plain and simple." He smiled. "At least, modern as in the last century or so."

Zack stood. "We've got work to do. We'd better get to it."

By this time the sun was high, the air uncomfortably warm. Zack closed up the Jeep and turned on the AC. Rolling along Interstate 40 at 65 mph the big tires rumbled, the engine whined, and the AC hummed. Zack had to speak loudly to be heard.

"Somebody doesn't want us hanging around here."

Eagle Feather raised an eyebrow. "The warning call to Susan?"

"That, and the rattlesnake in my wardrobe last night."

Zack watched Eagle Feather's reaction; for once he'd caught the Navajo by surprise.

"Something you had not planned to wear, I assume." He stared at Zack.

"I almost did, but I closed the door just in time. It slithered under the bed. I let the motel people deal with it."

Eagle Feather's eyes stayed on Zack. "How do you think it got in there?"

Zack's laugh lacked humor. "I think it had a little help. I found my motel door wasn't latched securely when I returned last night." He glanced at Eagle Feather. "Is that how you and Susan got in to surprise me with Blue?"

Eagle Feather's eyes went forward to the road. "Yes. The door was not latched. I thought you had been careless, I meant to mention it."

Neither man spoke for a moment.

"This person means business," Eagle Feather said.

CHAPTER TWENTY-THREE

That night Kella slept with Col in his tent. Their lovemaking was sweet, tender, awkward and clumsy, each anxious not to hurt the other, neither expecting nor wanting anything beyond this single moment of intimacy and exploration. When dawn came, Col awoke to tousled brown curls across his arm, the sweet smell of perfumed soap in his nose. He lay exalting in it, feeling the warmth of Kella's body next to his, responding in his heart to the trust bestowed upon him by this wonderful being. When he could stand it no longer he disengaged himself from warm limbs against disapproving groans and pulled on his jeans and shirt. Outside the tent, Julio had the breakfast fire roaring. He looked up as Col appeared and grinned.

"Good morning, lover boy. Ready for some coffee?"

Col smiled shyly. "Oh, yes."

As Julio poured the boiling water through the filter into a cup, he said, "I've been studying the map we drew from that slab. I think I've figured out what some of the signs mean."

Col squatted down and accepted the hot coffee from Julio. "Tell me."

"Well, this group of four vertical lines, for instance. They are grouped close together, but curve away slightly at the top. Etching stone with a knife blade, or whatever Juan used, isn't easy. You take shortcuts, you carve representative markings instead of full scale drawings, yes?"

"Okay."

"So vertical grouped lines curved away at the top suggest motion, maybe even flowing, to me."

"Like water."

"Yes, exactly. More specifically, like a spring."

Col raised his eyebrows. "That would narrow down the location."

"Yes it would, if we could establish which spring."

Col took the pencil drawing from Julio's hand. "What other signs have you deciphered?"

"Well, there are the obvious ones we've already discussed. The dotted lines, for instance, maybe represent strides or steps, specific distances from one location to the next."

Col nodded, sipped his coffee carefully. It was burning hot.

"This round egg shape—I think that's the treasure, whatever it might be. It seems to be the endpoint of all the other signs."

"Okay."

"These parallel lines, intersected with three vertical lines, suggest a fence."

"Well, that narrows it down. Not too many of those around."

Julio glanced at Col. "Very funny."

"Sorry."

Julio took back the map. "I can't figure out this thing, though, two Xs, one on top of the other."

Col looked over his shoulder. "Two of something right next to one another, like two trees or two rocks?"

"Maybe. Whatever they are, it is an end point for stepping off the distances. We are missing two critical bits of information: the particular spring, and what these Xs represent. Once we know that, we can start the search."

A slender arm came between them and took the paper from Julio.

"Good morning, miss." Julio looked up, smiling.

Col felt an arm slide over his shoulder.

"Could these two Xs be the tower of a windmill?" Kella suggested. She picked up an empty cup and held it toward Julio. "Coffee, please."

Col snatched back the map. "Of course. That's why the Xs are right on top of each other, to indicate trusses."

"Here's your coffee, genius." Julio filtered the dark liquid into her cup. "If it is the windmill tower, it tells us not only the starting place for stepping off the distance, but also which spring it is."

"Hidden Springs," Kella said, with a nod. "It's the only one I know with a windmill tower of any kind still standing."

"There are other windmills around the range," Col pointed out.

"Yes, but they pump from drilled sites. We think this sign indicates a spring." Julio pointed to the vertical curved lines on the map.

Col nodded agreement. "It does look like it."

"Well, it gives us a starting place, at any rate," Julio said.

Col turned to Julio. "You're figuring to go right at it."

"Sure. Why not?"

"Well, for one thing, I keep wondering what happened to Old Juan."

Kella took the cup from her lips, turned her head toward Col. "You don't think he just up and left?"

Col shrugged. "Why would he? Like we said before, everything he's done around here suggests permanence, like he loves the place, his work, the dogs.

And now we see he was about to find a treasure. Why on earth would he suddenly leave?"

Kella stared at Col. "Unless he was scared away."

"Or worse..." Julio said.

"Bronc," Col whispered. "The papers he wanted."

"If we go down to Hidden Springs and start digging around, he'll know exactly what we're doing," Julio said.

"And we'll end up missing, like Juan."

"I can't believe he'd just kill someone, can you, really?" Kella looked at each of their faces.

Both boys shrugged, didn't speak, faces impassive.

"What will you do?" Kella asked.

"I for one am not about to let some gun-toting bully scare me away from a treasure. I mean, what do we really know?" Julio put both hands in the air. "We don't really know if there is a treasure. We don't actually know what happened to Juan; he's probably in Vegas right now drinking coffee with bourbon and kissing some dancing girl on her pasties. We don't really know what papers Bronc wanted from Juan; could be from the sale of a sheep or something." Julio looked at his friends. "What do we really know?"

"Show me Juan and the girl with the pasties and I'll feel better about the whole thing," Col said.

Julio groaned.

"Whatever you decide, I can't join you today," Kella said with a smile. "I have to get started back, I promised dad I'd be home tonight." She leaned into Col, looked up at his face and gave him a quick kiss. "Don't do anything foolish, you."

She rose, went into the tent to begin packing.

"How about some breakfast?" Col called after her.

159

"Great."

Minutes later bacon snapped and fried in the pan, bread toasted in the rack and Julio mixed his famous salsa and eggs. As they ate, little was said about the treasure, and less about Kella's imminent departure. After the meal, Kella made her final preparations, looked over her tightly packed horse, and said soft goodbyes to Col while Julio finished the dishes.

When she said her goodbyes to Julio, he handed her a stamped, addressed envelope. "Would you mind?"

"I'll mail it as soon as I get home," she promised.

Her final words to both boys came as an admonition. "Stay away from Hidden Spring. Don't do anything about that treasure until I talk to dad about it. Promise me."

CHAPTER TWENTY-FOUR

Susan was caught up in research at the Needles Public Library for another two hours. There was no doubt in her mind she had found the cause of the murders at Hidden Springs. The tale of gold on Table Top Mountain, so close to both the sheep encampment and the double murder site was too coincidental not to play a part. The question was, what part? And how did the reputed discovery of gold on a mountain a mile away come to effect events at Hidden Springs?

She concentrated on newspaper clippings. The Kelso Times newspaper became extinct in 1946, when troops and munitions were no longer gathered and shipped by train from Kelso after World War II ended. She looked now to the archives of the Needles Desert Star. Slowly accounts came together to offer the shape of a story.

There had long been contention for water rights at Hidden Springs, she learned. The gunfight resulting in the death of both participants in 1905 was said to have been about just that, with settlers aligned against the big cattle outfit. But was it really? There had been three men with nefarious reputations as gunmen in the area. Two of them had shot it out at Hidden Springs. The third gunman was one of the partners who stumbled upon the "Iron Door" and the mine's reputed lode of rich ore on Table Top Mountain, a man named Bob Simmons. Coincidence? Susan didn't think so.

Was there another connection with Hidden Springs? Maybe. Susan went back to her original water sluice theory, in which the miners needed to wash the gold ore out of the soil. She found a detailed map of the area, located Table Top Mountain. She grinned in triumph. No doubt about it—Hidden Springs was the closest water to the mountain. If the men found gold, and wanted to separate ore from soil, they needed the water at Hidden Springs.

Suppose there was a sluice set up at Hidden Springs in 1905. Why was it never mentioned? Susan answered her own question: gold required secrecy. Simmons needed a way to disguise the operation to prevent everyone in the territory from descending upon it. He and his partner, a man called Andy Skaggs, must have taken the Winslow Cattle Company foreman, Curt Johnson, into their confidence, probably offered him a cut.

She thought about the windmill within the branches of the large cottonwood tree. It pumped the water into the large cattle tank, might it have pumped water to a sluice arrangement, something hidden in a building? She remembered Tav's account relating how Johnson had moved into a cabin or shed of some sort located right at the spring. What if that shed was built specifically to hide a gold ore sluicing operation? What if Johnson had moved into it not to guard the well against sheep and small cattle ranchers, but to guard the hidden gold operation?

Susan chuckled at how things were coming together. The gunfight, for instance: why had Curt Johnson called out from the hut to Skowler to "come on in", an invitation which immediately precipitated the gunfight? Had Johnson been pocketing gold, for instance; did he fear Skowler suspected him? Had Skowler actually come there to snoop around, try to catch Johnson in the act?

One article suggested a rifle bullet was found in Johnson's spine. If that was true, it might have been a double cross. What if Johnson and Simmons arranged an ambush for Skowler, with Simmons hidden outside the cabin ready to shoot Skowler through the window with his rifle? Could Johnson have called the gunman up to the shed, planning to shoot him as he entered backed up by Simmons and his rifle? Or had there been a double-double cross? Did Bob Simmons see the opportunity to eliminate both an unwanted partner and a second partner he didn't trust—and keep the gold for himself? Did he wait with his rifle and watch the outcome through the window, shoot Johnson when it seemed he might survive the fight? Did he intentionally use the same .44 caliber bullet in his rifle that the men had in their pistols, so no one would ever know a third person was involved?

Then...then what? Susan read about the furor the shooting caused in the valley. Lawmen rode out to investigate; locals came by to gawk. How could Simmons have hidden the sluice and kept everyone from learning about the gold? There were no accounts to explain it. She could only speculate. Considering the distances involved, and the isolation of the place, Simmons could well have begun his plan far in advance of the incident; he might have convinced Johnson to help him clean up the place before the ambush, to hide the gold—bury the gold, and destroy the sluice.

Susan's eyes gleamed as her mind raced. Now she knew what the shepherd boys were doing there, what they hoped to find. Somehow they had learned about the hidden gold, about the sluicing operation. They knew everything was buried there at the spring. Somehow they knew, somehow they had an idea where to look...and it cost them their lives.

Bit by bit the pieces came together, the facts tumbled into place. Susan did not yet have all the connecting links, but they would be found. It was time to tell Zack. There was a murderer out there, a killer who knew what the boys were up to, someone protecting the gold, or searching for it himself. Susan was pretty sure she knew who it was.

Zack did not answer his phone. Susan remembered he planned to return to the murder site and the sheep encampment with Eagle Feather. Signals were iffy out there. He probably had his phone off knowing it was useless. The same would be true for Eagle Feather, no point in trying him either.

Susan decided to call Tav Davidson.

He answered on the first ring. "Susan. How are you?"

"Tav, listen, I've discovered some information critical to our investigation, but I can't reach Zack or Eagle Feather. Have they come by?"

"No, not today. Did they plan to come by here?"

"They intended to revisit the crime scene. From what I've learned, I'm concerned for their safety."

"You must have discovered something important."

"Yes. I think I know why the boys were murdered."

There was a short silence. "What did you learn?"

Susan hesitated. "It's rather complicated and long, and it still might not be the correct answer, but it all fits together perfectly, and if true, someone might kill again to protect his secret."

"Susan, this is very intriguing. You seem quite convinced. Where are you now?"

"I'm at the Needles Public Library. I've been researching lost treasures here. I've just finished."

Tav laughed. "Lost treasures, eh? Sounds very exciting. Look, why not come out here to Hole-in-the-Wall. You can tell me about it and we can go together to find Zack and Eagle Feather. Do you have transportation?"

"Yes, I have Butch Short's Subaru on loan. Thank you, Tav. I may be way off base here, but I'm worried. I'll come right out there."

There was a gnawing emptiness in Susan's stomach. She stopped by her motel room to change into slacks, and picked up a sandwich at McDonalds. She drove up the I-40 ramp with the burger in one hand and a coke in the cup holder. Her notebook with scribbled notes from her research was on the seat next to her. As she drove, her mind raced. If gold ore had been washed at Hidden Springs, the apparatus was long since gone, as was the shed. Nothing remained but the broken windmill tower. But somewhere, under the sand, would be the remains of the sluice. And if Susan's theory was correct, a lot of gold.

But why wouldn't Simmons have taken the gold when things died down, when no one was around? Susan had no record of what had become of Simmons after the gunfight. Had he become incapacitated in some way? Had he taken some of the gold and never returned for the rest? Had some people suspected him, watched him, so that he had no chance to retrieve it? But what if there was yet another person, someone who knew the gold had been buried, someone who prevented Simmons from returning to retrieve it? There was that other man, Simmons' partner, that man named Skaggs. What happened to him? Where was he during the shooting?

165

UNDER DESERT SAND

Susan saw her scenario left two loose ends—
Simmons and Skaggs. Had they retrieved the gold after all,
shared the gold between them, gone off to a new life?
Maybe there wasn't any buried gold after all, only the
rumor of gold. Yet men were still being killed. Susan
supposed it wouldn't be the first time men had died
chasing a phantom treasure.

And then there was Bronc. Everything he did,
everything he said brought him under suspicion in her
mind. He knew something, she was sure. He was
protecting more than water rights at Hidden Springs.

Susan's brain was still whirring when she reached
the turnoff for Hole-in-the-Wall. She pulled into the empty
parking lot in front of the Ranger Station, climbed out, and
ran up to the porch. Her footfalls rang hollow on the deck.
The screen door groaned open, but door itself was closed,
locked. There was a note taped to the window.

"Susan. I'm out on the loop trail doing some
maintenance. Come find me. Tav."

Susan studied the map on the wall of the porch. It
showed a mile long loop around the huge rock formation
rising behind the cabin. Glad she had put on her pants and
walking shoes, she walked across the parking lot to the
trailhead. The sun was lowering but the slanting rays
reflecting off the volcanic rock were still hot as she began
to walk. Soon she was sweating through her cotton blouse.
The trail consisted of cinder chunks, broken from the
igneous rock formation, hard and sometimes sharp
underfoot. Susan needed to concentrate not to turn an
ankle.

The trail skirted the rock formation and brought
her to a vista across a vast valley of desert pockmarked by
Joshua trees and clumps of Mojave Yucca. A fence line ran

166

down the center, buildings tucked among several cottonwoods suggested a ranch although the distance was too great to be sure. The trail faced west, the sun was full upon her and it was hot. She glanced at her watch; she'd been walking almost ten minutes now. Where was the man? She'd come out here to talk to him, to find a way to warn Zack, not to get her daily exercise. Annoyed, she picked up her pace.

Her course brought her around to the rear of the formation, where sandstone predominated. Wind and weather had carved isolated pillars, a series of grotesques to Susan's mind, with eyelike holes and tortured carvings, a Dante's inferno of lost souls standing in deep shadow protected from the sun within the embracing arms of high cliffs. The path meandered up among these stone figures, under their overhanging midriffs and around pedestals into deep shadow, toward a dizzying array of slot canyons. The path itself became confused, offshoots departed toward other formations, into other canyons. Susan struggled to stay on the main path, the one most traveled, as best she could.

She paused at a junction, less obvious than others, and studied it. Her thoughts were interrupted by a sudden mosquito-like whir by her ear. Instantly she heard the loud snapping crack of a gun, followed by a thousand snap-like echoes bounding off the stone pillars and cliffs. For a millisecond, Susan stood rooted in place, stunned, confused. In the next millisecond she dropped to the ground hard, lay cheek pressed against gritty stone and dirt, shocked. She felt her pounding heart thump against the hard ground. She lay still, her eyes closed, and waited to know her fate

.

167

CHAPTER TWENTY-FIVE

Not long after the boys established their camp, Col had found a spot near the summit of Hackberry Mountain where his cell phone had enough bars to call Kella. Because he had no way to recharge the phone, he used it sparingly. Both boys realized the importance of their phones for emergency calls. Because Julio never used his, Col felt freer to make more calls. Two days after she left, he climbed the mountain and called her.

"Did you talk to your dad?"

She groaned. "You won't like what he had to say. He's had his run-ins with Bronc, none of them pleasant. The man tried to prevent dad from bringing supplies to Juan."

"Did he threaten him?"

"Not really. But he was his usual unpleasant self."

"What did your dad say to you?"

"Well, first he told me to stay away from your treasure hunt. He's not going to let me come back if he thinks I'll take part. He told me to tell you he strongly recommends you leave it alone. He doesn't think there is a treasure, but he says it doesn't matter; as long as Bronc or others like him think you are interfering, you'll be in danger."

Col paused. "Well, that's pretty straight forward."

Kella was silent.

"He won't let you come out here again at all?"

"I think he might, eventually—once he's sure you won't be digging up Hidden Springs while I'm there."

"What if I promise him we won't do that while you're here?"

"I asked him that. He said you must promise not to search for it at all, because even if I'm not there when you search, if you upset someone like Bronc, the danger will still exist."

"Damn." Col thought about it. "He's right, of course. Frank must really believe there is something to this business."

Kella's reply was whispered. "I don't think dad believes Old Juan just went away on his own."

"Wow." Col's mind spun. "Okay, look. I'll talk to Julio; try to get him to drop this idea. It seemed exciting to me, fun, you know—but not if it means we can't see each other."

Col thought about it as he rode back down the mountain. Julio wouldn't drop the idea; he knew that, not even if it meant Kella wouldn't be allowed to visit. Col knew better than to try to convince him.

On the other hand, Col didn't really believe they would find anything. If there had ever been a treasure, it was sure to be long gone. By the time he rode into camp, Col had decided to say nothing about his conversation with Kella. He believed the best course, his best chance to see Kella again as soon as possible, was to go ahead with the treasure hunt and get it over with. Once they tried and failed Julio would drop the idea and things could return to normal.

When Col rode up Julio was sitting in the sun, studying the notes they had transcribed from the underside of the slab.

"Hey. I was just looking over these notes. It looks simple."

"Yeah?"

"Yeah. Too simple." Julio moved the paper toward Col when he sat down next to him, pointed to the sketch and some words. "If we follow this, we start at the windmill, walk due west for sixty paces, assuming the tiny number means paces, then step due north forty more paces. Then there's another right angle, back east for forty paces. Is that how you read it?"

Col studied it for a moment, nodded. "I guess so."

"But the egg shape isn't at the end of that last set of paces. It's drawn in the middle of that area. Why do the dashes keep on going?" Julio looked at Col.

Col shrugged.

Julio continued. "Here's another question. Why make us walk all that way west, only to end up going back east again? Why not step directly to the spot from the windmill?"

Col took the paper from Julio, grunted, handed it back. "Maybe whatever is buried there isn't in an exact location, like right at the end of the dashes. Maybe the treasure is somewhere along the continuum."

Julio stared at Col. "Shit. You may be right." He looked back at the map. "I shouldn't have expected it to be that easy. This means we have to explore every inch of a line half a football field long."

"At least it's all sand there. We might be able to use a probe."

"You mean like a long skinny stick."

"Yeah." Col grinned. "Then after we find the zillion dollars in gold we can roast marshmallows with them."

Julio eyed Col, not amused. "You don't really believe there is anything to this, do you?"

Col gave a shame-faced grin.

"I think you should begin to take it more seriously, my friend," Julio said. "Let me tell you something I haven't told you before. I don't believe Old Juan went away voluntarily at all. I think he's dead."

"We've all wondered about that, but there's no real reason to think that way."

"Maybe there is." Julio reached into his pocket and retrieved a creased, dog-eared plastic card, about the size of a driver's license, folded in half. He handed it to Col. It was a photo card, with a green banner and blue-green image of the statue of liberty. A Hispanic face looked earnestly back at him. Next to the photo were dates and a name: Juan Domingo.

Col gasped. "This is Old Juan? I mean is this his Green Card?"

Julio nodded, his face grim. "I didn't want to show you this before, especially not when Kella was with us. I found it two days ago caught in some rocks where Juan had kept his horse. It must have dropped out of his pocket."

Col didn't understand. "Okay, he dropped the card, lost it. What does that prove?"

Julio pointed a finger at the lower right hand section of the card while Col held it. "Look at that expiration date. Look at the "Resident From" date. This card was issued the same year he disappeared. It's good for another nine years."

"I still don't—"

Julio gave a short, humorless laugh. "You've never been an immigrant, so you don't get it. I have. These cards are very hard to get, often you have to enter a lottery for them and get lucky. You hold on to these things." He cocked his head toward Col. "You and I don't carry around our wallets out here, we keep them with our special belongings in the tent. If we need our driver's license, say, or a medical card, we get the wallet and take it with us to wherever. Working here, you never know what you might have to do, so you don't risk having the wallet in your back pocket. Right?"

"Yeah, so—"

"Not this little guy." Julio took back the card, looked at it. "You keep this on you at all times. You never know when someone may challenge you. You keep it deep in a pocket, a watch pocket, or a zippered pocket; somewhere it can never slip out so you never lose it. This little guy is your life."

Col felt a sudden rush of understanding, and with it fear. "He didn't lose it. Someone took it from him."

Julio gave him a thin smile. "Yeah, or it came free while he struggled, or was dragged, or stripped, or—"

"Okay, okay, I get it. Jesus!"

"I've been asking myself, why would anyone want to treat an innocent old guy like Juan that way? I have seen no evidence the sheep ever left this mountain, so they were never a threat to the water or the grazing of the Kellogg Ranch cattle. Even out here"—Julio waved an arm—"a man would have to trespass in a serious way to deserve death in someone's mind. My guess is they found he was after something they considered their own."

"The treasure."

"Yep."

Col looked hard at his friend. "So despite all this, despite the danger, you still plan to look for whatever is hidden at Hidden Springs."

Julio nodded.

Col sighed. "Okay. When do we start?"

R LAWSON GAMBLE

CHAPTER TWENTY-SIX

Susan stayed down, her eyes closed. She became aware of footsteps, sand crunching underfoot. Her arm was grasped; she was pulled to a sitting position.

"Susan, is that you? Are you alright?" It was Tav. "You aren't hit, are you? You couldn't have been hit."

Susan opened her eyes, felt the blood begin to flow through her body. "No, I'm not hit." She became conscious of Tav holding her, supporting her back. She pushed away, struggled to her feet. "I'm okay."

"I never expected you to come this way, the long way. I expected you to come directly in from the picnic area. It never occurred to me you might come this way."

Susan felt anger. "What difference does it make which way I came here? What are you shooting at, anyway?" She glanced at his rifle, which lay on the ground where he left it when he reached her.

Tav shook his head, his look earnest. "Ground squirrels. It's the maintenance job I mentioned. The little buggers constantly burrow under the paths and around signs and cause a hazard. I have to keep them under control." He nodded toward the rifle.

Susan shook his arm off her shoulder. "I'm okay, I'm startled. I'm not used to hearing bullets whistle by me."

"Well, it wasn't that close."

Susan glared at him.

"Okay, okay, you're right. It should never have happened. I never saw you until after I fired, but I should have been much more cautious."

Susan was somewhat mollified, but didn't respond.

"Come on. Let's go back up and get a nice cup of tea. You'll feel better. Then you can tell me why you're so concerned for Zack's safety."

Susan reluctantly agreed, was cajoled into following Tav up the trail. Once opened, the door to fear closed slowly, however, and suspicion followed. She began to imagine it was Tav's voice on the telephone, warning her away. She noticed he carried no game bag, had no ground squirrels. The slot canyon steepened, ended at an abrupt climb of forty feet up sheer-faced boulders, aided by iron rungs sunk into the rock. Tav moved up easily, the rifle cradled in one arm, his other hand grasping rungs. Susan found it much more difficult. She tried to imagine climbing down the opposite way, as Tav had apparently expected her to do. She doubted she would even have attempted it.

Her head full of these thoughts, Susan felt less than comfortable when they emerged from the canyon into the full afternoon light. It was an easy stroll down the road from the picnic area to the ranger station. Tav gestured her to a chair on the tiny porch and went inside to brew tea. She wanted to leave, but felt trapped.

Tav was back in moments with a tea tray and set it on a small table.

"Sugar?"

"No, thank you. I like to experience the full bouquet."

"That seems like you, to want to experience it all."

Susan glanced up at him. "How do you mean?"

"You don't pull back from a new experience, in fact you charge toward it. Take that iron ladder we just climbed; you didn't seem dismayed in the least bit." After a moment he said, "It's why I expected you to come from that end of the trail."

UNDER DESERT SAND

It seemed to Susan he was trying to regroup, to excuse his actions. "I think you overestimate both my curiosity and my courage," she said.

He sipped his tea, looked at her over the lip of the cup. He set the cup down deliberately, carefully. "What is it you have learned causing you to worry about Zack and Eagle Feather? You mentioned something about lost treasure."

Where Susan had once been ready to bring Tav into her confidence, she was now hesitant. The whir of a bullet passing so near her, even if accidental, gave her pause. "I spent today in the public library at Needles, looking for any historical reference to Hidden Springs, any occurrence which might offer an explanation for the way those two boys died."

She glanced at Tav.

He nodded, waited.

"If those boys were not there to shoot each other, in some romantically inspired moment of nonsense, what were they doing? I think the most likely answer is they were looking for something."

"A buried treasure, you said."

"Well, why not? Young guys, adventurous, romantic ideas; they may well have heard some of the legends I read about today."

"Such as?"

"Well, such as the Kokoweef underground river of gold, where black sands are permeated with gold dust. That's no more than fifteen miles from Hidden Springs."

"I've heard of it." Tav shifted his position, stretched out his legs. "If that's what they were after, why were they at Hidden Springs?"

176

Susan shrugged. She hadn't touched her tea, she realized—that might make her appear anxious. She picked it up now and sipped.

Tav studied her. "Susan, you are not yourself. I'm afraid my carelessness has put a barrier between us. I am truly sorry."

Susan gave a quick, bright smile. "I'll get over it. To get to the point, my research today revealed a number of possible mineral deposits, valuable resources that have been discovered and lost over time in this region. While I sat at the desk in the library, the thought came to me the boys might have been searching for gold, or silver—that somehow they learned of it, and that someone else was also hunting it and wanted to prevent them from finding it. Then I thought about Zack and Eagle Feather out there combing the area and I began to worry for their safety." Susan looked at Tav and gave a wave of her arm. "Now that I'm out here in the open air, my fears seem unfounded."

Tav's eyes searched her face. "Do you still want to go find your friends and warn them?"

Susan stood. "Not warn them, maybe fill in some spaces for them. I'm not sure they see any angle beyond the sheep versus cattle scenario." She turned to go.

Tav rose to follow her.

Susan put up her palm, smiled warmly. "I was panicked before. You have helped. But there's no need for you to babysit me any further."

Tav stared, paused. In a few seconds he shrugged, then smiled and resumed his seat. "As you wish."

Susan drove north over dusty hard-pack with the radio's single speaker groaning a comforting Country/Western song. She barely noticed it while she

177

examined her feelings. If the mosquito buzz of a bullet passing so near her had done anything, it brought to her a new sense of reality. Out here, people used guns like tools. They used them for 'maintenance', to clean up messes, to control their landscapes. What was the value of human life in this place? She guessed it depended upon the man wielding the weapon. For some, it might just come down to whether one can take a life and at the same time safeguard one's own.

Susan didn't think Tav was that way, although in fact she didn't know him at all. Her instincts had caused her to hold her cards close to her chest with him, a reaction to his carelessness. She'd probably be a lot less open with the people of the desert from now on.

Despite four-wheel drive, the Subaru lacked the clearance to drop into the dry creek bed on the road to Hidden Springs, so Susan parked it, removed the keys, and began to walk. It took her ten minutes to reach Hidden Springs, the sand so deep in the ruts at times it was like trying to climb a dune at the beach.

She was disappointed when the gate came in sight, but not the Jeep. The gate appeared secured, the lock in place. She turned to go, saw a flash of movement. Big Blue careened toward her through the blackbrush. She braced for impact.

As Blue enveloped her face with his tongue she heard Eagle Feather call a greeting. There he was on the far side of the fence. She went over to him.

"Where's Zack?"

"He went on to the sheep camp. I stayed to give this place another look. How'd you get here?"

"I have Butch Short's old Subaru, but it couldn't make it this far."

178

Eagle Feather studied her face, seemed to read something in it. "Maybe I should ask why are you here?"

Susan leaned against the fence, her legs a little weak. Now in the comfort of Eagle Feather's presence, she let down her defenses. "I think we're in more danger here than we realize."

"Why do you think so?"

Susan told him her findings.

Eagle Feather listened without comment; let her finish. When she was done, he looked across the crime scene, up the slope to the windmill, at the blackbrush and sage where the old cabin foundation stones rested. He lifted his eyes to look beyond, down the valley toward the higher hills. He pointed.

"That would be Table Top Mountain. We cannot see the flat summit from this angle. Those cliffs could be where they found the shaft." He glanced back at the windmill and the nearby terrain. "They may have used a rocker to sift the gold. If they found a vein and needed to separate ore from other materials, this would be a good place." He glanced behind them. "They could have shipped the gold from here by wagon; it's isolated, yet not far from the Fairfield Road junction. From there, the road went directly north to Vegas."

Susan nodded, feeling her excitement return. "If we accept that possibility, we can't ignore the connection between the men involved in the gunfight and the discovery of gold on Table Top Mountain. Remember, the man Simmons, who found the gold with his partner Skaggs, had once been a foreman of the Winslow Cattle Company. He would have known Curt Johnson, the current foreman, and the de facto guardian of this well. If the gold came here, Johnson had to be in on it."

UNDER DESERT SAND

Eagle Feather gave Susan a searching look. "Your theory is the 1905 gunfight had nothing to do with water rights, and a lot to do with gold."

"It's one theory," Susan said. "But if it's true, we have to wonder what happened to the man Bob Simmons and his partner Andy Skaggs. We know Johnson died in the gunfight. But what happened to Simmons and Skaggs after that? And to the gold?" She turned to face Eagle Feather, hands on hips. "What if the gold is still here? What if some friend or relative of Simmons or Skaggs is trying to locate it and is ready to make sure no one else finds it first?"

CHAPTER TWENTY-SEVEN

They decided to make their first visit to Hidden Springs at dusk, when fewer people were about, and before full darkness made the search too difficult. When three hours of full daylight remained, they packed water, energy bars, headlamps, a folding shovel, and the map copy. They dressed in the darkest clothing they owned and strapped on their gun belts.

Col argued against the guns. "Why do we even need them?"

Julio waved a hand in frustration. "You saw Bronc coming out of our tent, the look on his face. Was there any doubt in your mind he would have shot us if we challenged him?"

Col, remembering, had no reply.

"Besides, it'll be night, we should have some protection. Rifles won't help us, we can't see far enough in the dark."

Col shrugged. He couldn't argue that point either. Despite the discomfort of the weight of the handgun and ammo belt, he strapped it on.

They mounted up, checked on the sheep, instructed the dogs, and rode down from Hackberry Mountain toward Hidden Springs. Their route took them along the outflow of Watson Wash and through the blackbrush scrub along the Woods Mountains. The final leg was parallel to the imposing rise of Table Top Mountain, the last two miles along a dry creek bed and across the cactus and yucca valley to the spring. Shadows were long now; they hoped to meld into their surroundings despite more open terrain.

UNDER DESERT SAND

They came upon the dirt track from Kellogg Ranch to Hidden Springs. From this point forward they faced their greatest risk of discovery. Although they were on what was technically free range, some might regard their presence with suspicion. But here at this time of day they were unlikely to meet anyone—and they didn't.

At Hidden Springs they dismounted on the rise above the well and tied their horses to the fence. The ghostly outline of the broken down windmill dangled its perforated blades into the upper branches of the cottonwood. West of them, the slope was mottled with blackbrush, dark patches over the sand. Below them, the ground sloped to a level area, beyond it the shadowy smudge of the concrete holding tank. Whatever they sought must be somewhere under that level sand.

Now was the blue-grey liminal moment of twilight; no birds sounded, no insects buzzed, no breeze stirred. With careful movements submissive to the silence, the young sheepherders found their headlamps and unloaded the shovels and probes.

Julio held the map; Col stood next to him and illuminated it with his headlamp. Julio lay the compass on the map, oriented due west. His eyes moved from map to slope and traced a route.

"That's it. We step off sixty paces," Julio whispered. "Ready?" He led off.

The direction took them straight through the tough dense scrub. Julio ploughed through oblivious to spines, trying to keep constancy to his step and not forget his count. Col followed.

At sixty paces Julio stopped, stood, rotated his body and faced north. After a breath and a swipe with his sleeve across his forehead, he plunged on. The downslope leg went faster. When Julio's count reached thirty paces, they stood on level sand. It was easier to keep their strides even once out of the clingy scrub. At forty paces Julio stopped, turned, and faced east.

He reached out a hand. "Let me have the compass."

Col gave it to him.

Julio oriented the compass due east, looked up and picked out a focal point. He glanced at Col. "I'll take two steps and then probe. You probe the alternate step. That way we save time."

"Okay." Before handing Julio the probe, Col held both sticks out like a divining rod and made them vibrate.

"Very funny." Julio grabbed his probe, paced two steps, and sunk the stick deep into the ground. The sand was soft; it penetrated easily. He took two more steps, repeated his action. Col followed and probed the alternate steps, as instructed.

There were several false alarms, including an old tin can, so rusted the original contents could not be discerned, a chunk of hard wood, and three stones—but no treasure.

Julio looked back at their tracks in the sand. "Maybe we should go back and probe where we didn't probe before."

"How small do you think the treasure is?" Col said, and chuckled. "Let's go back to the windmill and try again. I'll lead this time. My steps are longer than yours."

His laugh and his voice came louder than intended. As the echo of it died away, he thought he heard another sound. He glanced quickly at Julio who was staring up the slope, his mouth agape.

Col followed his gaze, saw a flash of movement, something indefinable had disappeared into the shadows.

"What—the fuck—was that?" Julio said, his voice hushed.

"What was what? What did you see?"

"I don't know. I don't know what it was."

"Is somebody up there?"

"Something is up there." Julio's eyes were huge. "I don't know what the fuck it was."

"What did you see?"

"It was something walking up there, walking like a human but it wasn't human, it couldn't have been human."

"Hold on, let's not panic. I saw something move near windmill, but it disappeared before I could see what it was."

Julio held up a hand, hushed Col. "Listen to the horses."

Col became aware for the first time of frightened neighs, stomping hooves. "It must be a bear." He was concerned for the horses. "We'd better get up there."

Julio grabbed his arm. "Wait. It wasn't a bear. Believe me, it wasn't a bear. You don't want to go up there now."

Col turned, studied Julio. "I think we better get out of here."

"How can we? We have to go right past where it was to get to the horses."

Col couldn't believe his ears. His friend had always maintained control of himself in the past, no matter the circumstance. Now he was a mess.

Col took Julio by the arm and spoke calmly. "We'll walk a wide circuit around the slope, way over there, and loop around to the horses."

Julio hesitated, nodded. He took out his pistol, cocked it.

"Whoa," Col said. "You lead. I don't want to get shot."

He urged Julio forward. They walked back along their steps, made a wide arc around the patch of blackbrush, their eyes on the shadows around the windmill the entire time. When they reached the horses, they found them calm now, ears perked, nosing the boys for treats. There had been no movement, no sign of any creature near the windmill, as far as Col could tell. But now it was true dark, mystery cloaked everything.

The boys mounted quickly and rode away at a fast trot. Not long into their journey the moon rose and their way grew easier. Now their surroundings seemed friendlier. Neither boy uttered a word the entire way home.

It was well after nine when they began the climb up Hackberry Mountain. They greeted the dogs, checked the sheep and rode up to camp. In the tent, Julio placed his pistol in the holster near the doorway within easy reach. Not until both were snuggled in their sleeping bags did Col repeat his question.

"What did you see?"

His friend did not reply at first. Col waited. At last Julio said, "I really don't know what I saw. But whatever it was, it was huge, it walked upright like a human and it had red glowing eyes that glared right into mine."

CHAPTER TWENTY-EIGHT

Eagle Feather stared across the creosote and cholla landscape to distant Flat Top Mountain and pondered Susan's theory. As always, her logic was unassailable. If gold was involved, few white men could just walk away. If the gunslinger Simmons and his partner had stayed around, and they knew gold was buried nearby, they would have tried to retrieve it by now.

He did the mental math. The gunfight took place in 1905. The men were probably not much older than forty at the time, but even if they were shy of twenty it was unlikely they were still alive. But a younger relative, a grandchild, even, might have learned about the gold and the failed attempts to retrieve it over the years. It was less likely to be an outsider, Eagle Feather thought, because secrets involving great wealth tended to stay within families.

He turned to Susan. "I like your thinking. I think we should do more research, check the genealogical records of the families who settled here, find out which of our new friends is a branch on a local family tree."

Susan grimaced. "My first suspect is Bronc."

"His actions are suggestive."

Susan looked at Big Blue, relaxing in the shade of the windmill cottonwood. "Have you learned anything new here?"

Eagle Feather shook his head. "Blue and I retraced the steps of the boys one more time. There is no doubt in my mind they were searching for something when they were killed. I found these." He walked to the fence and picked up two sticks from the ground. He held them up for Susan to see.

"Sticks?"

Eagle Feather nodded. "I found these near the location of each body."

He handed them to Susan. "What do you see?"

Susan took them, studied them. "Someone cut off the appendages, like they were making an arrow or something."

Eagle Feather nodded. "They are not straight enough for arrows. These were cut from juniper, which occurs at a higher elevation than here. Someone stripped them with a knife after they were cut, as you noticed. The maker wanted them to move easily through a substance."

"Through the air?"

Eagle Feather shook his head. "No, not the air, through sand. Look where the sap resides at the cut nodules. See how the fine particles of sand have stuck to it, and not just on one side where they landed when tossed or dropped; on all sides. These were inserted into the sand as probes." He held Susan's eye. "The boys were searching for something deep under the sand."

Susan inspected the wands. "They could have been used for markers."

"Sure. But why then go to the trouble of stripping every little branch and knot?"

"Then haven't we proved my...our theory? Someone buried valuable ore of some kind here, ore they found nearby, probably Table Top Mountain. The 1905 gunfight was all about possession of the gold. Someone still alive today knows about it, or at least recently learned about it and is looking for his opportunity to remove it. Somehow these boys also learned about it, and when they went looking they were murdered." Susan pivoted, searched the horizon. "Take it a step further, someone is

187

going to be just as worried we might stumble onto this hoard, meaning, someone is as likely to shoot us, like they shot up Zack's Jeep."

"I think that is possible."

"I think we need to go warn Zack, tell him our suspicions."

Eagle Feather agreed. "We can take these wands to the Sheriff's office in Needles, see if they can get prints or DNA."

"And I can do some genealogical research back at the library."

Eagle Feather whistled to Big Blue, who rose up and lumbered after them. At the Subaru, the dog stretched out on the rear seat across Susan's maps and notes.

Eagle Feather looked at the little car doubtfully. "This won't leave us stranded somewhere, will it?"

Susan laughed. "It's four wheel drive. It can get us through all but the deepest stuff."

"If you say so."

Susan took the wheel and Eagle Feather slid into the passenger seat. It took them 25 minutes to reach the mouth of the Watson Wash. The Subaru tackled drifted sand and potholes with ease. They found Zack's Jeep up the slope where they had parked last visit.

Susan pulled just off the road, turned off the ignition. "I don't think we need test our luck that far," she said, nodding toward the Jeep and the deep sand and brush surrounding it. She started to step out her door, hesitated.

"What's that popping sound?"

Eagle Feather listened. It came again.

"That's gunfire." He looked at Susan. "Do you have a weapon?"

Susan's eyes were large and round. "No," she whispered.

"Neither do I. This may be tricky." Eagle Feather slid out of the car and closed the door quietly. Another pop sounded. "That's rifle fire, off toward the sheep camp. It might be someone hunting, it might be someone shooting sheep, or..."

"It could be someone shooting Zack," Susan finished for him, in a rush.

Eagle Feather nodded. "Unfortunately, that is the most likely scenario." He began to remove his shoes. He placed them carefully on the floor of the Subaru. Reaching into his daypack, he removed a pair of moccasins bound together with leather lace. He put them on.

"We don't know how many shooters there are. We have to assume there could be a second one watching for people like us to interfere. If they scouted us, they know Zack left me behind at Hidden Springs. They would also know I did not have a vehicle. We might surprise them." Eagle Feather drew a breath. He wasn't used to talking this much, to explaining himself, but it was important Susan understood. "Zack may be hunkered down, which explains why they are still shooting. I know he has his handgun, so they won't try to get too close. The question is, does he have his rifle with him?"

Eagle Feather stood. He was ready. A brown bandana held his long hair tight to his head under his hat. "We'll leave Blue in the vehicle, no point to risking him." He motioned Susan to follow, moved immediately up to the edge of the wash where there was cover. When they came opposite the Jeep, Eagle Feather told Susan to stay put and eased across the wash to the vehicle. As he returned, Susan saw he held a rifle.

189

Back with Susan, Eagle Feather shook his head. "I don't know whether to be happy or pissed he didn't take his rifle with him. Bad for him, good for us."

They continued up the narrowing wash, then moved east toward the sheep camp, keeping low in the sagebrush. The sporadic popping sounds came louder, the sharp reports better defined as they drew nearer. Then came a different sounding shot.

Eagle Feather paused. "That is Zack's pistol," he whispered. "He is keeping them honest."

Susan breathed out. He was alive, at least.

They came to the end of the thickest of the sage and creosote, now tundra-like sparse grasses and occasional boulders offered them little cover. The arroyo where the shepherd boys' had established their camp was before them, several hundred yards away. As Eagle Feather studied the terrain, another rifle shot sounded.

"I think the sniper is upslope over there." Eagle Feather pointed for Susan. "Zack must be in that jumble of rocks just beyond the arroyo." He touched Susan's arm. "Stay close."

Eagle Feather wormed along on the ground. Susan followed, tried to stay as low. They came to a halt behind a large boulder, just sufficient to hide them. It was no more than three feet at its highest point, about the same in width.

"We are now in line of sight for the shooter," Eagle Feather whispered. "You will stay here and stay down. I will try to work around behind him." Susan stared at him, waited.

Eagle Feather touched her arm again. "I will need you to draw their fire. Stay flat on the ground. Wait five minutes after I am gone, then shake this bush right here.

190

Do it once, wait one minute, do it again. Continue until you know you have drawn his fire."

Eagle Feather took his hat from his head, placed it on top of the boulder. "He will shoot at the hat. He will not come closer, if he tries, Zack or I can shoot him. Just stay down." Eagle Feather emphasized each of the last words. Then he was gone.

Susan did as she was told. When her watch told her five minutes had elapsed, she shook the bush several times and waited. Nothing happened.

She looked at her watch, watched the minute hand crawl its way around, reached out and shook the bush again. This time she heard the mosquito-like whine of a bullet, heard the crack of a rifle, something hit her on her back. Panicked, she rolled tight to the base of the boulder, felt something under her. She reached for it, came back with Eagle Feather's hat. It now had a tidy round hole through each side of the crown.

Susan decided she did not like the feeling of bullets passing close to her. She also decided not to move any more bushes. She was quite confident her presence had been noticed.

CHAPTER TWENTY-NINE

An entire week passed before either boy mentioned the map or Hidden Springs, Col out of consideration for Julio, and Julio from reluctance to revisit the image in his mind.

One night, without preamble, Julio spoke about it. "I wonder if that thing had anything to do with Old Juan leaving so abruptly—the monster, I mean."

Startled, Col stared at his friend, then into the fire. "I didn't see what you saw, but if it was so terrifying, you could be right."

"I wonder about Bronc."

"What do you wonder?"

"How much he actually knows. He was looking for papers left by Juan. They were important enough he came here and went right into our tent uninvited. What papers could he mean other than the map?"

"Maybe he owed Old Juan money, wanted to destroy the records." Col shrugged. "He seems like a person who would intrude for less reason than that."

Julio was silent for a while. "I saw that monster thing as a silhouette against the sky. It was very scary, impossible to believe I was seeing it." Julio stirred the fire. "Still, I can't help wondering if it could have been staged." He looked at Col. "You know, Bronc in a costume, to scare us away."

"Where did he go, then? You said it walked right to the windmill, then disappeared."

Julio's eyes went back to the fire. "Yeah, I know. That is sure the way it looked."

"But?"

Julio grimaced. "I guess I have to check it out, to be sure, to stop being afraid. Maybe there is a hollow near the tree we didn't notice, or some way to disappear through the brush. I'd hate myself if I thought I allowed Bronc to scare me away with a trick like that."

"So we're going back?"

Julio shrugged. "I have to, you don't." He stared into the coals. "I've been thinking about Juan. There are two possibilities; either he ran away or he was killed. If he was murdered, his stuff has to be somewhere. We found his Green Card, so I believe he was killed. Otherwise, like we said, he'd have come back to look for it."

Col nodded. "It seems a strong possibility."

"Yeah, but we haven't found his stuff—tent, clothing, saddle, cookware; we're talking about a lot of stuff. We've been wandering around this place for over a month now and we haven't found another thing, not even signs of digging. So if we figure Bronc or someone else killed Juan and buried his stuff, where did he do it?"

"Couldn't Bronc just take the stuff home, hide it there?"

Julio shook his head. "I don't think so. Would you? If you murder a guy, you want the evidence to be in a neutral place, not where it could be associated with you." Julio shook his head again. "No, you bury the stuff and the body somewhere you think it will never be found, somewhere no one else would think to look."

"Okay, Sherlock, where do you figure that is?"

"I don't know. But I do know this: if I thought someone was going to dig near the place I'd buried him, I'd try to scare him away."

Col turned to stare at Julio. "Wait a minute. Are you saying you think Old Juan is buried at the springs, not a treasure?"

Julio stirred the fire. "Maybe it's both. Think about it. What if there is something valuable hidden, and Bronc knows about it, but he doesn't know how to find it. Then he figures out Juan maybe knows, somehow. So he follows him to Hidden Springs, watches him search. Maybe Juan spots him, or maybe Bronc gets impatient and tries to make Juan tell him what he knows. We'll probably never know that part. Things go wrong; he kills Juan without finding out his secret. There he is at Hidden Springs with a body. Juan probably had a shovel with him, so Bronc uses it to bury him around there somewhere. He can't risk hauling the body away, right?"

Col stared at his friend, amazed. "You've really thought this all out."

"Yeah. It's what I've been doing instead of sleeping. Anyway, here is Bronc in the middle of the night with Old Juan's horse. He knows he's got maybe four, five hours of darkness to make it look like Old Juan just decided to go away. So he rides to Juan's camp leading his horse, collapses his tent and somehow loads up all his stuff on both horses." Julio turned to point to the rocks where they found the Green Card. "Right there, the card falls out from somewhere, Bronc doesn't notice. Even if he did, he wouldn't know its importance. Now he has to walk back to the springs, leading both horses, 'cause it would be a lot of stuff. He digs a big hole next to Juan's body, dumps the stuff in, probably including the saddle, and covers it all up." Julio cracked a dry smile. "It's a long night for Bronc. After that, he leads the horse off somewhere, probably puts a bullet in its head on some lonely mountain top."

"What about the treasure?"

Julio's laugh was harsh. "If there is one, Bronc has now effectively screwed himself. He can't be hanging

194

around Hidden Springs, digging or what not, without arousing someone's curiosity. If someone gets curious, begins to dig around and finds the body, well...it's Katy Bar The Door for Bronc."

Col stared at his friend. "Man, it all fits together perfectly."

Julio nodded.

"But Bronc can't let go, right?" Col said. "He came here to see if maybe we had the map."

Julio nodded.

"But if he can't go there and dig for it anyway, why—?"

"Why would he still want the map?" Julio glanced at his friend. "I don't think he does. I think he wants us to find the map. He talks about papers so we'll wonder about it, and look around for ourselves, and—"

"And then we go hunt the treasure for him." Col felt a shiver pass over him. "All Bronc has to do is watch and wait. If we find something, he takes it and buries us next to Juan."

"That's about how I see it."

Col sat thinking about it, his brain straining to understand the implications. "But what about the monster, the creature you saw? Why would Bronc want to scare us away if he wants us to find the treasure?"

"I don't think he wants to scare us away," Julio said. "Maybe he put on that getup in case someone else saw him, to scare them away. There are legends about that spring, apparently." Julio shook his head. "Or..." He hesitated, glanced at Col.

"Or the thing you saw is real?" Col laughed. "I like the other scenario better."

The two boys stared silently into the fire.

Col shifted his legs, cleared his throat. "What now? Do we play into his hands? Or give it up?"

Julio's face pulsed red in the firelight; his brown eyes glistened. "Do you think there is something buried there? Other than Old Juan, I mean?"

"I dunno. Juan or someone went to a lot of trouble to scratch that map onto the rock. Why would he have done that unless he was convinced?"

"That's the way I see it. So the next question is, how much do we want to risk to find a treasure?"

Col shook his head. "I don't want to give my life for it. But I don't want Bronc to get away with murdering Old Juan, either."

"Same here. So maybe we can kill two birds with one stone." Julio's eyebrows raised. "Sorry, poor choice of words under the circumstances."

"You're thinking we draw out Bronc and find the treasure at the same time?"

"In a way. Maybe we get some help. We recruit someone to watch Bronc while he watches us."

CHAPTER THIRTY

Eagle Feather crawled up the slope within a tangle of creosote, taking pains not to disturb the brush, a skill well developed while hunting game as a guide. The wind was a mild breeze out of the west, swaying the upper branches. Ten minutes into his stalk he heard the rifle bark again, raised his head enough to orient to the sound, judged the sniper had not changed position and had just fired at Susan. That was good. The shooter would be worried now, believing he faced two adversaries. He would have to decide whether to attempt to keep both pinned down, or begin a retreat. Eagle Feather watched for any indication of either, but saw none. He knew Zack would realize the sniper had fired in a different direction, would know someone else had joined the party, might try to take advantage.

Eagle Feather continued his stalk. Every few minutes, he raised his head, looked toward the shooter's position for signs of movement. He was well up the slope by now, but wanted to reach a position above the rifleman if he could. His eye caught movement, the tip of a creosote bush swayed slightly when its neighbors did not. The breeze had not moved it. The sniper was near a large boulder downslope from him, much nearer than Eagle Feather expected. He let his breath out slowly.

There was little cover where he was now; glancing around, he saw a smallish boulder ten feet upslope and moved toward it with great caution. It would not do to reveal himself now. Once there, he rested his rifle across it and waited.

A bullet cut through the brush near Eagle Feather, surprising him. It hadn't come from the sniper; the report sounded more like a pistol. So Zack was on the move. This was a dangerous game. Zack did not know where the sniper was concealed and might mistake Eagle Feather for his adversary.

More movement of brush; the sniper was retreating toward the ridge. Eagle Feather aimed a few feet ahead of the disturbed branches and pulled the trigger. He heard a grunt. He'd hit his target.

He stood, aimed his rifle at the same place, and waited. He saw Zack rise from concealment downslope and move cautiously up toward him, his pistol aimed in the same direction. Zack neared the spot, crouched, moved in close, peered into the brush.

Eagle Feather knew from the way he stood and lowered his pistol the sniper had eluded them. He watched Zack examine the spot, glance up the hill toward the ridge, raise an arm to motion Eagle Feather and continue up the slope.

Eagle Feather angled toward him. When he arrived, Zack gave a slow shake of his head. "You came along at a good time."

"I spend a lot of time saving your skin, White Man." Eagle Feather crouched to study a small patch of blood. "I only grazed him."

They followed scuffmarks in the sand on toward the ridge. "He moves well, and he's a good shot—knocked your hat right off the rock," Zack said.

"He's made it up and over the ridge by now." Eagle Feather turned downslope, cupped his mouth and shouted to Susan.

Zack swung toward Eagle Feather. "Susan's down there? I hope she's okay."

"I gave her strict instructions not to move."

198

Zack's face showed anger. "You used Susan as a decoy?"

Eagle Feather raised an eyebrow. "Well, yes, I did."

"How could you do that?"

"There wasn't much choice."

"You'd better explain."

Eagle Feather remained calm, explained patiently. "The shooter had you pinned when we arrived, pistol against rifle." He held up the rifle. "I knew that because you seem to have forgotten it. The shooter was upslope, didn't know we were there. If I could get above him, we would have him in crossfire. Susan could not move up the slope without exposing herself. The safest place for her was right there behind the rock. I put my hat on it, asked Susan stay down and tug the creosote bush one time to draw fire." Eagle Feather shrugged, stared at Zack. "She did a good job, exposed the rifleman; we drove him away."

They watched as Susan brushed dirt from her clothing and climbed toward them. Eagle Feather's hat was in her hand. She waved it when she drew near. "You have a hole in your hat," she called to Eagle Feather, and grinned.

Zack's expression softened. "Thank you, friend. You were right. I was in a bind."

Eagle Feather took his hat from Susan, examined the bullet hole, put the hat on his head. "I need a new one anyway."

Susan saw the patch of blood. "Where is the sniper?"

"Gone, likely," Zack said. "Eagle Feather nicked him, but he escaped up to the ridge."

Susan grimaced. "I don't want to hear another bullet pass by me for the rest of my life. Two in one day is two too many."

Both men turned to stare at her.

"Two bullets? I only heard one fired in your direction," Zack said.

Susan sighed. "I hadn't meant to tell you. I stopped by to see Tav. He was exterminating ground squirrels, didn't see me coming, and a bullet came a little too close. It was scary but no big deal."

"You did not tell me that," Eagle Feather said.

"It was an accident. It wasn't worth mentioning. Tav felt really bad."

Zack didn't say anything. He watched Susan's face, glanced at Eagle Feather.
Their eyes met for a moment.

"Can you read any sign here?" Zack said, changing the subject.

"It was not a woman this time," Eagle Feather said. "This one has bigger feet. Now we know two people do not like you. That is closer to your usual average."

Zack grinned. "Yeah, that's about right."

Susan glanced at both men. "Well, it couldn't have been Tav. I was just with him. We were on his porch. He might have had time to follow me, but he wouldn't have had time to circle around here and ambush Zack before we arrived."

Zack sighed and turned back. "Let's go back to the sheep camp. I was interrupted before I could finish searching."

They walked down the slope to the stones where Zack had taken shelter.

"It's fortunate I happened to be right here," Zack said, glancing at the rock surface. "The first shot didn't miss me by much, it hit right next my hand." He pointed out the bullet pockmark. "I was just able to scramble behind this boulder. I had been about to investigate that." Zack pointed to slab of rock fifty feet away, half a foot thick, shaped like a coffin. "I had noticed it just before the sniper shot at me."

They walked over to it. Zack stared down at its surface. "Well, look there."

Susan knelt for a closer look, breathed in. "I think you found the map."

CHAPTER THIRTY-ONE

The following morning, as Col and Julio enjoyed their coffee by the fire, Shep's low growl warned them they had a visitor. Col stood to look. A man was climbing toward their camp.

Fifty feet away, the stranger stopped to wave. "Hello the camp. Mind if I come up?" He wore an official uniform.

"Come on up," Col shouted back.

The boys watched the man stride up the hill. He moved with the ease of one accustomed to the terrain. When he drew near, Col saw he was a stocky man with a broad, swarthy face and large brown eyes—a Native American, he thought at first glance. The man's expression was impassive.

"Care for coffee?" Julio stirred the embers under the pot.

The man nodded. "Yes, please."

Col extended his hand. "I'm Col."

The man took it. "My name is Tav." His grip was strong; fit the look of him.

Julio added water to the pot. "I'm Julio."

The man nodded to him. "I work for the Preserve. I've been meaning to get over here to say howdy to you boys and see how you're gettin' on."

"That's kind of you. Fact is we're doing just fine." Julio grinned over his shoulder.

"I'm glad to hear it." The man squatted near them, looked comfortable that way—another Indian trait, Col thought. "What's your job with the preserve?"

Tav gave a slow shake of his head. "Just about everything. You might say I am six park rangers rolled into one."

Julio passed a steaming cup of coffee to Tav. "Where's your office?"

Tav took the cup, carefully sipped the hot liquid. "Ah, that's good." He raised his eyes to Julio. "I work in the little store at Hole-in-the-Wall, issue permits, sell camping items, books on nature, and give lots of free advice." He took another sip.

Julio grinned. "Got any advice for us?"

Tav wiped his chin. "Sure do. Stick to tending sheep."

Col felt a twist in his stomach. "What do you mean?"

The boys stared at Tav.

"Hey, I'm not trying to scare you. No offense meant."

"But what did you mean by stick to tending sheep?"

Tav took his time. He held his empty cup out to Julio. "Mind?"

Julio took it, refilled it, handed it back.

"I don't guess you boys ever got to meet Old Juan, the man who worked here before you."

They shook their heads.

"Nice old guy. I came out here like this to see him several times. Very hospitable." He gestured with his cup. "Like you boys. We had good chats, the old guy knew a lot about a lot of things." He took another sip. "Thing is, sitting out here, just him and the sheep, you get lonely, start to get strange ideas. He used to talk to me about them sometimes."

"What sort of strange ideas?" Col asked.

"Well, fantasies, sort of, things right out of kids' books like ghosts and treasures and whatnot. Came on him slow, first thing you know he was all over these hills, lookin' for dragon hoards or who knows what."

"Do you have any idea what happened to him? From what we heard, he just disappeared," Col said.

"You think he went crazy?" Julio asked.

Tav frowned. "Not crazy, so much as stir crazy. Too much solitude." He flicked his gaze at Col. "What do I think? I think he had enough and just rode off."

Col kept his face still, stared into the fire. Tav apparently believed what everyone else believed, had no reason to think otherwise.

"Now you boys," Tav went on, "You have each other. Makes a big difference."

Julio's chin jutted slightly with the stubborn look Col knew well. "You advised us just now to stick with our sheep. Why'd you say that?"

Tav regarded each of them in turn. "Old Juan stirred up some folks with his wandering. He'd show up at night in places people didn't expect him, came near to getting shot more than once. I got a bunch of complaints about him. Just don't want to start hearing the same things about you fellas."

Julio's chin jutted even more. "We're on a lease on a National Preserve. I thought that meant it was public land."

Tav shrugged. "You're not the only ones on a lease. There's others have properties grandfathered, their ranches and camps been here since before the Preserve. Those properties will turn over to the government soon as the lessees die or quit the area, meanwhile we take some responsibility for keepin' up those lands. But that don't mean it ain't private, to their minds."

Col felt he knew where Tav was going. "So if it's got a fence around it, then—"

"That's right. A fence means keep out, in any language." Tav gave them a brief smile, without humor. "Look, I'm not trying to tell you boys how to lead your lives, just want you to know you're not in the city anymore. Wasn't that long ago people out here were shootin' each other over water rights."

He stood, handed the cup across to Julio. "Much obliged for the coffee. Nice to meet you two."

After Tav disappeared from sight toward the wash, Julio fed the dogs and the two friends walked down to the sheep.

Col put his thoughts into words. "He didn't just happen to turn up today. I wonder who complained?"

"No one could've known we went down to Hidden Springs, except maybe Bronc. Maybe we were wrong about him; maybe he doesn't want us to find the treasure for him after all and told Tav to warn us off." Julio grinned. "Maybe Tav is right, maybe we are leading too solitary a life, creating mysteries where they don't exist."

"The Green Card?" Col reminded him.

'Yeah, I know. That's the one piece of solid evidence that says Juan didn't just up and leave."

Col watched a lamb limping among the ewes. "That little guy's leg seems better. I think he'll recover."

"I don't see we have any choice."

Col glanced at Julio. "About what?"

"About checking out the map, seeing if we're right about Juan. I know it'll keep bothering me."

Col sighed. "I know. Okay, then, let's do it, get it over with. Let's do it tonight." He started back up the hill.

Julio followed. "Who will we get to watch our backs?"

Col felt a rise of impatience. All he wanted now was to get this over and done. If they finished with it tonight, he could call Kella tomorrow and make plans to see her again. He cared more about that. "I think we can both agree Tav didn't show up here today by coincidence. The only one who could possibly have seen us leave our camp is Bronc, there's just nobody else around."

"So?"

"So I think it had to be Bronc who complained to Tav. He'll know Tav was up here to warn us off, give us a scare. The last thing he'll expect is we go down there tonight, right after the warning." Col grew more confident about his logic even as he tried to convince Julio.

Julio shrugged. "I can't think of anyone around here to help us, anyway. If we locate Juan, we can get the authorities involved. If we locate the treasure—"

Col looked at his friend, waited.

Julio grinned. "Well, we'll figure that out when it happens."

CHAPTER THIRTY-TWO

They gathered around the slab. Susan traced a finger along the etched lines. Eagle Feather scraped off some caked dirt.

"We are not the first," he said. "You see how someone scraped away that layer of dirt as I am doing here. It is caked on, it did not just drop off."

"The shepherd boys must have discovered this," Susan said.

"How would they know to look for it?" Zack asked. "It had been resting face down, you can tell by that depression."

No one had an answer to that.

"The better question might be who carved this in the first place, and why?" Eagle Feather said.

"Maybe the one who buried something to begin with?" Zack suggested.

Susan shook her head. "If someone found gold ore on Flat Top Mountain, as my research suggests, and used Hidden Springs as part of their production and then buried the gold until they could move it, why come all the way over here, completely in the opposite direction and carve a map on a rock?"

Zack was confused. "Whoa, what's all that about?"

Susan gave an apologetic smile. "I haven't had a chance to tell you what I learned in the library. There is good reason to suspect the gunfight in 1905 was about gold, not water rights. I'm theorizing the publicity surrounding that event prevented the gold from being recovered. I suspect there was a third person involved, and maybe that person's relations are still trying to find it."

Zack tried to assimilate all that. "I guess we do have a lot to talk about. So who do you think did this?"

"I think it had to be a shepherd or cowboy, someone who had plenty of time to do the carving without being observed." Susan shook her head. "What I can't figure out is why anyone would go to all this trouble."

Eagle Feather grunted. "I think he did it to preserve his memory. Memory is uncertain; symbols carved on rock can revive them, as my people know. This person wanted to remember every detail. I see two reasons he might do this: one, if he wrote it down on paper the map might get lost or stolen; two, if other people found him with the map they would know he knew too much. I think he had seen the map somewhere, scratched it here before he could forget it, so no one would know he had it."

"But where is the original map? Where could he have seen it to memorize it? Who did he think might steal it from him? "

Eagle Feather shrugged.

"He saw it somewhere he wasn't supposed to see it," Zack said. "He remembered it and etched it on this stone, his own perfectly hidden map. It would be here when he needed it."

"I still don't get it. Why not just write it down on a piece of paper later on at home where no one would know?"

"Maybe too risky," Eagle Feather said.

"Right." Zack spoke as he thought. "This person must have known possessing the map would put him in danger. He must have figured if he etched it out here, no one could tie him to it. A tent is not a very secure place."

"Okay, let's be straight forward," Susan said. "We're talking about Juan, the old shepherd. His disappearance caused the boys to come here in the first place. The private investigator told you Jim Hatchett found the map in his attic. He actually showed it to Old Juan, hoping to get help locating the place it represents. Juan pretended he didn't know, but memorized it. One day he saw this slab and decided to carve it."

Zack stood, stretched. "I think we can guess Bronc was skulking around, saw Hatchett talking to Juan, maybe even watched Juan carving out the map. I'll bet Juan disappeared not too long after that."

Susan studied the etched slab, frowned. "From the caked dirt and disturbed ground, it appears this slab had been left face down, as you said. So how did Juan flip this thing over all by himself after he scratched the map on it?"

"Horsepower," Eagle Feather said.

"Oh."

Zack glanced at Susan. "We've still got a few blanks to fill in."

"Here is one," Eagle Feather said. "The two boys were at Hidden Springs to look for something under the sand when they died. Susan and I found wands they cut from branches to probe with."

Susan nodded. "Maybe the boys had learned about the treasure. They had to have a map to know where to look. Maybe they found this stone."

Eagle Feather rose from a squat and stood next to Zack. "Too many questions. What is next, White Man?"

"First I'll make a copy of this map. Then we'll find some excuse to visit Bronc and see if he's got a fresh wound." Zack stood at the end of the slab and snapped a picture with his phone. He studied it, nodded. "That's got it."

They headed back to the wash and their vehicles. Zack's memory was triggered. "I hope we don't find our tires flat again."

"That's another blank to fill in," Susan said. "Where does a woman sniper fit into the picture? We've been focused on Bronc. Do you think he has a female partner?"

"He doesn't strike me as the type to partner with a woman," Zack said.

"How do you plan to visit Bronc, White Man?"

"I think we'll just drive right up to the ranch and knock on the door," Zack said, grinning. He presented his plan to Eagle Feather. "From the little I've seen of Bronc, he has a prejudice against most things, but particularly against Native Americans. Susan and I will go to the Kellogg Ranch. Eagle Feather, you can take the Subaru and take Blue back to the motel. No sense in stirring up feelings needlessly."

Eagle Feather's eyes twinkled. "You are most considerate for I do not want my feelings stirred up."

Zack turned his eyes to Susan. "I don't expect us to be in any danger. From what Jones said, Hatchett is just as eager to get to the bottom of the killings as we are. I've been meaning to have a chat with Hatchett, anyway." He glanced at Eagle Feather. "My guess is Bronc will not show up there."

Eagle Feather took the Subaru keys from Susan. He let Blue out for a stretch, poured him some water. Blue sloshed up the liquid.

Zack spread a map across the hood of the Jeep, studied it. "The shortest way to get there is from Hidden Springs. From there, we can take this dirt track and save a lot of mileage." Zack folded the map. "That must be how

210

Bronc and Hatchett got to the spring the first day we saw them."

Eagle Feather tooted his horn and drove off.

The ride to Hidden Springs was by now very familiar. At the well, Zack climbed out and swung the gate open.

"I thought Bronc had a lock on that gate," Susan said, when he climbed back in the Jeep.

"He had no right. I had Butch Short remove it."

"Bronc isn't going to like that," Susan said.

Zack shrugged. "I can't spend time worrying about what Bronc likes."

The track wound around the windmill and continued on south. The road was primitive, but well packed. They were headed into the heart of Round Valley, an area of sparse pinyon and juniper with an occasional solitary Joshua tree. The going was slow; they had to watch for occasional deep sand. They came to a fence line, passed over a cattle guard. Beyond it were outbuildings. A large sign warned that trespassers would be prosecuted.

"Shot, more likely," Susan said, under her breath.

Zack grinned. "Let's not approach this with attitude. I suspect Mr. Hatchett will supply plenty for all of us."

Susan smiled back. "I see there's no attitude on your part either."

211

CHAPTER THIRTY-THREE

The Hatchett ranch house was a single floor home built in typical California style, with large windows and a sense of openness. A wide porch swept all the way around the building. The place had an air of bachelorhood about it, the chairs held stacks of leather harness, old lariats lay on the porch floor, toward the rear of the house beer bottles lined the rail like soldiers. Zack's boots clumped on the porch floor. He dropped the heavy brass knocker several times, heard it boom inside.

The door opened a minute later. Jim Hatchett, hair tousled, a look of surprise on his face, regarded them. He had old jeans on, a T-shirt, and bare feet. "Not too many people come knocking at this door," he said, almost as an apology. "Tolliver, right? And Dr. Apgar? C'mon in."

He led the way through a spacious entrance hall to a vast living room with a few leather chairs scattered about like so many cattle, without rhyme or reason. The portraits of stern old people on the walls, the red velvet border trim, the lace sheers at the windows presented a decayed Victorian look. The room seemed the antithesis of the house exterior.

"Sit," Hatchett said, and pointed to the nearest chairs. "Can I get you a drink?"

"Just water for me, if you don't mind," Susan said.

"I'm fine," Zack said. He lowered himself into a chair, admired the smell of the leather and the feel of the soft cushion. He noted the lace curtains were yellowed, the Oriental rug faded and torn by spurs. He figured the place hadn't felt a woman's touch in a long time.

Hatchett walked to a sideboard, reached into a small fridge and removed two water bottles, poured the water into whiskey glasses, brought them over. He looked at his watch. "By my reckoning, it's almost cocktail hour. Sure I can't find you something stronger?"

Zack smiled. "No thanks, I'm still on company time. But don't let us stop you."

"I doubt you could." He smiled, poured an ounce of Bowen's Whiskey into a glass. He carefully replaced the bottle before he spoke again. "This is when I'd ask you what brings you to this poor old rancher's home, way out in the middle of nowhere, but I got a fair idea." He turned to face them, lifted his glass. "Cheers."

Zack and Susan raised their glasses, sipped the water.

Hatchett turned another chair to face them, sat down. "I'm guessing either I'm a suspect in the shooting of those two boys, or you think I can tell you who is."

"We do have a few questions," Zack said.

Hatchett took a long swallow, set his glass down on an end table and twisted to look at Zack. "I need to get a few things squared in my mind before we go much further. First, just exactly what is your capacity in this investigation? What is your official standing? Should I give a holler out for my lawyer?"

Zack looked down at his glass, back at Hatchett. "Fair question. As of this moment, I am no more or less than a consultant to the investigative arm of BLM. My responsibility is to Butch Short. This conversation is not official, in that sense, but of course I could be required to repeat it under oath at some future time. Just as Mr. Jones could be, for instance."

"So you know about Mr. Jones."

"We have met, in fact." Zack glanced at Susan, then at Hatchett. "I should say, given that we've

213

established there's been murder committed on federal land, a likelihood exists I could be assigned officially to this case." He took a sip, peered over his glass. "It hasn't happened yet, though."

"Well, I see no reason to hold back what little I know. I see myself on a parallel path with you, hoping to learn the truth. That's why I hired Jones." Hatchett grimaced. "There's a long history in this area of conflict between cattle ranchers and sheep owners. I don't want the deaths of those two boys laid at my door."

Susan raised her eyebrows. "You think that could happen just because of the history of the region?"

Hatchett pondered her for a moment. "I'm sure you've done your homework. You must know a duel over water rights occurred at that very same spring over a hundred years ago. You may even know of my family's connection to that event."

Zack shook his head. "Not precisely."

"My grandfather was a cowboy with the big cattle concern that used to graze their beef through all this area, called the Winslow Cattle Company. That's how he came to be out here in the first place. At the time he rode for them, the ramrod's name was Skowler, a mean guy with a reputation as a gunfighter. There was a bunch of those type fellas out here in those days. Skowler was a hard man, difficult to work with. My grandpa quit the company, tried his hand at homesteading; that's when he built this place." Hatchett waved his arm, sloshing his whiskey in the glass. "Wasn't like this then, of course. But he did well enough, raised some beef cattle, stayed on good terms with the big outfit, not an easy thing to do."

"Why was that?" Susan leaned forward in her chair.

214

"Well, the Winslow outfit was losing calves pretty often. This was all open grazing, like it used to be in the Old Spanish days. No fences. You branded your calves soon as you could at rodeos, but they happened only once or twice a year. A lot of calves were born, stayed unbranded until you could get to it. So calves went missing, and at the same time some of the small sheep and cattle outfits would show up with a lot of calves, kind of an amazingly high birth rate. The Winslow cowboys naturally assumed those extra calves came from Winslow stock. Things got touchy.

"The settlers were afraid of Skowler. He was a bully, he'd drive cattle right through someone's newly planted field, claim it was Winslow land, dare them to do something about it. About the only guy in the valley not afraid of Skowler was Bob Simmons.

"Simmons came to the area long ago, well before my grandpa. He was no stranger to the outlaw trail, had a reputation with his gun as well. He worked a few cattle, but his heart wasn't really in it. He spent more time scouring the hills looking for precious minerals."

"What was Simmons like?" Susan asked.

"I never met him, of course, but my grandpa used to call him "a bit tetchy". He had lived by his gun for a long time, held his own with some pretty bad hombres. My grandpa, he wasn't a gunman, he was a farmer, but he did have an adventurous spirit." Hatchett sipped his whiskey, looked up, grinned. "Had to be, to come out here to make a living." He stared at the floor, remembering. "Anyways, the settlers sort of banded up behind Simmons. That's how my grandpa got thrown in with him."

"How'd they get along?" Zack asked.

"Surprisingly well. Simmons was a cowboy, knew about cattle, but not much about raising goats or pigs, not much about growing hay and vegetables. He'd come by, get advice from grandpa. They'd help each other with chores that needed two people to do. Grandpa was an easygoing guy, most folks got along with him. He knew something about geology and that got Simmons all excited. Pretty soon he got my grandpa to go along on his mineral hunts from time to time."   Hatchett paused, shifted his weight in his chair. "Then, to everyone's surprise, Skowler quit Winslow Cattle Company. Some say he got in a feud with the owners, but I don't buy that. I think Skowler just figured he could just help himself to Winslow cattle and there'd be no one to stop him. So he found himself a spot, homesteaded it, and his cattle herd grew faster than weeds after a rainstorm.

"Well, the Winslow Cattle Company couldn't stand for that, so they brought in yet another gunfighter to lead their outfit, name of Curt Johnson. He was rumored to be real fast and had more than a couple of killings to his name. That's when it became a war zone around here, with rifle sniping and bullet holes through windows; it was dangerous for folks just to work their farms." Hatchett lifted his palms. "It went both ways, mind. Johnson had settled into a cabin at Hidden Springs, to set guard over it. More than a few times he'd return to find bullet holes in his walls. Pretty soon most settlers and sheep herders were packing up and moving off to safer places."

"What did your grandpa do?" Susan asked.

Hatchett waved an arm to take in the entire ranch. "Obviously, he didn't leave. Funny thing was, he apparently ignored the whole thing. He spent more and more time up in the hills, sometimes with Simmons, sometimes alone. This was the time before grandpa met my grandma. He could disappear for days at a time if he wanted. I was told he was off some place when that gunfight broke out between Skowler and Johnson, didn't even know about it until he got back. "

"Jones told me about a map," Zack said. He saw a look of surprise pass over Hatchett's face. "That got anything to do with your grandpa and Simmons bein' up in the hills?"

"He told you about the map, did he?" Hatchett's eyes flickered from Zack to Susan. "Guess he might as well have taken out an add in the local newspaper." He sighed. "It doesn't really matter. I don't think that old map is more than a curiosity. Just don't want to see a bunch of treasure hunters running all over these hills tearing up the place."

"Why don't you think it's authentic?" Susan asked.

Hatchett shrugged. "First I heard of any map was when I came across it going through the old attic. Something like that, I'd expect it to be talked about in the family, if it was worth anything. God knows, the family sure could 'a used some treasure back then."

Susan leaned forward. "What did you do with the map?"

"Nothin'. It's in my safe." He smiled. "Not that I think it's got value, I just don't want it floating around."

"Sounds like you don't trust someone around here." Zack watched his face for a reaction, got none.

Hatchett kept on. "After my wife passed away, there was just me and my foreman, Bronc, plus any cowboys we hired that particular year. The cowboys don't generally come into the house—they stay in the bunkhouse. But you never know, one of 'em could drift

217

through when I'm out on the range." He shrugged his shoulders. "Not that it matters."

Zack became aware of someone in the doorway. He glanced over, saw it was Bronc. Zack wondered how long he'd been listening.

Bronc came on into the room. Zack watched him move. If he had any kind of wound, he gave no sign of it.

"I thought I heard my name mentioned," Bronc said.

CHAPTER THIRTY-FOUR

Late that afternoon Col and Julio rode down the slope to the floor of the wash to the flatland. Joshua trees projected grotesque shadows. The sun above the flat summit of Table Top Mountain hung precariously, vanishing then reappearing when they passed beyond the mountain's vast bulk and descended into Round Valley. Here the touch of the sun's rays still burned on their skin, in their eyes the intense glow of the orb low in the west was like a train headlight.

Julio reigned in, waited for Col to come alongside. "Let's give it a minute or two before we ride out into the open ground."

The boys sat quiet on their mounts, each with his thoughts, the tension already in them for the night to come. The tools for their task were bundled behind or slung from their saddles; two shovels this time, the probing wands, headlamps, two large canvas bags to transport treasure back to camp, should fortune smile. Their revolvers were belted to their waists.

As Col looked out over the raw beauty of the sun-dappled desert, he was overcome by a premonition of loss, and a wave of sadness swept over him.

The sun edged lower, shadows crept longer, finally merged. Without a word, Julio urged his horse forward, Col fell in behind. They moved snail-like with no unnecessary motions, hoped to blend as black silhouettes with the pinyon pine and tall yucca.

At the spring, they tied their horses to the rail fence and unpacked their tools. The cottonwood tree and windmill were married together in shadow, discernable only against the lighter night sky. The boys spoke in low whispers, kept their headlamps off. They stole toward the tree and huddled at the base of the windmill.

"Don't turn on your light. I remember the directions and the number of steps," Julio said in a whisper.

The compass hands glowed blue phosphorescence. Julio moved off through the blackbush, stepping deliberately with a consistent stride length, Col just behind. At the end of the first leg Col waited while Julio turned, lined the glowing compass hand once again, stepped down the slope through blackbush, then onto level sand. At the end of his count he stopped, faced right, aligned the compass again. Col came up beside him. They stood for a moment without speaking.

"Stay here." Julio's voice came low. "I'll move ahead, probe at each step. When I'm done, I'll turn to face you. You probe along a path parallel to mine and I'll return by a yet another. We'll cover as much ground as possible. If we don't find something after that, there's nothing to find."

"Okay," Col whispered. He watched Julio take a stride, stop, plunge his wand into the sand two or three times, take another step and repeat the motion, slow and methodical.

Col waited. The temperature dropped rapidly with the sun buried behind the horizon, a trickle of sweat felt cold as it ran along his spine. It was difficult to see Julio at a distance in the growing dusk; he sensed his friend had stopped. Col waited for the shadowy figure to turn and face him, the signal for Col to advance. It never happened.

A strong beam of light came full in Col's face, blinded him. He heard Julio's voice, urgent, panicked, yell, "Col! Shoot!" The light moved from Col, lit up Julio.

220

Blinded, Col saw only a halo of light around the dark outline of his friend, like an aura. There was motion. A line of fire spewed from Julio toward the windmill, a long red flame came back toward him. The percussive slap of almost simultaneous gunfire roared in Col's ears.

Col's pulse raced, his temple throbbed, his hand groped for the handle of his revolver, tugged the awkward heavy weapon from its holster, the entire movement much too slow, like a film shown frame by frame. The pistol came free; the light came into his eyes again. His revolver jerked in his hand, he felt punched backward, the bright light faded, blackness took its place.

CHAPTER THIRTY-FIVE

"Hey Bronc, glad you're here," Hatchett said. "You remember Dr. Apgar and Agent Tolliver. I've been giving them a history lesson, about my grandpa and the old days. I don't want them to think I had anything to do with the death of those two boys."

Hatchett swung his eyes away from Bronc back to Zack and Susan. "You may not know this, but cattle ranching out here dies along with me. We're just goin' through the motions these days. The government is moving all the cattle and sheep out once the current grandfathered leases expire. They want the land to revert to how it was before people came to live here—sort of a time in a bottle kind of thing."

"So the Kellogg Ranch..." Susan asked.

"Gone, all gone. Three generations of Hatchett family ranching this territory, all gone. You'll be reading about us in the Park brochures."

"Do you have a plan for your family?"

Hatchett shrugged. "I'm the only one left. The Hatchetts, like the Kellogg Ranch, are destined to fade into obscurity."

"How about you, Bronc?" Zack asked. "Will you fade into obscurity?"

Bronc's eyes were expressionless. "Don't you worry, I'll be around."

Zack shifted the topic. "I recently spoke with the chief of the Chemehuevi Band of Indians, man named Dan Singletree. You know him?"

Both men shook their heads.

"He told me about sightings of a strange creature at Hidden Springs, made it sound like some sort of supernatural being. You ever hear anything about that?"

Bronc snorted. "There's always been tales of mythical creatures around that spring. Used to be a good way to keep enemies away, back when the Indians infested the area."

"He spoke of a sighting just a month or two ago." Hatchett stared at Zack. "A month or two?"

Zack nodded. He relayed the story Singletree told him.

Bronc laughed. "A super sized Indian. Perfect."

"He didn't say Indian," Zack said quietly.

"All those old stories talk about a monster with a tail."

"Why would you bring that up, Agent Tolliver?" Hatchett asked. "Do you connect the sighting with the boys' death in some way?"

"I found it curious, is all. Like Bronc here says, its a good way to keep folks away from Hidden Springs, especially after dark."

Kellogg looked pensive. "You think someone is trying to hide something at the spring? You think there might be another motive?"

Zack shrugged. "We have to look at every possibility."

Bronc snorted loudly. "There's nothing there but desert. Even the buildings are gone."

Zack gave Bronc a thoughtful look. "Someone took exception to those boys for some reason. Someone's taking exception to us as well."

"How is someone taking exception to you?" Hatchett's eyebrows were raised in surprise.

223

"Someone shot out my Jeep tires while we were investigating the shepherd camp. I saw that as a warning." Zack glanced at Bronc.

Bronc gave Zack a hard look. "If you got something to say, say it."

Zack raised his palms, denying. "You know the people around here. Maybe you know why someone might have done that."

"Lots of folks don't like outsiders snooping around."

Zack stood. He turned to Hatchett. "I'm grateful for your hospitality and willingness to answer my questions. You can reach me anytime through Butch Short." He glanced at Bronc. "If you think of anything, give me a call."

"I'll be sure to do that."

A few minutes later as they climbed into the Jeep Susan said, "There's a very angry, troubled man."

Zack nodded, backed the Jeep around. He glanced at Susan. "He's got something to hide, for sure. But I saw no sign of a wound."

"I didn't either, and I was watching his movements very closely." She gave a disparaging laugh. "I would've anyway, he's like a coiled snake."

Zack thought about Hatchett, the calm reasoned way he spoke, his willingness to speak freely. "I don't think Hatchett is involved. He rang true to me."

"What I don't get is how he can get along with Bronc, they seem so different."

"Maybe he wasn't always that way, Bronc, I mean."

"Hard to imagine," Susan grumbled.

Zack opened his mouth to comment— his phone rang. He stopped the Jeep, glanced at it, picked it up. "Hey, Butch."

"Hi, Zack, where are you?"

"Susan and I are just leaving the Kellogg Ranch, headed to Needles."

"Do me a favor and stop by my office when you get in. The boy's uncle is here, he'd like to talk to you."

It was an hour before Zack climbed up the steps to the BLM office. He had dropped Susan at the motel to change, was now conscious of his own dusty, sweaty clothing. It couldn't be helped.

Julio's uncle Roberto turned out to be a small man, short, slender, athletic looking. He was richly yet tastefully dressed in creased black trousers, white shirt with silver eagle bolo tie, black short-waist vest. His boots, exposed by crossed legs, were glistening black leather with gold embroidered stitching. He jumped to his feet when Zack entered, extended his hand.

"Agent Tolliver, thank you for meeting with me," he said, without a trace of an accent. "I am very anxious to know the progress of the investigation into the death of my brother's boy."

Although Castro appeared composed, Zack saw the glimmer in his eye and felt the underlying emotion.

Zack nodded to Butch, sat down. "I wish I could tell you something definitive. We're still trying to identify a suspect."

"You have no doubt it was murder."

"None whatsoever."

"Have you uncovered a motive?"

"Not yet."

"None at all?"

225

Zack sighed. "There are a number of possibilities, ranging from water rights to hidden gold, but nothing definitive."

"Why hidden gold?"

Zack shifted in his chair, crossed his legs. "Well, there is talk, there are legends, all that. The boys were young, curious, would have been drawn to the idea of hidden treasure. We found evidence pointing to the existence of an old map, handed down from early days. That's about it, really."

Roberto considered this, looked thoughtful. He reached into his vest pocket, removed an envelope. He held it up. "I received this letter from Julio a few weeks ago. Can you read Spanish?"

"Not very well."

"Permit me." Roberto lowered the envelope, extracted a letter. It was two pages, crumpled from frequent reading. "I'll read only the parts that seem relevant." He slid the back page to the front, cleared his throat.

"*We have some new excitement to occupy our minds beyond the sheep (although that responsibility is foremost, of course). We had a visit from a local man who was eager to find some papers he claimed Juan left for him. We knew nothing about that, but the man seemed to suspect that we did. His manner was quite rough. After he left, we talked about what might have happened to Juan. I feel uneasy about his disappearance after meeting this other man. We wondered whether Juan might have happened upon something the other man wanted.*"

Roberto folded up the letter, replaced it in the envelope. "That's all there is, I'm afraid. Do you suppose this man might have had a part in the murders? Is there a way to identify him, do you think?"

Zack thought about it. "That certainly is interesting. It does raise some possibilities in my mind, maybe adds to some suspicions, but not enough to even mention what they are, I'm afraid."

"Perhaps it goes toward motive," Roberto said. "I know Julio enough to suspect he understated the discomfort of that meeting, the roughness of the man. Perhaps they went on to discover what it was the man hoped to find."

Roberto's gaze grew intense. Zack began to sense the powerful personality of the man.

"There is also the question of Juan's disappearance," Roberto said. "I thought little of it before, shepherds tend to be itinerant. But now?"

Butch coughed, nodded. "I think Mr. Castro has a good point, Zack. I'll make it a priority to learn what happened to Juan."

Roberto stood. "Thank you for your efforts, Agent Tolliver, and you, Mr. Short. I intend to take possession of my sheep tomorrow. It will take several days to gather them and arrange transport. I intend to take them back to Mexico." He gave Zack a sad look. "There is nothing left up here for me." At the door, he turned. "I'll be staying at the Sheraton the next several days. Please, spare no expense, and keep me informed."

CHAPTER THIRTY-SIX

The Wagon Wheel Restaurant throbbed with the hum of low voices, stirring hunger cravings from the light smoky scent of burger and bacon. Zack had showered, put on fresh clothing. He even had time to speak on the phone to little Bernie following a good conversation with Libby. He felt on top of the world.

He leaned back in his chair, beer in hand, and described his meeting with Roberto Castro to Susan and Eagle Feather.

"Roberto strikes me as the kind of man who makes things happen. Here's a guy just lost his nephew, the only son of his dead brother, yet somehow he's got everything moving forward: the sheep transport arranged, all his bills and obligations settled, even added some ideas to our investigation."

"It sounds like he's pulling out for good, poor man," Susan said.

"So he said."

"What ideas did he offered?" Eagle Feather asked.

Zack set down his beer. "It wasn't much, just a paragraph he read from one of his nephew's letters. The boy described a visit to their camp, a local man, as he described him, who was looking for some sort of papers left by Old Juan. Julio felt the man suspected they had these papers, but in actuality they didn't know what he was talking about. Apparently the fellow was none too subtle; Julio described his manner as rough. After that visit, the boys began to wonder what really happened to Juan."

Eagle Feather lifted an eyebrow. "That adds fuel to my suspicions."

"It sure sounds like Bronc," Susan said.

"We can't leap to conclusions, naturally, but I'd have to agree with both of you. Unfortunately, suspicions don't advance our investigation."

The waitress arrived with their meals. The next quarter hour was spent managing overflowing burgers and filling taco shells.

With a happy sigh, Zack wiped his mouth with his napkin. He steered their thoughts back to the case. "Let's take another hard look at motive. The only real reason we have found for someone to kill the two boys is to prevent them finding buried gold, a motive based entirely on a string of coincidental circumstances uncovered by Susan. We have found a map that seems to point to Hidden Springs, where the boys' bodies were found."

"We have not seen the original map," Eagle Feather observed, dipping a French fry into a pool of ketchup.

Zack gave a slow nod. "Very true. Everyone has spoken of it, but we've never actually seen it. We can't even tie the etching on the stone directly to the Hatchett map."

"We should have asked to see it when we interviewed Hatchett," Susan said.

"I notice he didn't volunteer it." Zack glanced at his watch. "I'm meeting with Butch Short in an hour to go over our progress. I'll ask him to arrange for us to see it."

"Do you see any other motive to kill the boys?" Susan asked.

Zack looked from Susan to Eagle Feather. "I suspect we all agree the boys were killed because they were getting too close to something. Susan's research suggests gold. But what if they were getting too close to something else?"

"Like what?" Eagle Feather asked.

229

"Like Juan's body," Zack said. "Think about it. If the killer thought the boys were close to finding the treasure, wouldn't he kill them after they had found it for him? On the other hand, if they were close to finding a murdered body, he'd kill them before they found it, so it would not be exposed."

Susan shivered. "You think Juan has been under the sand all this time?"

"It's possible."

"When can we access the crime scene to look for ourselves?"

"That's another good question for Butch," Zack said. "Now let's talk about suspects. I think our top suspect is Bronc. Whether the motivation to kill was buried treasure or Juan's hidden body, Bronc is connected to both situations. Agreed?"

"Bronc was at the crime scene practically every time we went there. He seemed to be trying to keep us out. He likely knew about the map. Finally, Bronc could come and go from the shepherd camp anytime he wanted. He has access to all those areas." Susan crossed her arms, tilted her head for emphasis.

"More so than Hatchett?" Eagle Feather asked.

Susan glanced at him, frowned. "Well, maybe not."

Zack raised his hand for the check. "On the face of it, we really can't eliminate anyone as a suspect. It could have been some tramp just wandering through."

"We do need solid evidence. All we have now is a web of theories," Eagle Feather said.

"I plan to spend tomorrow morning at the library again, this time on genealogical research." Susan glanced at Zack. "We know Hatchett's ancestry, he told us about it. I wonder if anyone else is around here we don't know about who has connections to the 1905 gunfight."

Zack stood. "Good idea. I've got to go meet Short. I'll try to get an okay to dig up the crime site. If Short agrees, and the sheriff is all done with it, Eagle Feather and I can take shovels out there tomorrow."

When he peaked his head around the door, Zack found Butch Short buried in a file folder with several more stacked near him.

"You don't get out much, do you?"

Butch gave a weak smile. "Not nearly as much as I'd like." He sighed, closed the file. "But it's feast or famine, you know? Either I'm out in the hot sun so much I wish I was back here, or I'm here so much I wish I could be back in the field. Never satisfied, I suppose." He motioned Zack to a chair. "What've you got, anything knew?"

Zack gave a shake of his head, sat down. "Not much. Did you have any luck with the boys' rifles? Were they purchased locally? Anyone trying to sell them?"

Short looked discouraged. "None of the above, I'm afraid. Apparently they were not bought locally, and whoever has them is keeping them."

"I didn't expect a lot from that. Sometimes you get lucky, though. I do need to ask you a couple of things."

"Go ahead."

"First, we'd like to get a look at the old map Hatchett has in his possession. I thought a request coming from you might fly better."

"What map is that?"

Zack told Butch the story of Hatchett finding the map in his attic.

231

"This is turning into a Robert Louis Stevenson novel," Short said, shaking his head. "Sure, I'll float a request by him. What else?"

"We'd like to dig up the crime scene."

"Looking for treasure, or bodies?"

"Maybe both."

Short smiled. "Well, in fact, that's up to you. Sheriff Connelly told me they were done out there. I been keeping it closed until I was sure you were done with it."

"Thank you."

"No—thank *you*." Short's grin broadened. "It's your investigation now. Your supervisor, Luke Forrestal just called, said the case belongs to the FBI and you are the lead investigator. You can do whatever you want." He laughed. "And I just saved myself some money."

Zack was caught by surprise. Such a turn of events was natural, even inevitable, given a double murder on government land. He just hadn't been thinking about it. Now he'd have to change the way he handled reports, expenses. More work for him, but more freedom of action on the ground.

Short had another interesting question. "How does the FBI view spirits, officially?"

"Why do you ask?" Zack was suspicious.

"There's been another sighting of that big hairy creature at Hidden Springs."

Zack was caught by surprise for a second time. "By whom?"

"By Roberto Castro. He drove up there last night to see the place where his nephew died. He was almost too late, got there around dusk. Said he was right at the yellow tape, trying to figure out our flags when something made him look up the slope at the windmill. He says a large bipedal creature was standing there staring back at him. He couldn't see much detail—the light was behind it. He says it turned away as he watched, took a couple of steps toward the windmill, and vanished."

Short watched Zack's reaction to the story.

"You should see your face," he said, laughing. He spread his hands wide. "This case? It's all yours now."

CHAPTER THIRTY-SEVEN

That night Zack found another surprise waiting when he returned to his motel room. A large gift basket of fruit was on his bedside table. He tore open the attached note.

Dear Mr. Tolliver,
Please accept this gift as an expression of our deep regret. While we have no idea how the snake came to be in your room, we accept full responsibility and assure you we have taken steps to see it never happens again. Please also accept one free night, which we have removed from you bill.
Sincerely,
The Management

Zack was amused. He wondered what steps the management might take to keep human killers out of his room. It's fortunate they had no idea what was really going on, but he intended to enjoy the fruit and those little chocolates, regardless.

The fact the investigation was now a federal case changed little, to Zack's mind. Butch had more or less let him run the show up to now, anyway. He'd simply continue on the same way, the real difference was he could make his own decisions without consultation, thus move more quickly.

As he changed for bed, his mind grappled with the case. They had solid evidence the shooting was a double homicide by a perpetrator or perpetrators unknown. Beyond that, they had suspicions but not much more. With men like Bronc and Hatchett, who spent solitary lives herding cattle and mending fences, he couldn't expect alibis for the time and place of the murders. Zack hoped they'd find something under the sand at Hidden Springs to point them in the right direction.

The team gathered at the Wagon Wheel for breakfast. Susan had Short's Subaru and would be at the library. She'd call Zack if she learned anything helpful.

After breakfast, Zack and Eagle Feather went to the hardware store to rent a metal detector and buy a couple of shovels. They planned to stop off to see Tav on the way out to see if he had any new thoughts. After that, they'd go on to Hidden Springs and start digging.

When they carried the two shovels to the counter, the clerk said, "You boys are lucky. Those are my last two. There's been a real run on them recently."

"You don't say."

"I do say. Those two shepherd boys who killed each other out there, they bought two of 'em. The Kellogg Ranch ordered up three of 'em."

"How long ago did the ranch order the shovels?" Eagle Feather asked.

"That was a couple 'a weeks ago" the clerk said. "We dropped 'em out there a week last Thursday."

Zack and Eagle Feather left the store with a half dozen bamboo wands, the metal detector, two shovels, and a 100-foot measuring tape.

"It's good to be back on a budget," Zack said.

Blue leaned in from the back, gave each man a welcoming lick behind the ear as they settled into the Jeep.

"So the Kellogg Ranch bought three shovels. That seems to point a stronger finger at Hatchett and Bronc," Eagle Feather said.

Zack reversed out of the parking space, spun the wheel and turned out into the main road. "It's a ranch, don't forget. They need shovels from time to time, I'd imagine." He glanced at Eagle Feather. "But, yeah, it's a bit of a coincidence."

The morning had been lazy; it was close to noon when they drove up to the Hole-in-the-Wall Information Center. Several vehicles with bicycles attached to them were parked outside the building. Inside, they found Tav busy serving an assortment of tourists, answering questions. Zack and Eagle Feather waited.

When the last visitor drifted away, Tav turned to them. "Sorry for the wait. Folks drive out here from the city and have no idea what it's about. They expect a McDonalds over the next rise. You'd be amazed how many people drive in here without enough gas, food, or water. The Preserve is so accessible from Las Vegas and LA people just don't understand how wild it is."

"You seem busier than usual," Zack said.

"Middle of the day, like now, tends to be busiest. People drop by here on their way somewhere else. The ones who come later in the day are generally the campers, and don't need as much hand-holding." He peered at Zack, then Eagle Feather. "What's up?"

"We stopped by to let you know this is now an official FBI case. I wondered if you've had any new thoughts about the murders."

"If you mean do I have any new suspects in mind, the answer is no. I can think of no solid motive, either. Maybe those two young guys had some trouble of their own, like a bad debt, or were involved in something that has nothing to do with anyone around here." Tav put a sales receipt in a tin box under the shelf, glancing up at Zack. "They could have brought their own problems along with them, you know."

"Very true." Zack turned away. "If you learn anything helpful, you know how to reach me."

Familiar as they had become with the route, the drive from Hole-in-the-Wall to Hidden Springs seemed to take no time at all. For Zack, the barren beauty of the landscape had not lost its enchantment. At the well enclosure, the gate was shut, the lock was on it, but unfastened. The yellow police tape was in place, the site undisturbed.

The sun was high, a breeze helped allay the heat. Blue bounded out of the Jeep the moment it stopped and went to visit a nearby mesquite.

Eagle Feather pulled out the two shovels. "Where do you plan to start?"

Zack unwedged the map sketch from his shirt pocket, studied it. "I don't know where this map starts or finishes. Let's assume the boys had it figured out correctly, and start to dig in a direct line between the spots the bodies were found." He folded up the map. "I'll start to the right, you start to the left. We'll work toward each other."

Eagle Feather nodded. They went to work.

Work it was. Despite the breeze, the sun beat down, and the men were soon covered with sweat. The sand was dense, packed down like soil. Shovel-loads were heavy. Blue found shade nearby and watched the men work.

They dug holes two feet deep, a foot apart. They pushed the probes down in the bottom of the pits to search deeper. Other than the occasional perforated food tin or small piece of unidentifiable rusted metal, they found nothing. Later in the afternoon the breeze died completely and the heat draped over them like a living thing. Eagle Feather dropped his shovel and went to the Jeep for a long drink of water. He stared at the line of holes across the level sand. Zack flipped out a last shovelful, dropped his shovel, and joined Eagle Feather in the shade of the Jeep.

"I guess its time to move over a few feet, dig another line of holes."

"I've got a better idea," Eagle Feather said. "Why don't you take the metal detector along the line where you want us to dig. Maybe we can save some time."

"If it's treasure down there, maybe so. A body, maybe not."

Eagle Feather passed the water to Zack. "I'd rather find treasure than a body anyway."

"Okay, we better get at it. It'll be dark in another few hours."

Eagle Feather waved a hand. "Be my guest, White Man."

Using the metal detector, Zack moved along the projected line at a slow pace, far faster, however, than it took to dig the pits. Eagle Feather followed behind with a probe. In another hour they had covered much more ground, but had found nothing. They set the depth on the detector lower, tried again. Still nothing.

By now the entire area of level sand was covered either by probe holes or pits. "That's it," Eagle Feather said. "We've perforated the entire area."

The sun hovered above the hills in the west as if undecided. It would drop quickly after this.

Eagle Feather studied it, calculating. "Another two hours and we won't be able to see what we're doing here without flashlights."

Zack leaned against the Jeep fender, reached two fingers into his shirt pocket, and pulled out the map yet again. He studied each leg of dashes.

"I expect if anything had been buried recently in the patch of blackbush, it would be evident," he said, thinking aloud.

"Not if it was buried a hundred years ago. To be certain of that, we'd have to tear it all out."

"The map does not show those area as destinations, just passages," Zack said, hoping he was right.

"Why do you suppose the map maker drew those zigs and zags? Why not simply measure paces from the tree directly to the place of burial?"

"I dunno, to throw people off? To make it more difficult?"

Eagle Feather took the map from Zack, turned it this way and that. "What if there were obstacles, say here and here, at the time the map was drawn." Eagle Feather pointed to the space enclosed by the three legs. "Obstacles you had to walk around, like buildings."

Zack stood up straight. "I think you're on to something. Let's think about how a building might have fit in that space. Maybe we can approximate its size—draw it on this map. Theoretically, we can eliminate that area from our search and concentrate on what remains." He took back the map. "Look here," he said, feeling his excitement grow. "Another cabin might have fit—"

He felt Eagle Feather grip on his arm, looked at him. Eagle Feather was watching Blue. The big bloodhound's nose pointed toward one of the holes they had just dug, his whole body was tense.

"He's fixed on a scent," Eagle Feather said.

239

CHAPTER THIRTY-EIGHT

The big bloodhound crept toward the hole the men had just dug. Blue was trained to hunt humans, and only humans, whether runaways or rescue victims. He had caught a scent from beneath the sand that was drawing him to the hole. The scent must be strong and it had to be human.

Blue thrust his nose down into the pit, whined, dug away at its edge and widened it, his huge forepaws as efficient as shovels. The hole grew to twice its size in an instant. Blue's eager whines grew louder, then halted as if by command. The big dog stopped digging, turned to look toward Zack.

Zack glanced at Eagle Feather. "I think Blue found something, and I don't think it's a treasure." He walked toward Blue with measured steps, reluctant, knowing what he would find. He patted the great bony head and peered into the hole.

A face was exposed in the depth of the pit, eyes and mouth filled with sand. Zack saw a high forehead, a patch of black hair. Even in the dusky hole, he could see the dark complexion, wrinkles from age near the mouth and eyes.

Eagle Feather was next to him. "That must be Old Juan."

Zack reached down, carefully nudged sand from the hollows of eyes and mouth. The eyes were rolled up, whites exposed, a mustache came into view, then a chin covered with white day-old beard. A prominent scar, light against dark skin coursed from right eyebrow to near the right ear.

"That scar should make an ID simple, " Zack said.

"It must be Juan," Eagle Feather said, again.

Zack glanced at his phone; saw he had no signal. He turned to Eagle Feather.

"Get your shovel. We need to dig him out as best we can without messing up forensic clues. I'd like to know how he died. After that, I'll drive out to where there's a signal and call in some backup."

The sun edged beyond the far hills, the shadows lengthened and deepened, the songs and chatter of birds ceased The silence of the night settled in as the two men set about their grim task.

* * * * *

Susan returned to her room after breakfast, satiated and sluggish. She opted for something more comfortable than the spring dress worn for breakfast with the men, settled on slacks and a blouse with flats. She peered in the mirror for a final hair adjustment.

Susan had no expectations from the men's plan. The ground at Hidden Springs had been covered quite thoroughly with the metal detector. Even with the limit set to a foot to obtain a stronger signal, if some large metal resided even a foot or more below that, the machine would have reacted. Oh, well, let them mess about.

Her phone found the nearest Starbucks several miles north on Route 95 at Fort Mojave. She wavered, but the taste of the hot bitterness came to her memory and edged her toward it. The directions took her across the bridge over the Colorado River and on north. Forty-five minutes later she was back in Needles nearing the Needles Public Library, this time with a large lidded brew in hand.

241

UNDER DESERT SAND

The same librarian was at the checkout desk. When
he opened his mouth to object to food in the library, she
tried on her most beguiling sultry smile and blew away his
defenses. Soon after, she was ensconced in her most happy
situation; a coffee at hand, several books nearby, and a
computer screen open to a search engine.

The hours passed unnoticed. The Styrofoam cup
now empty sat neglected and cold. Susan was completely
engaged by the information supplied at Genealogy.com,
where she tried different combinations of birthdates,
spouses and parents. Her search had narrowed to an
attempt to trace the lineage of just three names: Simmons,
Skaggs, and Hatchett, but so far with limited success. If
anyone alive today in southeastern California could claim
those three men in a family tree, it wasn't obvious.

Susan wasn't as concerned about Hatchett. She felt
assured he had been truthful in his description of his
parents and grandparents during their interview. Her
search of Simmons was short, and disappointing. The
results came in the form of an obituary, printed in the
Arizona Sentinel, circa 1915. Robert Simmons, age 45, of
Yuma, AZ, previously Fairfield, California, died from an
accidental self-inflicted gunshot wound. No known family
members. That lineage ended before it began.

Somewhere around two o'clock she found a family
tree posted by Eleanor Skaggs Roper. She read with
growing excitement the name and date for the woman's
father, and then her grandfather, Andrew Lionel Skaggs,
occupation farmer. No location was given. Susan looked
for accompanying documents, found a census report from
1900. She opened it; her eye scanned the surnames,
handwritten in columns yet legible. There he was—listed

with no family members in his household, his property evaluated at $500. But where was this?

Susan scrolled to the top of the page for the location. The place given was—San Bernardino County. Eureka! Susan tabbed back to the family tree, found a 1910 census with Andrew Skaggs, head of household, spouse Emily, child Peter. The location given was Los Angeles. So he had married and moved. Susan plugged in more variables; found the same family members in the same location a decade later. No other child was present. That made things easier, she need only follow Peter's branch. Peter did not remain in LA, she found, but moved at some point to Flagstaff, Arizona. Further search found Peter married to someone named Alicia, with three children: Eleanor, the oldest, James, and a baby sister, Aretha.

Well, she knew about Eleanor. James had married a Susan Pfeiffer. Aretha married—Susan drew in her breath, unable to believe the name she read neatly typed on the appropriate line of the tree. She glanced at her watch—four o'clock.

Susan dug in her purse for her phone, dialed Zack's number despite the library admonishment not to use cell phones. She had to warn him.

Zack's phone rang and rang.

CHAPTER THIRTY-NINE

Dusk cloaked the desert, isolated shadows merged; yucca and barrel cacti were lonely black sentinels against a fading sky. The two men, first with shovels then with hands unearthed Old Juan's body. He lay on his back, arms folded across his chest. Blood caked with sand marked where two bullet holes had slammed into his chest, near his heart.

The digging done, Zack and Eagle Feather stood together next to the impromptu grave, and stared down at Juan.

"The shepherd boys got too close to finding Juan, and Juan got too close to finding something else," Zack said.

Eagle Feather nodded. "So they all had to die."

Zack scanned the sand near them, glanced up at the slope, toward the windmill, the tree. "We can't count on any support until I make my call. I'm gonna have to get to high ground for that to happen. Before I do, let's make one more attempt to find whatever else is buried here at the springs before it gets too dark."

"How do you plan to do that, White Man?"

Zack studied the slope. "My hunch is the bad guys would not bury Juan's body near the treasure."

"They figured if you find one, you find the other, you mean?"

"That's what I think. They also want access to the treasure, but they can't leave fresh signs of digging near the body, or it would be discovered. So—" Zack studied the slope, pointed. "I think it's up there."

Eagle Feather folded his arms. "How can it be up there when the map leads down here?"

Zack turned, looked behind them. "I don't think it does. Let's go back to our missing buildings theory. If there was a cabin, or some sort of structure between us and that slope, the map maker would have to draw his map around it." Zack took out his phone, pulled up the photo of the stone slab. "We assume the map begins at the tree because the windmill structure is drawn there but what's this up at the other end of the dotted lines?"

Eagle Feather glanced at it. "It looks like an X."

"But it's not a complete X, is it? It's just two of the four parts of an X, and the angle isn't even right. Our brains fill in the rest of the X because we expect it. I think he etched exactly what he intended to indicate, an angle representing a corner, like a corner of a building."

"A cabin, maybe," Eagle Feather said.

"Exactly. If you approach this place from the Mojave Road, as most people would, and if a building is standing right here, where would you think the map's starting point is?"

"White Man, now I remember why I hang around with you. The map begins here; the buried treasure must be up there near the tree. Everyone has looked at the map wrong way around."

Zack's eyes glowed. "I think that's it. I don't think anyone has located it yet, or we'd have seen some sign of digging up there. It's still there."

"That's real helpful information." The voice came from behind them. It was Bronc's voice.

Zack and Eagle Feather swung to face him.

Bronc stood near the well, rifle cradled in his arm. Zack saw Bronc's horse, tied back at the fence. In the heat of their discovery, Zack never heard the man ride up. He was angry at his own carelessness. Now he remembered

245

he'd left his own rifle in the Jeep, yet again. Here they were, unarmed, facing the man who very likely killed Old Juan and would now have to kill them to hide his crime. They could not expect any help.

"You boys got any weapons on you? If you do, I'd just as soon you drop them on the ground."

Zack lifted palms upward. "No weapons."

Eagle Feather opened his vest, nothing under it, nothing in his belt.

Bronc indicated for both men to turn all the way around.

They did, Eagle Feather lifting his vest at the same time.

"Whatever you got in mind, you should know this is now an official FBI investigation and I am lead investigator. If you hinder our work, you'll be hunted down." Zack hoped he didn't sound too desperate.

Bronc smiled. "Would that please you even if you're not here to see it?" While Zack mulled that one over, Bronc straightened up, raised the rifle slightly. "I'd like you boys to pick up those shovels and walk over to that pit you just dug."

Zack and Eagle Feather turned, picked up their shovels, walked back to the edge of Juan's grave and stood over it.

The next voice they heard wasn't Bronc; it was Tav.

"Well, now, looks like we got us a social gathering. What's happening here, Bronc?"

Zack turned around. Tav sat on horseback just inside the corral fence. His rifle rested on the pommel of his saddle, the business end toward them. Zack felt a swell of relief.

"Howdy, Tav. These boys went and dug up Old Juan's body," Bronc said.

"What was your plan, Bronc?"

"Well, I thought they should cover him over again."

"I see, let the old guy resume his peaceful sleep."

Bronc gave a crooked grin.

"What was your plan after that?"

"Let them dig their own holes."

"I see," Tav said. "Got it all figured out, I reckon. Nice and simple."

Bronc gave a worried looking smile. "Tav, you and I—" He never finished the sentence.

Tav's rifle came up, an almost indiscernible movement, and fired. Bronc dropped like a stone, a round hole in the middle of his forehead.

Tav lowered the rifle. "I believe he was about to shoot you boys."

Zack fought the shock and astonishment he felt, didn't speak.

"It did not look that way to me," Eagle Feather said.

Tav sat easy in the saddle, staring at them, the rifle still resting across the pommel. "Well now, he as much as said so, didn't he?"

Eagle Feather stared.

Zack found his voice. "Bronc didn't even raise his rifle."

Tav looked unflustered. "He moves quick as a snake, that one. Got to kill a snake before it strikes." Tav climbed down from the saddle, rifle in his right hand. He walked his mount back to where Bronc's horse was tied.

Zack and Eagle Feather remained where they were, uncertain.

Eagle Feather spoke in a low voice. "Something doesn't add up here."

Zack gave a slight nod.

Tav tied his own horse to the rail, walked back toward them, his rifle resting in the crook of his right arm. He stopped ten feet away, face expressionless. "What do you figure to do now, Mr. FBI?"

Zack stared at the man, tried to read his expression, failed. "Nothing we can do for Bronc, now. I've got a message out for sheriff's deputies and forensics. We'll figure out what we can from the crime scene; forensics will take Juan's body and see what they can learn. The man was shot twice; we'll find a bullet, likely, since he was shot in the chest. We'll match it to Bronc's rifle there, see what we get."

Zack took a step toward Tav, reached out his hand. "You'll need to surrender that rifle. We have to take you in for questioning. Likely a court will find for self-defense, but we—"

Tav's rifle barrel came up, pointed at Zack's chest. "I don't think I like that plan. Just sounds to me like a lot of fuss and bother over a couple of people not worth the space they took up."

"It's procedure."

Tav gave a humorless smile. "I got my own procedure in mind." He waved his rifle at Zack. "Step back where you were."

Zack did as he was told.

Keeping his eye on them, his rifle trained, Tav stepped back to Bronc's body. He reached down with his free hand, picked up Bronc's rifle. He glanced at the load,

248

back at them. "Here's the sad story, gentlemen." Tav switched Bronc's rifle to his right hand. "Poor Bronc here, his back was against the wall. He knew it was all over when you boys dug up Old Juan. He knew you'd match the bullets in Juan to his own rifle. So he's got one choice—to shoot you two and bury you next to Juan, then get out of the country before they figure out what happened to you."

Tav grimaced. "Pretty good plan, actually." He motioned toward the shovels. "Grab a shovel. We're gonna need to widen that grave a bit."

CHAPTER FORTY

Susan held the cell phone clamped against her ear—
reference books, computer, personal notes, all forgotten.
She listened for the fourth time to the laconic message
from Zack's answering service. She had tried Eagle Feather
three times—it was no use; they were both out of signal
range.

The name she discovered, the name of the man
Aretha Skaggs, who was the direct descendent of Arthur
Skaggs had married, ricocheted in Susan's brain like a Ping
Pong ball. His name, his antecedents, his relationship to
people past and present thrust everything into focus,
snapped everything into place. Her friends were in grave
danger.

Susan tossed her phone in her purse in panic,
gathered her things, rushed past the receptionist without a
glance, pushed through the door into the bright sunlight.
She tried yet again to call Zack as she walked to the
Subaru. Failing again, she called Butch Short. She was
already in the car, the engine started, when Butch
answered.

"Bureau of Land management, Butch Short
speaking."

"Butch, it's Susan—Susan Apgar. I'm on my way to
see you. Zack and Eagle Feather are in great danger, we
need to drive to Hidden Springs right now."

"Right now? Whoa, Susan, what's going on?"

"I was doing genealogical research and found the
name of the man I believe is the killer. Zack and Eagle
Feather have no idea, and they are out at the crime site
right now doing the very thing that will get them killed. We
must get out there."

After a short silence, Butch said, "Okay, Susan, I'll be ready when you get here."

Susan swung into the BLM parking lot where Butch was waiting, stopped next to him. He was barely in the car when she hit the accelerator, spun her tires, and lurched out of the lot.

"Are you armed?" Susan's eyes were on the road.

Butch patted his jacket pocket. "Yes".

"Good."

"We can pick up Tav Davidson along the way," Butch said, and pulled out his phone. "I'll give him a call."

Susan reach out, grabbed his arm. "Don't."

Butch gave her a long look, said nothing. They rode in silence.

"Are you planning to tell me what's going on?" Butch said, finally, with a touch of annoyance.

Susan gave him a sidelong look. "I apologize for acting in such a mysterious manner. It was imperative you come with me. If I mentioned the name earlier, you may well have doubted me. I would have had to try to convince you, with precious time lost."

Butch gave her a sardonic grin. "Well, that crisis is past. Do you think you might tell me now?"

Susan nodded, staring at the road ahead. They were on the freeway, the old car rocketing along at 80 mph, the best it would do. It sounded like a concrete mixer. She waited for her pulse to slow before speaking.

"There were four men important to our story. Two died in the original 1905 gunfight—Jake Skowler and Curt Johnson. The third man was Bob Simmons, also a gunman who had ridden the outlaw trail. The fourth and final man was Andrew Skaggs, a rancher who managed to keep his head down during the range disputes. Simmons had left the Winslow Cattle Company to take up ranching, but it didn't hold his interest for long. Soon he turned to prospecting, scouring the local hills in search of mineral wealth."

Pausing for a moment, Susan put on her blinker, slowed for the ramp to Essex Road. They flew down it, spun right without stopping. She glanced at Short. "It was really not such an oddball idea. There were mines in the area already. But Simmons lacked expertise. First he took Hatchett's grandpa out with him, but soon found the man's knowledge was limited. Another neighbor, Andrew Skaggs, had more expertise, so Simmons enlisted his help instead. Skaggs didn't give up the farm, but he spent many days out with Simmons. According to a newspaper article, they found an old mine and brought home a sample of gold ore. After that, though, there were no more articles, no more references to their find. One might have assumed their discovery was a bust."

The Subaru lurched in and out of a large pothole. "I don't believe it. I think they kept their silence because they had actually found a source of gold ore. I believe they mined it, transported the ore on horseback to Hidden Springs, sluiced it and prepared it for shipment by wagon."

Short stared in wonder. "That's an amazing story, Susan, and might even be true. But it doesn't explain why we're hurtling at death defying speeds toward Hidden Springs."

"Be patient and listen, it will all become clear. As you know, the Winslow Cattle Company hired gunfighter Curt Johnson as foreman to intimidate the sheepherders and small ranchers. Johnson occupied the cabin at Hidden Springs. That posed a dilemma for Simmons and Skaggs. They had no alternative but to take Johnson into their confidence, probably had to give him a share. On the positive side, enlisting Johnson gave them a 24-hour guard over the gold. All went well until another gunfighter turned rancher, Jake Skowler, became suspicious of the activity at the spring. He began asking pointed questions, stirring things up. Simmons and Johnson realized they had to eliminate Skowler."

Susan glanced at Short. "Hence, the famous gunfight, you see. The idea was Johnson would call Skowler into the cabin next time he brought his cattle to the spring. Simmons would hide nearby with his rifle to make sure Skowler didn't get the upper hand. But Skowler knew how to handle a gun, and although Johnson had the element of surprise, and managed to kill Skowler, he received several wounds in return. Simmons watched all this from the bushes and saw his opportunity to increase his share. He assured Johnson's death with a rifle bullet to the chest, which lodged in his spine." Susan gave an abrupt laugh. "And then there were two."

They flew past the turnoff to Hole-in-the-Wall. Short glanced at the sign, then at Susan. "You're sure we shouldn't bring Tav along?"

She grimaced. "I'm sure." The car flew off the end of the pavement and bounced onto the packed dirt roadway leaving a sandy wake like a motorboat speeding across a lake.

"Almost there," Susan said.

"Hidden Springs, or the end of your story?"

"Both. After the gunfight, Simmons dropped out of sight. Skaggs eventually married, moved off. You see the murder plan had backfired. The gunfight gained such notoriety tourists were constantly showing up at Hidden Springs. The men buried their gold ore there prior to the gunfight, planned to retrieve it later, but now that was out of the question. So they moved off to wait their opportunity, secure in the knowledge no one else could possibly know it was there. And they were right, at least until Hatchett's map appeared, and Old Juan got a peek at it. But Simmons and Skaggs were dead and buried by then."

"So the threat was gone."

"As it happens, not so much. I set about my genealogy research with the assumption the murders of Juan and the two boys were not random acts, but were related somehow to rumors of hidden gold. It meant someone had to know about it. These things pass down within families, so my objective was to see if anyone in the valley today was a descendent of one of the original four. I could eliminate Skowler and Johnson, of course, dead before they could have any progeny. They might have had siblings or cousins, but it is most unlikely those two would have shared a secret like this with anyone else. So I was looking for a descendent of either Skaggs or Simmons, or both."

They had arrived at the Mojave Road. Susan braked with one or two quick jabs, turned the wheel to the right, spun the rear end and resumed her speed. This road surface was rougher, with occasional washouts; Susan had to slow down. Frustrated, she pushed the speed as much as she dared, continued the story.

"I soon learned Bob Simmons never married. He had relocated to Yuma, Arizona, waiting there, no doubt, for things to die down around Hidden Springs. But it was not to be. I found his obituary. He died at age 45 from a self-inflicted gunshot wound." Susan glanced at Short. "If you buy that, I've got a bridge to sell you." She negotiated around a deep trough. "So that left Skaggs. Seems he too moved away within a decade or so, went to LA. He married, had a son. His son married, had three children, two girls and a boy. They all married. The oldest girl's husband had the surname Pfeiffer, unrelated to anyone here. The son, of course, had the surname Skaggs, another blank. But the youngest daughter, named Aretha, married a man whose surname was..." Susan paused, looked at Short..

"Okay, come on, what was his name?"
"His name was Davidson."

CHAPTER FORTY-ONE

"And if I refuse?" Zack stared down the barrel of Bronc's rifle, held in Tav's all too steady grip. An unnatural silence surrounded them; no insects sounded, no birds sang, there was no breeze. Dusk hovered at the threshold of darkness, its thickening cloak not yet sufficient to hinder visibility.

"I will shoot you and let your friend do all the work." Tav waved the rifle barrel in the direction of the shovels. "Now get going."

Zack and Eagle Feather picked up the shovels. In unspoken agreement, they separated and began to dig at opposite ends of the pit, hoping to spread the target. They shoveled the dirt toward Tav's side so not to rebury the sheepherder. Their two mounds of dirt grew, gradually began collapsing toward each other to form an embankment.

Zack paused to wipe sweat from his brow.

"No resting," Tav said, jabbed the rifle barrel toward him. "You'll get all the rest you want soon enough."

Zack resumed shoveling with deliberate slowness.

They dug, and the shadows increased. Zack knew their only hope was darkness deep enough to make aim uncertain. He decided he would stall as best he could, judge the right moment, throw a shovelful of dirt toward Tav and run. He knew Eagle Feather would react quickly and follow his lead.

They never got the chance.

"What the—!" Tav's sudden outcry was full of shock and fright. Both diggers looked at him in surprise. Even in this low light, Zack could see the man's face had turned white. His eyes were round white orbs fixed on the ridge near the windmill.

Zack turned, followed his gaze. Something stood on the ridge ten feet from the tree. Human-like but not human, thick bodied, wide shouldered, huge; its penetrating red eyes glared down at them, its body looked impossibly large backlit against the sky. The creature's angry eyes conveyed a wave of almost tactile hostility; Zack smelled the mephitic aura emanating from it.

Everything happened at once.

Tav's rifle spoke repeatedly in fiery darts, with each report he exclaimed: "Shit...shit..."

Zack and Eagle Feather dove into the unfinished pit. Even before he landed, Eagle Feather's knife was in his hand, drawn from its hiding place.

Tav appeared at the rim of the pit, not seeing them, eyes fixed on the ridge, muscles of his face taught, reflexively firing and cursing. Eagle Feather tensed to leap——before he could, there was a report from a different rifle. Zack saw Tav's head jerk, blood spurt, and the man fell from sight.

Zack rose to a half crouch, stared through the shadows toward the sound of the shot. He saw an outline of someone, rifle dangling toward the ground. He glanced back at the ridge; the creature was gone.

Eagle Feather was out of the pit, crawling toward Tav's body on the opposite side from the shooter. He picked up Tav's fallen rifle, rolled behind the dirt mound, rested the rifle barrel on it, and aimed at the distant figure.

"Drop you weapon," he shouted.

The rifle slid to the ground.

"Walk this way with your hands in the air."

The figure moved toward them.

257

UNDER DESERT SAND

Zack stared through the gloom. As the shooter came into view, he saw long hair under a cowboy hat, a slender build, delicate features—the killer was a girl.

CHAPTER FORTY-TWO

The Subaru surrendered to the terrain at the dry riverbed. Susan and Butch climbed out and hurried through encroaching darkness along the light sand ribbon of roadway. It took ten minutes to reach the open gate, the red Jeep just beyond it.

They ran past two saddled horses tied at the fence, and around the well. Susan faltered, stopped, stared at the tableau of figures portrayed in chiaroscuro before her. A body sprawled nearby; another lay on the sand at the feet of two men who faced a third figure, a young girl.

"Zack?" Susan cried. "Are you alright?"

A head turned, it was Zack. "Susan? Is that you? Who is that with you?"

"It's me, Butch Short."

"Thank God. Come on over here." Zack turned back to the girl. "Who are you?"

The girl's voice was edged in bitterness. "My name is Kella Darnell. My father is Frank Darnell. My family owns the Circle Ranch near Fountain Peak." She pointed to the body of Tav Davidson. "That man murdered Col Budster and Julio Castro."

Susan and Butch came up to the group.

"How do you know that?" Zack asked.

The girl saw Susan, seemed to find new courage from the presence of another woman. "I was with the boys when they discovered a map etched into a slab of rock. When I left their camp that day, the last time I saw them alive, I passed this man. He rode on by, acted as if he didn't see me. I wondered why he was there.

"I never heard from the boys after that. A week later I rode back to visit them but even before I reached

their camp I saw their belongings scattered everywhere.
When I came closer, I saw this same man digging through
their belongings, so I hid behind some trees and watched."
She pointed to Bronc's body. "That man was with him. I
didn't learn until later the boys had been murdered." Her
voice choked up. She waited a moment, gained her
composure and continued. "I knew it had to be these men.
I also knew the Julio and Col had intended to search
Hidden Springs for something buried here. I've watched
everyone who came here, ever since." She lifted her eyes to
Zack. "I intended to kill the murderers."

"You shot the tires on our Jeep," Eagle Feather
said.

Kella nodded. "I saw you digging among Col and
Julio's things. I didn't know who you were. I didn't want
you there."

Susan felt a surge of sadness for the girl. "You
poor thing. Was Col your boyfriend?" She touched Kella's
arm.

At her touch, tears overflowed, ran down Kella's
cheeks. "I loved him," she said.

* * * * *

Zack felt the weariness of a man just returned from
the battlefield. He forced his shoulders back, took
command. "Butch, I need you to secure this site until I can
get other agents in here. Eagle Feather will assist you until
I return. I will take the Jeep and drive somewhere I can get
a signal for my phone." He turned to Susan. "Where is
your vehicle?"

"We came in Butch's Subaru. We had to leave it
back at the riverbed."

"Susan, I'd like you to take Ms. Darnell here to the Sheriff's Office in Needles. I'll call Sheriff Connelly and tell him what happened here. Ms. Darnell needs to remain in his custody until I return for her. Have her call her father, ask him to come to the station."

Zack looked at Butch. "Okay if she takes the Subaru? You can ride back with me."

Butch grinned. "At this point, it's more her car than mine."

Zack turned to Kella, spoke gently to her. "I'll have the sheriff send a deputy to trailer the horses back. I think what you need most is to meet with your family and then get a lot of sleep. We'll deal with this later."

Kella and Susan rode with Zack in the Jeep to the dry bed where they transferred to the Subaru. With a nudge from the Jeep, the car regained its grip and the two women went on their way to Needles. Zack drove the opposite way on the Mojave Road and found a signal within two miles. He called Luke Forrestal, his supervisor. Luke promised to send available agents immediately.

"You know you'll have to recuse yourself, Zack," he said. "You're a material witness now."

Zack said he'd stay to support Butch Short and the sheriff deputies while they secured the scene and allowed the forensics team do its work. It promised to be a long night.

It was pitch black before the first deputies arrived. They brought battery operated work lights and the scene was soon transformed from night to day. The crime lab van arrived around midnight; like the Subaru, the large cumbersome vehicle was forced to halt at the riverbed. The forensics team hauled their gear in from there. A large tent went up over the bodies; the entire scene was lit up like Macy's at Christmas.

A deputy took Zack's statement while a second one interviewed Eagle Feather. Neither man mentioned the creature they had seen on the ridge that so successfully diverted Tav's attention. After their statements were taken, the deputies sent both men away.

"Go get some sleep," they were told. "We'll need to interview you more thoroughly tomorrow."

Zack knew the FBI team would be next in line to take their statements when they took over. Tomorrow would be a long day as well.

Zack and Eagle Feather compared notes on the drive back to Needles.

"Do you think the girl Kella told the truth?" Eagle Feather asked.

"It is a rather amazing story," Zack said, musing. "Such a young girl, and so determined to avenge her boyfriend's death. I'd not want to be the object of her revenge."

"Helluva shot with a rifle."

Zack glanced at his friend, grimaced. "Thank God for that."

Eagle Feather stared off into the darkness. "The partnership between Tav and Bronc was made in hell. How do you think they got together?"

"A marriage of convenience, likely. Bronc must have shared his suspicions about the treasure with Tav. But to do that, he would have to trust Tav, which suggests their relationship began even before Hatchett discovered the map."

"A disposable relationship in Tav's mind, I think. He did not hesitate to end it."

Zack stared at the twin cones of light illuminating the pale roadway ahead and creating ghosts of the dust-coated bushes that bordered it. "It upsets me to miss a cue. I should have picked up on Susan's story, when she was nearly shot by Tav." His palm hit the steering wheel in sudden frustration. "Susan underplayed that incident. There's good reason to believe the man tried to kill her with that shot, then changed his mind."

Eagle Feather nodded. "He may have realized he had better learn what it was she had discovered before he killed her." He paused. "He probably didn't think of that until after he took his first shot."

"No matter how long I work at this job, no matter how much experience I gain, I still make rookie mistakes." Zack shook his head. "It's very disconcerting."

They rode in silence after that, each wrapped in thought. Zack's were dark.

They turned up the ramp to Route 40, the Jeep gained speed. They were in their own world of darkness, no other vehicle or light anywhere in sight.

Eagle Feather glanced at Zack. "You do have a weakness, White Man, a big one. But it is not what you think. Your weakness is you are too hard on yourself. You dwell on your mistakes. I know I will regret this, but I will say you handled yourself well tonight."

Zack laughed. "Truth is, I was scared to death. For a while there, it seemed like there was no way out of that pickle." He glanced at Eagle Feather. "I got to hand it to you, though. Where'd that knife come from, anyway? And you pounced on that rifle like a terrier when Tav went down. You were impressive."

Eagle Feather looked at Zack, almost smiled. "I know, White Man, I know."

UNDER DESERT SAND

CHAPTER FORTY-THREE

Zack slept long the following day, although not as long as he would have liked. His phone began to ring around nine and it didn't stop. The Sheriff's office, Butch Short at the BLM office, the FBI agents who arrived to take over the case, Luke Forrestal back in Tuba City—everyone needed to be briefed, everyone needed his statement, everyone wanted his thoughts. The local press swarmed the motel by midday, soon joined by their colleagues from Las Vegas and even as far as Los Angeles.

Zack wasn't the only one who had a long day; Eagle Feather and Susan were equally in demand. They passed one another coming and going from various offices.

Kella had her first interview the night before, was then remanded to the custody of her parents. A sheriff's deputy went to stay at Circle Ranch to keep an eye on her until the hearing.

The story behind the multiple murders gradually came clear. It all began a century ago, as Susan had surmised. The secret of the buried gold remained with Simmons and Skaggs after the deadly Johnson and Skowler gunfight. It later died with Simmons, but lived on for three generations of the Skaggs family. None of the descendants took it seriously until Tav Davidson came along. He met Aretha Skaggs while in college; she was fascinated by his Indian heritage, he by her family's history in Fairfield. Tav continued his studies in geology and wildlife ecology and when the time came, made application to serve as a Ranger in the Mojave National Preserve. There wasn't a lot of competition for the post. By the time he assumed his duties at the Preserve, his wife had died, the circumstances unclear. The loss soured him.

Investigating agents guessed the gold story simmered in Tav's brain until it gained new life when Bronc told him of an old map Hatchett found in his attic. It leant credence to what he already knew, and stoked his fire to recover the rumored gold hoard.

Bronc was a range tramp. He attached himself to Jim Hatchett at the Kellogg Ranch. He was not a character of high moral fiber, or particularly loyal, and found no problem falling in with Tav's schemes to pursue a fortune in gold. Although the rest is theory, investigators believed Bronc was frustrated in his attempts to gain access to Hatchett's map. When he deduced Old Juan had seen it and apparently knew the location it described, he visited the old shepherd and tried to wheedle the information from him. He did not succeed.

It's anybody's guess why Juan decided to etch the map onto the stone slab; perhaps he didn't trust his own memory, or maybe he had a premonition of disaster. Either way, it was universally accepted Juan himself flipped the slab over with his horse to hide it. After that he must have ridden to Hidden Springs to try to uncover the treasure, unaware Bronc was shadowing him. Juan mistakenly read the map backwards, as Zack and Eagle Feather would later do, and began to dig in the wrong place. Most agree Bronc believed Old Juan was close to finding the gold, and shot him. But there was nothing in Juan's pit, so Bronc buried him there. The Sheriff guessed Bronc left Juan's horse dead on a mesa somewhere. Tav likely helped Bronc search through Juan's personal things later at the sheep camp, then took it all away to leave the impression the old shepherd had simply ridden off.

266

Before Col and Julio arrived, there was nothing Tav and Bronc could do without the map. Bronc may have tried to get a glimpse of Hatchett's map, but Jim Hatchett himself had no interest in it other than as a family curiosity and left it locked in his safe.

Kella described how Bronc visited Col and Julio to inquire about papers Old Juan might have left, still hoping to find a map copy, and how she and the boys found the map scored on the stone slab. The evening the boys decided to try out the map, Bronc was no doubt watching the camp, and followed them. Kella had gone home, her father had not let her return while the boys were on the treasure hunt, believing, correctly, she might be in danger. Bronc or Tav or both watched while the boys searched, saw they used some sort of map, possibly from Old Juan. While it seems unlikely they decided to shoot the boys to get the map, when they might simply have taken it from them at gunpoint, Bronc must have grown uneasy when it appeared they might have found Old Juan's body with their probes. The forensics lab would try to match the bullets that killed the boys to a rifle, to determine who actually shot which boy, but for now it didn't matter.

Zack suspected it was Tav's idea not to approach the bodies after they shot them, but leave the scene to look as if there had been a shootout, mirroring the historic one at the same place, and so disguise their crime, but their hopes for treasure were frustrated once again; they knew the spot the boys planned to dig held no treasure, only Old Juan's body. Where, then, was the gold hidden? They couldn't approach the boys' bodies to retrieve their map without compromising themselves.

Investigators believed the two men destroyed the shepherd boys' camp in an attempt to find other clues.

UNDER DESERT SAND

With the double murder, and the publicity it drew, they couldn't search for the treasure at Hidden Springs until it all died down. Once again, all they could do was wait. It must have been very frustrating. Tav could not have been pleased when Zack and Susan showed up; their presence was an indication of Butch Short's suspicions.

By the end of the second day the investigation was complete and the witnesses were free to go. Susan, Eagle Feather and Zack met one final time at the Wagon Wheel. They enjoyed house margaritas while waiting for their entrees.

"What will happen to Kella, do you think?' Susan asked Zack.

"I expect she'll be released, at most a short probation period. After all, she saved our lives when she shot Tav."

"What a hard beginning to a young life."

"She is made of sturdy stock," Eagle Feather said. "I think she will recover."

Susan peered at him, gave a teasing smile. "Do I sense some grudging admiration for the young lady?"

Eagle Feather didn't bother to answer.

Zack grew philosophical. "You know, there is a certain irony here. Think about the original gunfight in 1905. If it was about gold, as we theorize, two men died over it and the surviving two men were unable to collect it due to the publicity the gunfight caused. They had to wait, apparently both died still waiting. Then a second gunfight, albeit truly a double murder committed by new gold seekers caused more publicity, the place becomes a crime scene, and again the men must wait before attempting to recover the gold. Finally, here we come to try to locate whatever is buried there, another gun battle erupts, another crime scene and even more publicity, and again no chance to look for the buried treasure." Zack glanced at his companions. "Do you think anyone will ever recover it?"

"If it's even there," Susan said.

"It might not be the kind of treasure we think it is."

Susan and Zack swung their heads to look at Eagle Feather.

"What do you mean?" Susan asked.

Eagle Feather glanced at Zack. "Perhaps that thing we saw is guarding something of its own."

Susan stared from one man to the other. "What thing?"

Eagle Feather looked at Zack, waited.

Zack looked down at his glass, a little sheepish. "We didn't mention this to you before, we needed to wait until the interrogations were over. There was someone or something else at Hidden Springs during the shooting. Whatever it was, it helped to save our lives."

"It distracted Tav, gave Kella the chance to shoot him," Eagle Feather said.

Susan stared. "What was it?"

"Well, that's a good question," Zack said. "You remember I told you about my conversation with Chief Dan Singletree, and the witness he brought to see me who described the creature she saw at Hidden Springs? That thing."

Susan drew in her breath. "Really! What did it look like?"

Zack described what he saw. "It looked quite similar to creatures we have seen before," he added.

"Really!" Susan continued to stare. "What happened to it?"

"That's a very good question. A lot was happening all at once. First Tav was emptying his rifle at the thing; next Kella blows his head off. By the time I thought to look for it, if I even did, it was gone."

Susan turned to Eagle Feather. "You saw it too."

He nodded.

"Describe it."

"Like Zack says, just like the creatures we have seen before; very large, red eyes, lots of hair, a hostile beast."

"Did you see what happened to it?"

"I, too, was busy. I sensed it moved toward the tree. It seemed to disappear."

The three margaritas remained on the table, forgotten for the moment.

"And you bastards didn't say a word to me."

Zack put his hand on her arm. "Susan, we didn't say a word to anybody, not even each other. This is the first time we have spoken of it."

Eagle Feather raised an eyebrow. "Imagine how describing this creature would have complicated the investigation. We would still be in there talking to those guys."

Zack added, "I am sorry, Susan. I was going to tell you, until I thought how knowing might skew your own testimony. I didn't want you to have to obfuscate."

Susan was silent, then patted Zack's hand and removed her arm. "I suppose you were right not to tell me. You're telling me now, anyway." She paused. "Did Kella see it?"

Zack and Eagle Feather exchanged glances.

"I don't know," Zack said.

"Seems like she must have," Eagle Feather said.

Zack turned his margarita glass to the salty side, scooped some of it with a finger. "I know she didn't mention it. I read her testimony."

The three friends pondered this in silence.

Zack licked his finger. "Isn't it interesting how we seem to see these creatures each time the three of us are involved in a case like this? What do you think? Are we just lucky, or are they following us around?"

"If we knew the answer to that, we would know more about them. Now we can only guess."

After dinner, the friends climbed into the Jeep and drove back to the motel to pack and get some sleep for an early morning start. Eagle Feather took Blue out to the parking lot for a last stroll. Zack joined him.

"What now, White Man?"

Zack watched Blue leave a long message, lifted his gaze to the rift in the hills where the mighty Colorado flowed through, admired the barren summits backlit by the sun. He turned to Eagle Feather. "I'm going to quit."

Eagle Feather stared, taken aback. "Quit what?"

"The FBI."

"For Libby and Bernie?"

"Yes. I miss Libby every day, and I don't want to miss the entirety of Bernie's childhood."

"I can not fault you there." Eagle Feather put a hand on his friend's shoulder. "Have you told Susan yet?"

"No, not yet. I'll still help Susan from time to time on the lecture circuit. A few days away now and again won't hurt; in fact, it will probably help. It's time to slow my pace, though, minimize my risk. When we were digging our graves at the business end of Tav's rifle, it began to look like the end of the road. My regret was even greater than my fear. I don't want to feel that again."

271

UNDER DESERT SAND

"When will you break the news to Libby?"

Zack smiled, dug in his pocket for his phone, turned his back and walked away. "Right now."

CHAPTER FORTY-FOUR

By the fifth day, the last FBI agent, Forensics expert, Sheriff's Deputy, BLM Special Investigator, Park Ranger, Tribal liaison, hanger-on and spectator was gone, the yellow tape was down, the stillness of the desert reborn. The wind lost no time erasing footprints and shifting sand over refilled pits and graves. The windmill sagged a bit more, the splintered and trampled blackbrush on the slope rebounded, and the big lock on the gate remained securely engaged.

In the following years, time resumed its relentless, glacial transformation. The leases for sheep pasture and cattle grazing expired, and abandoned houses and barns crumbled and decayed, fences sagged and fell, roads grew over with weeds. With mineral resources exhausted, and the mines reclaimed by the Preserve, inhabitants could no longer make even a scratch existence and moved away, replaced by daytime tourists whisking past on the main roads from one historic sign to the next.

The tourist stops did not include Hidden Springs. The nearby Mojave Road fell out of use, barred to four-wheel drive enthusiasts to protect the fragile land. Its only access removed, Hidden Springs returned to the lonely, barren and unremarkable place it had once been.

To the Chemehuevi Indians, this location was and would always be a sacred place. Yet none visited, or even approached, for the pervasive sense of evil that blanketed the place remained and turned the adventurous away, as if all the dead from over the millennium stood as one in a protective ghostly barricade.

Yet reports continued, sightings from nearby hills or passing planes, strange flickering lights glimpsed in the darkness, large upright creatures black against the blackness, sounds of striking pickaxes and scraping shovels, even shouts of anger and pain in long forgotten languages.

Dreams of hidden treasure died with the dreamers that final night when the cursed spring claimed its own. After that, Jim Hatchett removed the map from his safe and burned it. On the lonely hillside, the etched slab cracked from freezing and thawing, and lichens fed and flourished within the fissures, until no sign of human work remained. No one was left to know of maps or treasure, or to care to brave the unnatural guardian protecting it.

Was there ever a treasure to be found? Or did rumor feed upon tall tales and idle speculation, as is so often the case?

And what glints and glimmers in the desert tortoise's deep burrow under the deserted windmill when a ray of evening sun enters at just the right angle?

fini

THE REAL STORY

I thought the reader might be interested to learn how my fiction grew from an actual gunfight, possibly the last of the Old West, between two outlaw gunfighters in 1925. I came across the story while exploring the Mojave Preserve region of the Mojave Desert in California. The story can be found in the October 22, 1956 issue of the **San Bernardino County Sun** on page 23, in an article entitled *Duel To The Death Drops Curtain On Farm Area*, and, closer to the actual event, in **The Billings Gazette**, Tuesday November 9, 1925, page 1, an article entitled *Gun Men Duel Till Dead In Desert Shack*. Here are the facts.

Few would suspect while visiting the bleak Lanfair Valley today it once was a populous farm and grazing area. At the time, the big player in the valley was the Rock Springs Land & Cattle Company. This outfit claimed a range extending thirty miles. Small farmers with herds of a few head disputed the outfit's claim to the grazing, while at the same time helped themselves to a calf or two.

The Hidden Springs in my novel is in actuality Government Holes, the plural a misnomer, for in its 100-year history there appears never to have been more than one well. At the apex of the Southern Piute Indians' inhabitation of the area, the well was one of many springs dotted across the desert which sustained an ancient road, later named the Mojave Road, a southern desert North American Silk Road of sorts, along which trade extended among tribes all the way from the Colorado River to the Pacific Ocean.

Government Holes was a key watering hole for the Rock Springs Land & Cattle Company, and it was here they would take their stand.

UNDER DESERT SAND

The first gunman to come to the region was Bob Holliman, who had roamed the Outlaw Trail, and who gave the name Hole-In-The-Wall to the rock formation in the southern preserve area from a resemblance to the original hideout of that name where outlaws took refuge in Wyoming.

My Jake Skowler was modeled after Matt Burts, whose history is given fairly accurately under Jake's name in an early chapter of this volume. He did hire on as foreman of the cattle company, largely to enforce its claims against the likes of Holliman, thought to be helping himself to beef. The active outlaw life I described for Jake Skowler in Arizona is very close to that of Burts before he moved on to Lanfair Valley. Even before Burts' arrival, there was "sniping and general gunplay" directed at the foremen of the cattle company, a position that became available with some regularity. The Rock Springs outfit brought in Burts largely to "get" Holliman, the most dangerous of their antagonists, but after a horse was shot out from under him in ambush, and his hat shot off, Burts also decided to retire from the foreman job and built a small ranch in the area, in effect joining the other team. The cattle company filled the vacancy yet again, this time with a known gunman named Bill Robinson. As described in my novel, Robinson took up quarters in a shack next to Government Holes and took control of the use of the water.

The talk in the valley was Robinson had been hired to kill Burts and Holliman. While rumors and gossip grew around this controversy, to everyone's surprise nothing happened for more than a year. Meanwhile, Holliman had gone off prospecting. His partner was Bert Smith (my fictional Skaggs), a war veteran who had moved to the desert to clear his lungs of poison gas. The legend of lost gold on Table Top Mountain is told much as I describe in the novel; Smith slipped and fell, momentarily grasped an iron door to save himself, and found an ore laden rock nearby at the end of his fall (**Lost Treasures of California - Map & Guide**).

On November 8, 1925 the inevitable came to pass. Burts arrived at Government Holes in a model T Ford, seeking water for the radiator. His passengers were Lucinda A. Riedell and her grandson. They were on the way to a local mine where the young man, Harold L. Fulton, had gained employment. The story goes Burts called to the shack for permission to access the water, Robinson shouted back granting it and invited Burts to come on in. Burts went, leaving Mrs. Riedell and Fulton to care for the car. As soon as Burts stepped through the door gunfire erupted. Accounts vary; however the November 9 article (**AP**) specifies 13 shots were fired. Both men died. Each had a .45-caliber pistol, loaded with six bullets. Some accounts suggest a rifle bullet was found in Robinson's body. A news article reports sheriff's deputies stayed on to try to determine if Burts had help from "his gang". All of this, of course, was grist for my mill.

When I visited Government holes in the summer of 2016, no buildings remained. The Rock Springs Land & Cattle Company trough is still there, as is the cottonwood tree sheltering a derelict windmill. I searched through the blackbrush and found the remains of a rock foundation for a building, possibly the one where the gunfight took place.

A great source for this story and more history of the area may be found in historian and author Dennis G.

UNDER DESERT SAND

Casebier's **Mojave Road Guide: An Adventure Through Time**.

Although my novel touches them but briefly, it would be wrong not to mention the Mojave, Chemehuevi and Southern Piute bands of Indians who frequented the area before the first Europeans stepped foot on the desert. The Mojave, a strong race, walked across the desert on the original Mojave Road all the way to the Pacific Coast to trade. They subsisted with agriculture utilizing the rich flood plains of the Colorado. On the other hand, the Chemehuevi were hunter-gatherers, carving a lean cuisine from nuts and berries and an occasional rabbit, lizard or tortoise. A rock face with Chemehuevi petroglyphs may be viewed at Hole-in-the-Wall information center at Mojave National Preserve.

If you enjoyed this book, please take a moment to review it on the book's page on Amazon or the site of purchase. Your thoughts are most helpful.
The Author

Zack Tolliver, FBI Crime Mystery Series By
R Lawson Gamble

THE OTHER
MESTACLOCAN
ZACA
CAT
CANAAN'S SECRET
LAS CRUCES
LOST OASIS

New Johnny Alias Western Series

JOHNNY AND THE KID
JOHNNY AND THE PREACHER

Made in the USA
Middletown, DE
11 October 2022

12506334R00170